An Old Sailor's Yarns

by

N. Ames

Double9
BOOKS

An Old Sailor's Yarns
by N. Ames

ISBN: 978-93-64286-96-1

Published by

DOUBLE 9 BOOKS

2/13-B, Ansari Road
Daryaganj, New Delhi – 110002
info@double9books.com
www.double9books.com
Tel. 011-40042856

ABOUT THE AUTHOR

N. Ames is the pen name of an author whose works often explore maritime themes and the life of sailors. Though specific biographical details about N. Ames might be limited, the author is recognized for contributions to maritime literature and storytelling. Ames's writing is characterized by vivid storytelling and detailed descriptions of nautical life. The author uses a conversational tone to narrate the adventures, making the stories engaging and immersive for readers. The portrayal of sailor folklore and nautical traditions adds authenticity and depth to the narratives. The themes in Ames's work often include adventure, bravery, camaraderie and the romanticism of maritime life. The stories reflect the hardships and rewards of seafaring, as well as the strong bond between sailors and the ocean. Ames's works provide a window into the historical and cultural aspects of maritime life. By focusing on shipwrecks, pirate encounters and other sea-related events, the author offers readers insights into the traditions and folklore of sailors. The book remains a valuable contribution to maritime literature, celebrated for its engaging narratives and portrayal of sailor life. N. Ames's contributions to literature offer a rich exploration of maritime adventures, reflecting a deep appreciation for the seafaring tradition and the life of sailors.

CONTENTS

THE PIRATE OF MASAFUERO

PREFACE

Mr. Buckingham, noticing the "Nautical Reminiscences" in the New England Magazine, says, no author ever stopped at the second book; and he very gravely proceeds to recommend that my number three should savor more of the style of Goldsmith or Washington Irving. I should have no objection whatever to writing like either of these distinguished authors, *if I could*; but as the case is, I must be content to write as well as I can. The whole article in Mr. B's magazine bore no faint resemblance to a dose of calomel and jalap, administered in a table-spoonful of molasses, in which the sweet and the nauseous are so equally balanced, that the patient is in doubt whether to spit or to swallow. I was, however, exceedingly flattered with the notice bestowed upon me by this literary cynic, as he was never before known to speak well, even moderately, of any author, except natives of Boston, or professors in Harvard University.

"Morton" is founded upon an old tradition, now forgotten, but well known when I first went to sea, of the exploits of some of our adventurous and somewhat lawless traders in the Pacific. A number of the crew of one of these smuggling vessels were taken in the act, and, after a hasty trial, ordered to be sent to the mines. The route to their place of condemnation and hopeless confinement lay near the coast. A large party of seamen landed from two or three ships that were in the neighborhood, waylaid the military escort, knocked most of them on the head, rescued the prisoners, and got safe off without loss. The story says nothing of female influence or assistance, but knowing it to be morally impossible to get through a story without the assistance of a lady, I pressed one into the service, and took other liberties with the original, till it became what peradventure the reader will find it. Many stories are told of the skirmishes, or as sailors call them, "scrammidges," between our "free-traders" and the guarda-costas in different parts of the Pacific. In particular, the ship D——, of Boston, is said to have had a "regular-built fight" with a guarda-costa of forty-four guns, that retired from the action so miserably mauled, that it is doubtful to this day whether she ever found her way back into port. An old sea-dog who was on board the D——, furnished me with many details of the proceedings of our merchantmen on the coasts of California, and Mexico, some thirty years since, but most of them have escaped my memory.

I have inadvertently, in one or two instances, called the inhabitants of Mexico, South Americans. The fact is, there is scarcely a perceptible shade of difference in manners between the Chilians, Peruvians, and Mexicans; there is none in their language, dress, or religion; and sailors, who pay but little regard to arbitrary divisions of continents, are in the habit of calling all the quondam possessions of his Most Catholic Majesty, that border upon the Pacific, by the general name of South America, upon the same principle, I presume, that they call the whole of that ocean the "*South* Sea," though they may be at that very moment anchored in Sitka, or cruizing in the chops of Behring's Straits.

"The Rivals," is built upon a strange story that was quite current among our men-of-war's-men some years ago, but I am unable to give any further account of the hero of *their* story than the reader will find in the conclusion of mine. There seems to be no doubt that the stranger was obliged to fly on account of a fatal duel; and sailors, who cannot conceive of a duel between two gentlemen, as they somewhat ironically call them, unless there is a woman in the case, have accordingly attached one to the quarrel that compelled the unfortunate officer to take shelter on board an American national vessel.

"Old Cuff" is a sketch from real life. He was a petty officer in the service at the same time with me, and notwithstanding his rambling life, was a man of good education and strong mind. His life was a striking illustration of the truth of the proposition that "there is no romance like the romance of real life." He proposed to me to take minutes of his adventures, which were extremely interesting, but before I could commence operations I was myself made a petty officer, and removed to a station in a part of the ship where I but seldom saw him, and the ship was soon after ordered home.

The reader need be neither a wizard nor a witch to perceive that "Mary Bowline" is a creation of my own brain, and is of course defective, and will disappoint. But if it is true that "Bacon, Butler, and Shakspeare have rendered it impossible for any one after them to be profound, witty, or sublime," it is equally true that Scott, Irving, and others have rendered it impossible for any one to be equally entertaining, interesting, or amusing. I hold, however, to another maxim, that "he is a benefactor to mankind who furnishes them with innocent materials for laughter and delight," a maxim that did not come exactly "ex cathedra," but is full as profound, and correct. If I have been so fortunate as to contribute to, or become the cause of innocent delight, I shall think that the "Forecastle Yarns" have not been written in vain.

It was objected to my two former works that they contained strictures, and remarks, upon what are commonly called orthodox principles. In the present volume, I have studiously endeavored to steer my footsteps clear of the tender toes of every religious sect except the Catholics; whom, in imitation of the Protestant clergy and laity all around me, I have handled without mittens whenever I could get a chance.

I cannot close without repeating that if I have succeeded in helping to make

"The wheels of life gae down hill scrievin',
Wi' rattlin' glee," —

I shall feel more gratified than if I had squared the circle, or drawn up a tariff that, like Shakspeare's barber's chair, should fit all parties.

N. A.

Providence, October 1, 1833.

P. S. More than a year ago the following pages were written and prepared for the press, under the title of "Forecastle Yarns," but a gentleman connected with the New York Mirror took a fancy to that title, and immediately appropriated it to himself with the most genteel indifference as to the prior right of another. In consequence, I have been obliged to adopt a new name. The "Pirate of Masafuero" was written after the above preface was prepared. "Old Cuff" has already been before the public in the columns of the first and only number of a new magazine[1] that expired for want of patronage, and support, having just survived long enough to give ample proofs that it deserved the patronage, and support, that were denied it. The very favorable notice that the Evening Star took of "Old Cuff," is proof positive that it is much higher than "fair to middling;" and if it is true that "the proof of the pudding is eating the bag," (and the reader will consider "Old Cuff" as the bag,) I think it follows that the pudding now set before him cannot be a bad one.

November, 1834.

[1] American Spectator and National Magazine.

MARY BOWLINE

CHAPTER I

"Nautaeque, per omne
Audaces mare qui currunt, hac mente laborum
Sese ferre, senes ut in otia tuta recedunt,Aiunt."

Horace.

Captain Robert Bowline, a retired sea-captain, occupied a snug little farm in the town of B— —, one of the many pleasant villages on the coast of New England. He had followed the sea for many years, acquired considerable property, married, and had a family. When he had attained his forty-fifth year, a relation of his wife died, leaving her heiress to a very handsome estate, part of which was the farm aforesaid. In consequence of this event he was easily persuaded by his wife, whom he tenderly loved, to retire to private life, and leave the "vexed ocean" to be ploughed by those who had their fortunes to make. They retired to their farm, when the first act of the old Triton was to pull down the antique house that had been erected "about the time of the old French war," and build another more "ship-shape," and congenial to the taste of a sailor. The dwelling itself was not, indeed, externally different from any other of the snug-looking and rather handsome two-story houses of substantial farmers, &c. in New England; but its internal economy was somewhat nautical, containing numerous "lockers" and "store-rooms." Its front gate-posts were composed of the two jaw-bones of an enormous whale; the fence was of a most fanciful Chinese pattern; and directly in front of the house was erected that never-failing ornament of a sailor's dwelling, a tall flag-staff, with cap, cross-trees, and topmast, complete; the last, always being kept "housed," except upon the 4th of July, 22d of February, &c. At the foot of the flag-staff, "hushed in grim repose," was an iron six-pounder, mounted upon a ship gun-carriage, ready for service, whenever any national holyday required its voice. The house fronted the sea; a most superb view of which it commanded, but was at the same time screened from its storms in great measure by being flanked by noble old elms, and a fine orchard, which almost entirely surrounded it;

while in the rear the ground swelled into a thickly wooded hill of moderate height. The ground in front sloped gently down to the water's edge, at the distance of half a mile from the house, but to the left gradually rose into a high point, or headland, terminating in a rocky cliff that strode far out into the sea, and formed the harbor.

The family of the old seaman, at the time he took possession of his "shore quarters," consisted of himself, wife, and daughter Mary—the rest of his children having died young. As we have no particular concern with the events of his life from that period to Mary's twenty-first year, we shall only observe that during that time he had the misfortune to lose his wife.

Mary Bowline was a young lady, confessedly of the greatest beauty in the little town of B——, and for many miles round; a trifle above the middle stature, sufficiently so to relieve her figure from the imputation of shortness; or, as she was a little inclined to be "fleshy," or "embonpoint," as our refined authors call it, from what is sometimes called "stubbidness;" her eyes were of deep celestial blue; her hair, a dark brown, and her complexion, notwithstanding her continual rambles along the beach in her girlish days, of exquisite purity. Her education, I grieve to say, had been most shamefully neglected; her mother, though a most exemplary woman, both as a Christian and a member of society, had never tied her up in a fashionable corset to improve her figure, nor sent her to a fashionable boarding school to improve her mind; the consequence was that she knew nothing of the piano,—Virgil seems to have had the gift of prophecy with regard to this part of modern education, when he said or sang,

"Stridente stipula miserum *disperdere* carmen,"—

and was equally ignorant of that sublime and useful art, working lace; she had no further idea of dancing than had been beat into her head, or rather heels, by the saltatory instructions of an itinerant dancing-master—I ask pardon, "professor"—who, with a bandy-legged dog at his heels, and a green baize bag under his arm, paid an annual visit to the town, to instruct its Thetises in the "poetry of motion;" an apt illustration of the

"*Bacchum* in remotis" choreas "rupibus
Vidi docentem
Nymphasque discentes,"

of Horace, with the alteration of a word; said fiddler having "forsworn thin potations" very soon after the commencement of his capering career. In the "serene and silent art" she was, however, truly fortunate; the clergyman of the place, a most amiable and intelligent man, and, to the credit of his amphibious parishioners, loved and esteemed with the utmost fervor and unanimity, added to his other accomplishments no mean skill as a draughtsman; an art, that he had full leisure to practise; one of his parochial duties, that of visiting the sick, being a mere shadow; for your fisherman, with his wife and his little ones, is but seldom on the doctor's list, and when he "files off," generally does it without beat of drum or flap of banner. He was a constant visiter at the house of Captain Bowline, whither he was attracted by the fascination of the seaman's stories of foreign parts. Charmed with the dawning beauty of the lovely little Mary, he readily undertook to give her better instruction than she could have obtained at the town school, to which he added drawing. Her mother had amply instructed her in the more useful and homely arts of cooking, sewing, knitting, &c. and she had even taught her to spin; for she lived before the establishment of any, or many, of those institutions for the increase of illegitimate children, ignorance, immorality, suicide, seduction, murder, &c.—I mean cotton factories. The comparatively affluent circumstances of her family had, however, rendered it unnecessary for her to practise this last accomplishment. With all these charms in her own person, and right in her father's strong box, it is not to be wondered at that the lovely Mary Bowline had suitors in abundance; but the only one that seemed to have made any impression upon her light heart, was a young seaman by the name of Kelson, who had now attained his twenty-seventh year.

Thomas Kelson was the son of poor parents, indeed it would have been extremely difficult, if not impossible, to have found a family in the whole town of B—— that could be called wealthy. He had followed the sea from early life, and had always returned home during the intervals of his voyages, at which times he had improved his education under the instructions of the clergyman aforesaid. His acquaintance with Mary had passed by a very natural transition from intimacy to affection; he was the constant companion of her rambles, and when she chose an aquatic excursion his sail-boat was always ready. To her father his company was always acceptable; the old seaman had none of the pride of "monied aristrocracy;" he saw no harm in his daughter placing her affections, and bestowing her hand and fortune, upon a young man who was fast rising to respectability and wealth, in precisely the same steps by which he had himself ascended, commencing as cabin-boy and ending as master and part owner; he lived on a part of the coast that lay entirely out of the track of "refinement," if indeed she had then begun her march.

Accordingly things were permitted to go on just as though consent had been asked and obtained; the young couple walked together, sat together, and Kelson being "free of the house," talked together upon almost every subject but love. Was there to be a fishing or sleighing party, or an excursion into the neighboring woods, Tom Kelson was invariably and by quiet agreement Mary Bowline's escort; was there a ball, no one, "louting low with cap in hand," solicited, or thought of soliciting, the honor of her company; that felicity was always supposed to be reserved for Tom Kelson; still, with all this constant and close intimacy, the young seaman had never talked of love, never offered himself as a husband, and Mary, the gay and light-hearted Mary, had never, as the New England saying is, "thought a word about it." Had Kelson suddenly presented himself to her with "Mary, shall we be published next Sunday?" she would have answered "Yes;" without the slightest hesitation; nor thought her assent worth the trouble of a blush or a simper; and such, I believe, will be found the case in most of our country courtships.

Captain Kelson, for he had attained that title some time previous, had been on *terra firma* some months; partly for want of a vessel, but chiefly in compliance with the earnest entreaties of the lovely Mary, who was terrified at the thought of his again encountering the frightful calamity that had so nearly proved fatal to him on his last voyage. On his return from St. Petersburg with a full cargo, he had experienced a tremendous gale near the Grand Banks, during which his vessel was struck by lightning and consumed. After undergoing most dreadful sufferings in their boats, the exhausted remnant of the crew were most providentially picked up and brought safe home. In consequence of losing his vessel, the owners had received him with coldness, as is invariably the case, as though a deep loaded brig, lying-to in a gale of wind, could dodge a flash of lightning! I have known many a good seaman kept "lying out" of a vessel for months, merely because the owners had thought proper to send him to sea in a *craft* whose bottom had "dropped out," as the sea phrase is, as soon as she had encountered bad weather.

Captain Kelson had accordingly remained on shore from April, till September; the time when we have thought proper to commence our story; during which period he contrived to kill time quite agreeably in fishing, shooting, surveying the harbor, and last but not least, in paying continual attention to the fair Mary. He had one day made a visit to Captain Bowline's house, and had accompanied him in a ramble over part of his farm. During their "cruize," the old sailor had detailed his plans for the season, and gradually extending his views, announced certain arrangements and alterations as about to be carried into execution "when Mary gets married." When Mary gets married! the words passed like the shock of a galvanic battery through the mind of the younger seaman; he soon took leave, and as he strolled, unconscious of the direction his feet were taking without admitting his head into their counsels, down towards the narrow strip of white sand beach at the foot of the headland already mentioned, her father's words, the last that he distinctly heard or recollected, continued to sound in his ears —

"When Mary gets married! well, she must get married some time or other, and who will it be?" he said to himself, suddenly stopping short. "She seems to prefer me at present, but I know that when I am at sea she appears to favor Sam Ingraham, or Ben Bass, just as much. Yet why should she be so anxious to have me stay on shore to avoid an accident that may not occur again in a century, if I should live so long, unless she does really prefer me to all others? I will certainly try to find out the state of her feelings towards me the first opportunity, and if she refuses me, I will never set foot in B— — again."

With this chivalrous determination he visited his lovely and all unconscious mistress the next day, but the fair lady was busy ironing. —"I shall see her again this evening," thought he, as he turned slowly towards the town; and see her that evening he did. They rambled out towards the cape, or promontory, almost invariably the scene of their summer evening walks; for lovers, after one or two strolls over a particular portion of ground, regard it as almost sacred; there are a thousand sweet recollections connected with every step —here they have paused to admire some particular feature in the prospect —under that spreading tree they have stood together in silence, busy with their own peculiar thoughts; and this walk is seldom, if ever, changed —it is almost like inconstancy to each other to propose a different route.

They had reached the high bluff, and were seated, as usual, upon a solitary block of granite, which, had they lived in heathen times, they might have worshipped as the ancient and much respected god Terminus. Mary, who had hitherto had the conversation almost entirely to herself, suddenly noticed her lover's abstraction.

"Why, what's the matter with you, Thomas?"

"Nothing; I was only thinking, Mary."

"'Thinking, Mary!' well, do speak to Mary once in a while. I believe," she continued, after a pause, and with a faltering voice and feeling of faintness that she could not account for, "I believe you are in love, Thomas." She had heard that day that Captain Kelson was making furious love to a sea-nymph in B— —, the daughter of one of the richest inhabitants.

"So I am, sweet Mary, most desperately so."

"I know it, sir; I heard it all this morning; I wish you joy," gasped the poor girl.

"Heard of it all! good heavens, Mary, what do you mean? it is you, my own dearest girl, that I love; who else *could* you think of?" as he spoke he held both her hands in his and clasped them earnestly.

"I heard," faltered poor Mary, "I was told that—that it was—Jane Wilson, O, Thomas!" and sinking her glowing cheek upon his shoulder, she burst into tears.

Kelson, inexpressibly delighted by this unequivocal testimony of her love, prest her to his bosom, and hastened to explain to her that the sole object of his seeking an interview with her that evening, was to make known his affection; that his silence and reserve were owing to the deep interest he felt in the issue of that interview; that his visits to Captain Wilson's were solely on business; that he scarcely saw his daughter Jane at any one of them; and a thousand other things. What a stupid, asinine creature is a lover, *before* the ice is broken, and what an eloquent, inspired animal, *after* the *explosion!* A lover may retire to his closet, and spoil a whole ream of paper with "raven locks," and "eyes' liquid azure," and "sweet girls," &c. Such an epicure creature as Natty Willis will befoul you a quire of foolscap before breakfast in that way—but let a stranger see the same lover in presence of his idol, and he would think that he was then to apologise for an assault and battery with intent, &c.

The walk home was the pleasantest they had ever enjoyed—both were too happy for conversation. They decided, however, before they parted, that it was altogether unnecessary to communicate to Captain Bowline what had taken place. "He has understood all along what was the state of your feelings," said Mary, "and I am sure has always regarded you with paternal kindness."

CHAPTER II

O! a most dainty man!
To see him walk before a lady and bear her fan!

Love's Labor Lost.

The next day, as the old seaman sat by a front window smoking his pipe after dinner, he suddenly started up with the exclamation of "Hey! what—what the devil have we here? Mary, love, hand me the glass—a mariner adrift on a grating, by the Lord Harry!"

The object that called forth this animadversion, and broke a delightful day-dream that Mary was indulging in, now appeared in sight, having hitherto been hidden by a thick clump of trees, that bounded the ocean prospect towards the right. It was a small sail-boat, with three men in her, that, at one moment directly before the wind, and the next, "all shaking," seemed rapidly approaching an extensive mud flat, that formed one side of the harbor, and towards which the flowing tide and fresh breeze seemed to be fast drifting her.

"There they are, hard and fast! and on their beam ends, too, by the piper," continued the veteran, and as he witnessed this last catastrophe, he sprang from his chair, forgetting in his charitable intention of hurrying to their assistance, that they were more than half a mile off, and in full view of the town.

"There is a boat going to them, pa," said Mary, slightly blushing as she recognised at the mast head of a very handsome, fast sailing boat, a blue "burger," with a large white M. in it, the work of her own fair hands.

"Aye," said the veteran, reseating himself, "aye, there goes Tom Kelson in your namesake, Mary; they'll get off with a ducking, and it will serve them right. Yes," continued he, applying the glass to his eye, "there goes two of them ashore through the mud, like a couple of pup-seals."

Kelson managed his boat with great skill, so as to approach the wreck, on board which still appeared one person half overboard, and apparently almost exhausted by his violent struggles to disencumber himself from the wet sail, and by anchoring immediately to windward, and carrying away cable, reached the boat and rescued the unfortunate man from a situation that was exceedingly uncomfortable if not dangerous. The other two, by dint of swimming, wading, and wallowing through the mud, reached the shore, which was about three hundred yards distant.

As soon as he had ascertained that the man on board the wreck was rescued, the old seaman, "on hospitable thoughts intent," hastened to the village to obtain intelligence and render assistance. It was evening when he returned to his snug dwelling, and then he was accompanied by a tall, slight made, very fashionably dressed young man, whom he introduced to his daughter as Mr. Millinet, of New York.

Mr. Millinet, or as he usually designated himself, George Frederick Augustus Millinet, Esq., was a "dry goods merchant," *par excellence*, in Broadway, who having a little more cash on hand than he had ever possessed before, made an excursion to New England, with the charitable intention of civilizing and astonishing the natives. His debut was, however, rather unfortunate; B—— was his first "land-fall" after quitting the high road from New York, towards the east. Fancying that a sail-boat in a sea-way, was as easily managed as a Whitehall skiff, off the Battery; he had "put to sea," in company with two little amphibious urchins that he had hired for the occasion, and who desired no better sport. They immediately perceived the ignorance of their commander, and began to play tricks upon him, as man-of-war's men do upon an ignorant and tyrannical midshipman. These pranks had terminated more seriously than they expected, and, fearful of punishment, they had betaken themselves to the water and made their escape.

Mr. Millinet being somewhat annoyed by the sly jokes and grave humor of mine host, of the hotel, concerning his misfortune, and the giggling of the waiters and chamber-maids, gladly accepted Captain Bowline's invitation, and was soon seated at his hospitable and well loaded table, for the old tar put no great faith in tea and bread and butter for supper. The knight of the yard-stick had, however, gulped down too much salt water, and been too seriously frightened to feel much appetite, and he retired to bed early. The next morning he made his appearance at breakfast, over which the fair Mary was presiding, and which might have excited an appetite in the gastric region of the most confirmed dyspeptic. There were bass and tautaug fresh from the water; oysters in different forms, broiled, stewed, fried, &c.; a noble ham, into which the stout seaman plunged his flashing carving-knife, and hewed it in pieces, as Samuel did Agag, in the valley of Gilgal; there was broiled ham, beef steaks, mutton chop, eggs, cheese, butter, honey, hot cakes; a pile of pilot-bread-toast a foot high, ditto untoasted, coffee, tea, and chocolate. To all this good cheer, their fashionable visiter paid but small respect, and the old commander, having pressed him to make himself at home, and help himself, attacked his own breakfast with vigor, feeling at the same time no small contempt for a man whose stomach could be so effectually unhinged by a simple capsize, and thorough ducking. The vender of tape and calico, seemed to feast his eyes, if not his appetite, by gazing on the lovely countenance of his young hostess; and after some slight hesitation, commenced talking to her of theatres, and balls, and assemblies, and fashionable intelligence in general; but Balaam's ass, if she had marched into the room and commenced an oration in the original Hebrew, or Chaldee, or Syro-Phœnician, or whatever might have been *its* vernacular tongue in which she formerly addressed her master, could not have been more unintelligible. The old gentleman made an attempt to drive a conversation, and asked a few questions relative to foreign politics, the state of navigation, and commerce, in New York, &c.; but finding his auditor as ignorant as though he had proposed a case in middle latitude sailing, he dropped him altogether.

He remained in the family three or four days, during which, his attentions to Mary were incessant, but managed with such fashionable tact as not to be annoying. She was exceedingly amused by his consummate vanity and self-conceit; that seemed to make up the greater part of his character. His descriptions of society and manners in the commercial emporium, though not altogether intelligible to his fair auditor, were new and amusing, and in spite of the contagious effect of her father's contempt, and the troubled looks of poor Kelson, she could not help listening to him with complacency. It was evident to every body but Mary that the retailer of ginghams was most seriously smitten with her, as much so, that is to say, as his idolatry of himself left him capable of being with any person. And so it proved, for in less time than she had any idea that it was possible to go to and return from New York, back came her Broadway beau. Mary opened her large blue eyes in most unaffected astonishment, as he came up to the door at which she was standing, equipped for a walk with Kelson. She made no scruple of consigning him to her father and continuing her walk. The old man received him, of course, with politeness, and after a short conversation, his visiter who seemed much embarrassed, observed that he was desirous of entering the holy state, and then went on to give an account of his prospects, expectations, possessions, references, hopes, fears, anxieties, &c. The seaman listened with attention to the whole catalogue, mentally exclaiming, "what the d—l does all this mean?"

"In short, sir," said he of Broadway, "I have seen no young lady who seems so well calculated to make a man happy as your lovely daughter

Mary; and if you have no objection, I should be happy to be permitted to pay my addresses to her, if her affections are not already engaged."

The old sea-dog, who had been rubbing his chin during the latter part of his visiter's harangue, observed that "his daughter was indeed a fine girl, and he (Mr. Millinet) had not and could not say any more good of her than she deserved; that as to her affections being engaged, he did not pretend to bother his brain about an affair that did not concern him, trusting that the girl had good sense enough to make a proper choice; that with regard to paying his addresses to her, he might sheer alongside as quick as he liked—he would without doubt find her at quarters and all ready for action; and finally that he, her father, would not interfere to thwart her wishes in so important an affair as the choice of a husband, for," (he repeated, with an internal chuckle as the thought crossed his mind, that his favorite Tom Kelson was beyond a doubt the man of her choice,) "Mary knew what she was about, and had wit enough to make a judicious choice."

This speech, an exceedingly long one for him, was listened to with great satisfaction by his fashionable guest, who thus armed with the father's consent, as he regarded it, never dreamed of the possibility of any difficulty on the daughter's part, and looked upon the whole affair as settled.

In the mean time Mary, regardless of her victory over the heart of her New York visiter, was quietly pursuing her evening walk with Kelson, to whom she had made known the presence, in the vicinity, of his rival. Her lover heard the intelligence with a feeling of dissatisfaction that he could not exactly define—he had unbounded confidence in his Mary's constancy and love just at that present time, but, like most men, he had rather a mean opinion of woman's constancy in general, and could not avoid applying the general rules that he had formed for himself, to most individuals. He dreaded the effect of an assiduous and sustained attack upon Mary's inexperienced mind, from a dashing, fashionable lover, who held out to her acceptance all the charms and glitter of a life of ease, and splendor, and dissipation. His uneasy sensations were by no means quieted by his companion's gaiety, who having at once surmised, or pretended so to have done, the object of the Gothamite's visit, promised herself much amusement from his wooing.

On their return to the house, they found the new visiter quietly installed in the parlor, and waiting their, or rather her, return. In high glee with the flattering prospect before him, he completely monopolized Mary's attention, and eventually put to flight the overpowered and mortified Kelson, who left the house with a heavy heart. For at least a week Mr. Millinet kept the field; he was Mary's constant companion, whether sitting quietly at home or walking out; and Kelson, finding it almost impossible even to speak to her, prudently kept himself out of the way, well knowing that Mary would soon miss him, if she had not already, and eagerly seek an interview; nor was he wrong in his conjecture. Calling at her father's house one Sunday morning, he found her seated in the parlor waiting for meeting time. In the course of conversation he asked her jestingly, though with a beating heart, "what she meant to do with her new lover?"

"I don't know," said she laughing, "he says that he has my father's permission to make love to me, and he seems determined that the permission shall not become a dead letter for want of use."

"Your father! I had no idea that he had given his consent."

"My father, Thomas, has given me free permission to do as I please in the affair of choosing a husband."

"Certainly," said poor Kelson, construing this last speech into sentence of death to *his* love.

"And I have already acted as I pleased," continued the lovely girl, holding out her hand to him.

It was impossible to mistake the meaning of the last words and their accompanying action, and the delighted seaman certified his full intelligence and gratitude upon her lips.

"I believe this fellow, my sweet Mary, has made me almost jealous and quite foolish; but, seriously, what do you mean to do with him?"

"Why, the creature can't stay here for ever, and if he offers himself to me, I shall say 'No,' in as plain English as possible."

Mr. Millinet soon after made his appearance, and attended Captain Bowline and his daughter to meeting, to the no small surprise of the good folks of B— —, who, regarding him as the favored lover of Mary Bowline, could not help expressing their regret that she should have slighted Captain Kelson, and accepted "that tape-measuring son of a b— —."

What a pity that sailors, and seafaring people at large, can seldom or never give vent to their indignation without at the same time attacking the parentage of the object of their resentment. This is decidedly an orientalism; and I have observed in another place that sailors resemble the Orientals in their fondness for tropes and figures. The most opprobrious epithet that a Persian can make use of, when in a passion, is to call his antagonist "a dog's uncle." No other degree of canine consanguinity is considered so degrading.

The retailer of dry goods dined at the house of Captain Bowline, and attended the family to church in the afternoon, but excused himself immediately after the service was over and returned to the town. Kelson made a visit to the house of the old seaman just at dark, and on entering the usual sitting-room he found it unlighted, and occupied only by Dinah, the black girl, who, arrayed in what the old captain called her "go-ashore bib and tucker," was probably awaiting the arrival of her woolly-headed suitor. The old gentleman had gone out visiting, as he usually did on Sunday evenings, and Mary was in a little back parlor, where she usually sat in her father's absence, and which was the winter sitting-room of the family. Kelson had been in the house but a very few minutes when he saw his rival approaching the front gate. With all that propensity for mischief that characterizes sailors on shore, he immediately formed, and proceeded to put in execution, a plan for the torment and vexation of his antagonist of the yard-stick. He promised the sable handmaid of his Mary a half dollar, if she would personate her mistress for a few minutes, which he imagined easily enough done in the dark, and instructing her "to behave prim and lady-like," went in quest of the boy Jim, whom he stationed in the entry to open the door for Mr. Millinet, and show him into the front parlor, and then went to the room where the fair lady herself was sitting. She was just on the point of coming to the front room with a light, having heard his well-known voice and step, but he easily engaged her in conversation; and when, at Millinet's knock, she was rising to see who it was, he as easily detained her by the assurance, that it was "nobody but her New York sweetheart." Every thing favored the mischievous plans of the seaman: Millinet never suspecting that any female but the mistress of the house would presume to seat herself in the front parlor, and feeling moreover the darkness and solitude of the room peculiarly favorable to courtship, seated himself by the side of the supposed Mary, and immediately commenced making love in pretty "rapid" style. Finding that the lady answered only in monosyllables, and seemed more than usually affable, he ventured to take her hand and gently squeeze it. He was at first somewhat startled at the hardness and roughness of the palm, but soon recollected that the country ladies in New England were in the habit of milking their cows, making butter and cheese, &c., and said to himself, "Never mind, when she is Mrs. Millinet her hard palms shall be well rubbed with pumice-stone and milk of roses, till they are as soft as any lady's in Broadway."

Enraptured by the gentle pressure with which the "black lily" returned his amorous squeeze of her hand, he ventured to raise it to his lips, and imprint a kiss upon the short, thick fingers. At this critical and rapturous moment the door flew open, and the real Mary entered, bearing a lighted glass mantel-lamp in each hand. With a profound curtesy she placed her lamps upon the mantel-piece, and gravely asking pardon for her intrusion, flew into the room which she had just left, and which immediately echoed with her laughter, lively and joyous, but most unfashionably loud, hearty, and prolonged. The sable *fair* one made her escape at the same time, and received from Kelson double what he had promised her. Mary, however, as soon as she had recovered her gravity, joined her new suitor, but all her hospitable attentions were lost upon the discomfited Broadway merchant, who soon took his leave, overwhelmed with shame and mortification, nor did he sufficiently recover himself to renew his visits for two or three days. When he did again visit her father's house, Mary, who thought the joke carried far enough, treated him with more than usual attention, by way of apology for her untimely and mortifying mirth, so that by the expiration of the week he had entirely recovered his spirits, his self-conceit, his vanity, and his talkativeness.

CHAPTER III

You are now within a foot
Of the extreme verge; for all beneath the moon
Would I not leap upright!

King Lear.

Shortly after this mad prank of Kelson's, Mr. Millinet invited Mary to walk out one lovely evening, to which she gladly assented. They took their way towards the "Whale's Head," a name given by the inhabitants of B—— to the high bluff already mentioned, that formed the eastern side of their harbor, from its real or fancied resemblance to the nose, or to speak more scientifically, "noddle-end," of a whale. A path descended obliquely from the upper part of the cape down to the beach at its foot. The whole cape and the land adjacent were comprised in the estate of Captain Bowline, who kept the paths in good repair, and had been at considerable pains, when he first took possession of the farm, to render it perfectly safe and passable, for the convenience of the fishermen, who were in the habit of digging clams on the narrow beach at the foot of the hill, and fishing among the sunken rocks at the extreme point. For the whole length of the path the hill was extremely steep, but not perpendicular, and covered with short dried grass, which made the surface so slippery, that it afforded an apt illustration of Virgil's "facilis descensus Averni;" for though any one might accomplish a descent safely enough by dint of holding on to the few shrubs and bushes, and sliding occasionally, no animal but a cat, a goat, or a monkey, could ascend, if it was to save his life. Near the middle of the path it was crossed by a deep gap, or ravine, caused by the constant wearing of a small spring of water that trickled down the face of the cliff, and which was generally swollen by the melting of the snow, or by occasional heavy rains. The beach, or rather marsh, at the foot of the hill, where the little rivulet joined the sea, was so soft and boggy, as to be utterly impassable. Across this ravine, which was known by the name of the "Devil's Gap," Captain Bowline had caused a narrow bridge, of two planks in width, to be built, protected on the outside by a light railing. On the side next the hill, it was sufficiently guarded by the crooked branches of a knurly and scrubby oak tree, that grew on the very edge of the ravine.

Down this path the fair Mary and her suitor directed their steps. They wandered along the beach as far as the point, the New Yorker in full chat and high spirits, and Mary's attention almost entirely occupied by a distant boat that seemed to be engaged in fishing, and which she recognised, notwithstanding the distance, to be her namesake, the Mary, belonging to her lover Kelson. Their walk occupied them till nearly sunset, when Mary suddenly recollected that the tide was flowing, and would soon entirely cover the narrow beach that they had just passed. By dint of walking fast, they reached the foot of the path before the beach was covered by the tide, and commenced their ascent just as the sun went down.

In the mean time, heavy black clouds began to muster in the north-west, announcing the approach of a thunder shower, and reducing the evening twilight to less than half its usual duration. Large heavy drops of rain were soon felt and heard, rattling in the few straggling shrubs and bushes, accompanied by short gusts of wind. Mr. Millinet, who was considerably alarmed by these indications of a violent shower, and who trembled for the safety of his new Broadway hat, and Broadway coat, hurried on with the most uncourteous and unlover-like disregard of his fair companion, who was too much accustomed to take care of herself, to be at all incommoded by his neglect. They reached the "Devil's Gap," and the lover strode on most rapidly; he was just upon the middle of the little bridge, when being startled by a sudden bright flash of lightning, he stumbled, and in the dread of falling off, laid violent hold upon one of the branches of the scrubby oak on the other side, recovered himself, and passed on. The oak, that had long since been partially undermined by the water from the spring, and which Captain Bowline had determined to remove before it did any damage, gave way before the violent pull of Millinet. Mary, whose feet were already upon the planks of the bridge, alarmed by the rattling of the loose earth and stones that fell from under the roots of the tree, ran hastily back. The next instant, the tree, with a ton or two of earth attached to its matted roots, came thundering down, sweeping away with it the bridge, and a large portion of the path beyond it. In the mean time, short violent showers, of but four or five seconds in duration, with equally short and violent gusts of wind, induced the Broadway gallant to increase his speed; he had indeed heard a loud crash, but it is no more than bare justice to him to say that he mistook the noise for thunder.

Poor Mary was thus completely insulated—it was impossible to go back, for the beach was long since covered by the rising tide—to climb up the hill was exceedingly difficult, if not absolutely impossible to an active man—to go forward was of course out of the question—there was every appearance of a cold, driving October storm of wind and rain, to which she must necessarily be exposed, with no additional clothing except a shawl, till the tide had ebbed sufficiently to leave the beach passible, and then the walk round the point was full three miles. In this dilemma, far from any human habitation, and exposed to the night wind, which now began to blow extremely chilly, poor Mary seated herself upon the bank and wept bitterly. After the lapse of a few minutes, she became more composed, and most fervently and earnestly commending herself to Divine protection, she endeavored to shelter herself as much as possible from the wind; for the rain had now ceased, and the clouds breaking away towards the south-west, gave indications of a clear, cold, frosty autumnal night.

Relief was, however, much nearer than she expected. Her father, alarmed at her non-appearance, and the threatening looks of the weather, sallied forth in quest of her. He had gone but a few rods, when he met Mr. George Frederic Augustus, with his pocket handkerchief tied over his hat, and his coat buttoned up to the chin, "striking out," as sailors say, like a man walking against time.

"Holloa," he shouted, "you Mr. What's-your-name! where the d—l have you left Mary? a pretty fellow you are to convoy a lady, to bear up before the wind as soon as the weather looks misty, and leave her to shift for herself! not but that the girl is a d—d sight better able to take care of herself than you are to take care of her." All this was said in perfect good humor, the old tar taking it for granted that his daughter had "made a harbor," as he expressed it, in one of the neighbor's houses.

But the abrupt question had startled Millinet, and he answered with much confusion and hesitation, "I—really, sir, I thought,—I am sure that is—I thought she was close behind me—she certainly was a few minutes since."

Captain Bowline, muttering an inverted blessing upon his fashionable guest, pushed on towards the path over the cliff. He was soon joined by Kelson, who had come in from fishing but a few minutes before, and who, hearing of Mary's walking out upon the beach, had immediately hastened to her father's house. He too had seen the hero of Gotham; but that gentleman, not deeming it wholesome to hold much conversation with men of so little refinement and fashion as Bowline and Kelson, when irritated, had made the best of his way towards B——.

Mary's father and lover accordingly hurried on, stopping at the house of old Haddock, the fisherman, who lived near the upper end of "Jade's Walk," as the hill-path was called, where they furnished themselves with a lantern, a coil of rope, and sundry other articles that they deemed necessary. Old Haddock and his two "boys," great two-fisted fellows of twenty and two and twenty years of age, also accompanied them. They soon arrived at the Devil's Gap, where they beheld the ruin caused by the fall of the tree. For an instant a thrill of horror ran through the hearts of two of the beholders; the idea that the object of their search and solicitude had been swept away by the fall of the bridge, and crushed in its ruins, or smothered in the mud and water at the foot of the hill, occurred instantly to both of them.

From this state of agony and suspense, they were soon relieved by the silver voice of Mary herself, calling from the further side of the gap, "Here I am, dear father, don't attempt to come to me, the path is all carried away on this side, and it is impossible for you or any one to get to me. Wait till the tide has gone down, and I will walk round to the point."

The sight of the dear girl in safety only stimulated them to greater exertions; the old fisherman and one of his boys departed to their house to procure a long plank, while Kelson and the other young man returned to the top of the hill, and, by sliding and supporting themselves by the bushes, safely descended to the spot where stood the lovely wanderer. She was so overjoyed to see them, and so completely chilled through, that she could scarcely speak. Kelson immediately stripped off his coat, and insisted upon wrapping her in it; and the young Triton, following the brilliant example of one whom he respected so much as Captain Kelson, doffed his "monkey-jacket," and with hearty but rough kindness forcibly enveloped her feet and ancles in its fearnought folds.

In a short time the other two fishermen arrived, bearing on their shoulders a long plank. An end of a rope was then thrown to Kelson, by which one end of the plank was hauled across, and firmly bedded in the bank. Its passage was then rendered secure by double "life-lines" on each side; and Mary, supported by her lover and the young fisherman, safely reached the other side, and was pressed, sobbing with joy, to her fond father's bosom. The whole party then returned towards Captain Bowline's house, where the old fisherman and his two sons were liberally rewarded, and treated with a good supper.

The next morning a messenger arrived from the village, bearing a note from Mr. George, &c. Millinet, in which he attempted to excuse his behavior the preceding evening. Mary declined opening it, however, and contented herself with sending word by the bearer that the writer need not give himself any further trouble on her account, an answer that was sufficiently intelligible. But the old commander shouted after the messenger, "Tell that lubberly *yoho* [2] that if I catch him within a cable's length of my house, I'll break every d—d bone in his tailor-built body."

This threat was duly reported to the crest-fallen vender of pins and bobbin, who settled his bills, and accomplished his escape, with as little parade and as much expedition as possible; a movement that excited full as much conversation as his first appearance and intimacy in Captain Bowline's family; and while one party were confident that he had only gone to New York to make preparations for his marriage, and another were equally sure that Mary had, in nautical parlance, "given him his walking ticket," the story of the accident and Mary Bowline's narrow escape at the Devil's Gap came out, with suitable additions and embellishments, and of course the whole affair wore a different face at once. Old Haddock, the fisherman, was seized upon one evening in a ship-chandlery and grocery store, that was the usual Rialto of the loungers in B— —, and rigorously cross-questioned. The man of hooks and lines hitched up his trowsers, and proceeded to enlighten his audience as follows:—

"Why you see that 'are New York chap and Miss Mary took a stroll down Jade's Walk as it might be about five o'clock in the arternoon, P. M. as the newspapers say. Well, they went down Squaw Beach, and so clean away out as fur as the pint; and when they was coming back, and got to the furder eend of the walk, the Yorker he kinder shinned up to her, and she didn't like it, for I knowed all along she meant to have Captain Kelson. Well, one word brought on another, till finally he conducted himself in a very promiscuous manner, and she told him to go 'long about his business, or she'd tell Captain Kelson of his doings. Well, that made him just about as mad as a hoe, and so when they come to the Devil's Gap he kinder kicked away one eend of the bridge, and then turned to and hauled down that 'ere scrub oak that growed clost to the bridge, so's folk mought think 'twas done by accident; and so there the poor gal was left by herself till old Captain Bowline and I and my two boys and Captain Kelson, come there and rigged a kind of trumporary bridge like, and got her safe over, and that's the whole consarnment of the matter as far as I know any thing on't."

This account of the affair, coming from an eye-witness, was considered authentic, being full as correct as the stories of eye-witnesses generally are. Mary at first attempted to contradict it, but finding her efforts fruitless, prudently determined to let the story die a natural death, which it soon did; a tremendous gale of wind and a shipwreck on the Whale's Nose having in less than a week most effectually turned the current of conversation into another channel.

Mr. Millinet reached New York in safety, and solaced himself for his defeat in New England by attention to his pretty person, and his pretty customers, balls, assemblies, and billiards; in process of time made a fashionable failure, a fashionable marriage, and commenced business afresh. To the questions of his acquaintance respecting his excursion "down east," he was shy and reserved; evading all questions on the subject by declaring that he had passed his time very pleasantly while he was in New England, but that the people had some very peculiar and odd notions of things. In process of time the story of his repulse reached New York with all its embellishments. Some of his friends were exceedingly shocked at the idea of his having made an attempt upon the life of a young lady, for such seemed the tenor of the story; but those who knew him best fully acquitted him of any thing of the kind, inasmuch as he had not courage sufficient to offer violence to a hen and chickens. A true version of the story soon after came out, and Mr. George Frederic was compelled to undergo the ridicule of all his acquaintance.

Mary Bowline became Mrs. Thomas Kelson on "Thanksgiving-day-night," as the New England folks call it, on which joyful occasion the flag-staff was rigged "all a-tanto," and the colors kept flying from eight o'clock in the morning till sunset; according to the regulations of the naval service, and were also hoisted the next day.

It was a leading article in Mary's consent to the marriage, that her husband should give up going to sea, which he and her father contended did not include or contemplate his probably making a coasting "trip," if business required, and Mary at last consented to admit the exception. The bridge at the Devil's Gap was substantially repaired, and was often visited by Mary and her husband; and Jade's Walk was long celebrated as a favorite evening stroll when the weather permitted, not only with young lovers, but even with "old married fudges," as young ladies who are husband-hunting very politely call them.

> [2] Yoho, an animal, probably the ourang-outang, in whose existence sailors are firm believers, and of whose courage, intelligence, cunning, malicious and mischievous disposition, they tell wonderful stories. The word seems to be a corruption of Dean Swift's "Yahoo."

OLD CUFF

"Qualia multa mari nautæ patiuntur in alto!"
Virgil.

What Yankee man-of-war's-man is there, ashore or afloat, who has "helped Uncle Sam," any time between the beginning of the "long embargo," and the year 1827, who does not know or has not heard of Old Cuff? His real patronymic appellation is nobody's business;—perhaps it would puzzle himself to give any account of it: nor is it worth while to inquire how the name of Cuff, generally bestowed upon the woolly-headed and flat-nosed descendants of Ham, should be given to a white man; and as for the *prænomen*, as the Romans would call it, of "old," it is well known to all my short-jacketed readers, that it seldom has, in "sea dic." or nautical language, any reference to antiquity on the part of the bearer thereof; but is merely a familiar or affectionate distinction; as the commander of a merchantman, although perhaps under twenty years of age, is invariably called the "old man," by all hands on board.

Old Cuff, when I knew him, was just turned of forty, and was, of course, of venerable standing; as it is I presume, well known to every body that a sailor's life does not average much more than forty years, from exposure, hardships, and privations. Though not stricken in years, according to the usual signification of the phrase, Old Cuff had certainly *lived a great deal*, and had seen a great deal, there being scarcely a habitable corner of the world that he had not visited, or of the private history and internal economy of which he could not relate many anecdotes; so that he might, without arrogance or vanity, have assumed to himself the proposed motto of the Jesuits:

"Quæ regio in terris nostri non plena laboris!"

He commenced his career as cook and cabin-boy on board a "horse-jockey;" one of those vessels which carry horses, mules, and other cattle to the West Indies; a title bestowed upon them by sailors, who are very much in the habit of indulging in that figure of speech called by rhetoricians metonymy; in this instance applying the genuine name of all Connecticut men, and some Rhode Islanders, to a fore-topsail schooner, or hermaphrodite brig, as the case might be. He was next, by a sort of metamorphosis, or rather metastasis, not uncommon with those of "steady habits," a travelling tin-pedler; and his adventures and hard bargains, during a visit or two to the western and southern states, might prove highly entertaining to my readers, had I not seen some twenty or thirty of them lately going the rounds of the newspapers, which Old Cuff has often very gravely assured us, in our "quarter watches" in the main-top, were actually perpetrated by himself. By a transition still easier, and perhaps more natural, from a tin-pedler he transmuted himself into an itinerant preacher, and from conscientious motives endeavored to repair the injury he had done to the pockets of his customers with his white-oak nutmegs, horn gun-flints, and bass-wood cucumber seeds, by supplying them with pure unadulterated orthodox Calvinism, fresh from the Saybrook Platform. Nor did he confine his usefulness to beating the "drum ecclesiastic;" during the long winters in the country, he "kept school," as it is somewhat perversely called; whereas, in nine cases out of ten, it is the school that "keeps" the schoolmaster.

But "the sow that was washed returned to her wallowing in the mire;" and in like manner Cuff left off steering the souls of sinners through the temptations and sorrows of this wicked world, or the infant mind through the intricacies of a—b ab, and once more betook himself to steering vessels across the ocean. He went to sea as mate, and shortly after as master, of a merchantman. He was chiefly employed in the West India trade.

It has been said, that all, or nearly all, the Americans taken on board piratical vessels in the West Indies and parts adjoining, are natives of New-England; and it is gravely stated as a reason, that in consequence of the immense trade between that section of the Union and those islands, and the neighboring parts of the main land, that are the chief scenes of piratical depredation and resort; the crews of the New-England vessels trading, and occasionally smuggling, in bye-ports, become gradually and imperceptibly acquainted with those of piratical vessels frequenting those bye-ports and obscure harbors, for the purpose of refitting their vessels or disposing of their plunder; and that these acquaintances ripen into intimacies, that terminate in a strong cord with a running noose in the end of it. The deduction is perfectly logical, and it only remains to substantiate the premises; and these, I fear, may be proved, in but too many cases, to be based upon too solid a foundation to be overthrown by all the incredulous writhings of national pride. Be that as it may, the atrocities of Gibbs and others have recently proved, that total depravity is approached as nearly by the natives of New-England as by any of our Christian brethren.

In process of time the subject of our narrative grew tired of stowing molasses, feeding horses, or throwing them overboard, and "dodging" from island to island, and entered the naval service of the United States. The vessel to which he was attached was stationed in the West Indies, and had been on her station but a very short time, before that scourge of no small portion of the western world, the yellow fever, made its appearance on board. Our navy certainly was not then under so good regulations as at present. The medical department might perhaps be almost as good then as it now is, or rather as it was when I was in the service; the disgracefully penurious compensation allowed our naval surgeons rendering their station contemptible and degrading in the estimation of medical men of any pride or ability. Besides this, the sick at sea can never receive assistance from female attendance; for although some may deem it altogether imagination, there *is* something so soothing to the sick or wounded man in those thousand nameless acts of kindness that none but woman can think of, and none but woman perform, that, after one or two visits from the doctor, the patient feels wonderfully inclined to dispense with his further attendance: nay, when languishing on that bed from which he is doomed never to rise, his pillow is softer when arranged by woman's hand; his parched and clammy lips seem to recover their healthy freshness when woman administers the cooling draught. When I die, grant, kind Heaven! that the last earthly sound that murmurs in my "death-deafened" ear may be the kind, soothing, pitying voice of woman. When this worn-out hulk, strained fore and aft by exposure and hard service, its upper works crank with vexations and disappointments, shall be hauled up high and dry upon the lee-side of death's cove, may the last that "shoves off" from alongside be woman—I care not whether wife or stranger.

In addition to the want of proper attention, a sick sailor is invariably an object of contempt and disgust to his officers: they cannot forbear regarding with contempt a man who is reduced to mental and bodily imbecility by a disease that *they* do not and perhaps never did feel: his pale, emaciated, and squalid appearance excites disgust. I have made these remarks to illustrate what, on the authority of Old Cuff, took place on board the U. S. ship——.

Owing to the negligence or imbecility, or both, of the medical department on board, little or no provision was made for the sick. They lay about on the forecastle or the booms, and the dead were collected, sewed up in their hammocks, "ballasted," and hove overboard, every morning before the decks were washed, that is, between day-break and sunrise. This duty was generally performed by the master-at-arms and ship's corporal, familiarly called throughout the service "Jack Ketch and his mate;" but in this particular ship, and for the time being, they received the more apposite title of ship's "turkey buzzards." I ought to have mentioned, that in obedience both to naval etiquette and the superstitious feelings of the sailors, the burial service of the Episcopal Church was regularly read over the result of the ship's turkey buzzards' researches above or below deck.

Old Cuff, who had been on shore with a watering party, where he had made a pretty heavy libation of new rum, came on board at sunset; but having a somewhat confused recollection of the "bearings and distances" down the fore-ladder, he wisely concluded to set up his tabernacle for the night upon the boom. Long before midnight he perceived the symptoms of the cruel disorder that had so fearfully thinned the — —'s complement. His distress increased every moment—he earnestly begged for a draught of water, but in vain, and before daylight he became insensible. In due time all hands were called; the resurrection-men commenced their examination, and receiving no intelligible reply to a sound kick upon our hero's ribs, the ship's corporal laid hold of him by the heels, and dragged him into the gangway, where the two functionaries declared him "dead enough to bury," and forthwith reported progress to that effect to the lieutenant of the morning watch. "Very well," said the officer. "Young gentlemen, have a couple of eighteen-pound shot got up; pass the word, there, for the sailmaker's mate. Boatswain's mate, call all hands to bury the dead. How many are there?" "Only one, sir." "Very well. Tell Mr. Quill to bring his prayerbook on deck."

The corpse was soon inclosed in its canvass coffin, with the shot attached to the feet. The captain's clerk commenced the funeral service in a hurried, monotonous tone, and had nearly got to the fatal "we therefore commit his body to the deep," the signal for launching, when the ceremony was interrupted, and the officers and crew horrified by a violent struggle of the supposed defunct, accompanied with angry ejaculations.

"What the devil are you about? Let me out, let me out; d—n your eyes, I ain't dead yet;—cut away your thundering hammock, and I'll let you know whether I'm dead or not. This is a pretty how-d'ye-do, to be giving a fellow a sea-toss before his time has come."

Half a dozen jack-knives were at work in an instant upon the stitches of the hammock that inclosed the dead-alive—their owners being in their eagerness utterly regardless of the risk of amputation to which their haste subjected Old Cuff's nose; who, having burst his cerements and shaken himself, was conducted below to the doctor.

Death, however, had not yet done with him. His next cruise was in the Patriot service. Nothing very particular took place, till being sent with a party "cutting out," as it is technically termed by seamen—that is, capturing and bringing out vessels lying at anchor in an enemy's port, he and several of his party were made prisoners, and, according to the murderous system of warfare going on between the Spanish royal forces and the insurgents, ordered to be shot. No great formality was ever used on these occasions, (the Catholic Church, of course, withheld her consolations from heretics,) and their preparations were nearly completed, when several dragoons dashed into the "plaza," bloody with spurring, fiery red with haste, announcing that the rebels were advancing in great force from the interior. The intelligence proved to be correct, but the executing party did not wait to ascertain that fact; they scampered off instantly, leaving the prisoners bound. The Patriots, of course, set them at liberty, and Old Cuff was thus rescued a second time from an "untimely grave." (By the way, I never saw any person, however old and infirm, who was willing to admit the grave "timely," at any age.)

After many wanderings and adventures, he entered another Patriot vessel, cruising off the mouth of the river Plata. After making some captures, they were one day suddenly surprised and completely hemmed in by a Spanish squadron, consisting of a frigate and four or five other smaller vessels. Finding escape impossible, the commander of the Patriot brig, an Englishman, determined to defend himself to the last extremity, at the same time using every exertion to escape, of which the swift sailing of his vessel held out some hopes. These hopes were, however, frustrated, in consequence of the brig losing several important spars, and being soon rendered almost a complete wreck. In this crippled and unmanageable condition, she drifted upon a small, low, island, at no great distance, but still kept up a fire from such of her guns as could be brought to bear, or rather such as she had men enough left to work, for, by this time, full two thirds of her crew were killed or wounded.—Finding it impossible to save his vessel, the commander, who was dreadfully wounded, and fast bleeding to death, recommended to the wretched survivors of his brave crew to save themselves by swimming. Old Cuff and eight or ten others, being all who were able or willing to try their chance, accordingly took to the water, and reached the island safely, Cuff himself being severely wounded. The island was very low, scarcely rising six feet from high-water mark, and completely covered with a species of wild vine, that, finding neither trees nor rocks to support it, had formed a perfect cover to the whole island, by twisting and interweaving its branches with each other, so as to form a vegetable carpet sufficiently firm and close, in nearly all parts, to support the weight of a man. Between this singular roof and the ground was a space of two or three feet, and within this space the unhappy seamen secreted themselves, not with the hope of escaping, but deferring the fate that they were certain awaited them. Accordingly, the Spaniards, after having boarded the wreck of the brig, and, according to custom, murdered the wounded and mangled the dead, landed a large party to complete the horrid tragedy by murdering the few unfortunate men whom they had seen swim to the island. These savages ran about the island, which it does not seem was more than a couple of acres in extent, yelling like wild beasts, and thrusting their swords and boarding pikes down among the vines, with the hope of piercing some of the objects of their revenge. One of them, who appeared to be an officer, stood for some minutes directly over and upon Old Cuff, and while giving directions to his men, repeatedly thrust his sword down through the sheltering vines. The weapon passed once between his arm and body, and once through his clothes, slightly grazing his side. His agony during these moments was horrible. To be dragged out, and murdered by inches, or stabbed to death where he lay, not daring to move, though the pressure of the wretch's weight who stood upon him was so painful, that he could scarce forbear crying out. Such seemed his inevitable fate. But he was doomed to undergo still greater agony. One of the unfortunate men was discovered and dragged out within a few yards of him. The incarnate demons were a full hour murdering him, stabbing and hacking him with their pikes and cutlasses in parts of the body where wounds would be exquisitely painful but not mortal. The shrieks of the unhappy man were dreadful, the more so, as every one of his companions expected every moment to share his fate. The approach of night at length put an end to the dreadful scene, and the disappointed hell-hounds returned to their ships.

The next morning, the Spanish squadron sailed round the island, pouring upon every part of it discharges of grape and canister shot, that proved fatal to several of the unfortunate men concealed upon it. They also landed again, and attempted to set fire to the vines and dry grass, but providentially without much effect. They continued, however, to blockade the little island for two days longer, when they were compelled, by bad weather, to stand out to sea. Having ascertained that the Spanish murderers were gone, the miserable remnant of the brig's crew ventured from their hiding-places, almost exhausted with hunger, thirst, and terror. The main land was in possession of the Patriot, or Buenos Ayrean troops, but was more than two miles distant; and they consequently had no alternative but to swim to it; which they accordingly attempted, being extremely apprehensive that the Spaniards would return. The passage across the straits was long and tedious; and their hopes of ultimate success for a long time doubtful. When about half way across, one of their number declared that he was too much exhausted to go any farther, and after a few words of encouragement from his companions, suddenly exclaimed, "good bye," and sunk for ever. The rest, five in number, succeeded in reaching the shore, just at sunset.

After wandering about a mile, they came to a sort of farm-house, the mistress of which was employed baking bread. Delirious with hunger, three of them tore the half-baked bread from the oven, and devoured large quantities of it. They all died in horrible agonies before day-break. The other two, more prudent, or having arrived at that point of starvation, at which pain had ceased, ate nothing but such light food as was provided for them by the humane Buenos Ayreans. In a few days they were quite recovered from the effects of such prolonged hunger, and made the best of their way towards the city of Buenos Ayres. Here Old Cuff found several Republican officers, by whose influence he obtained a commission as lieutenant of artillery. But, not altogether liking the land service in the first place, and having moreover ascertained that the Republic of Buenos Ayres, like that of the United States of America, was not willing to vouchsafe any thing but hard knocks, and no pay, to those who stood by her and supported her, in her fierce struggle for independence, he very deliberately disrobed himself of his regimentals, laid aside his epaulets, tore up his commission, and returned in a merchantman to his native country. Not long after his return, he entered in the United States service, and it was then, that I first saw him. He was made captain of the main-top before sailing, and I was, myself, shortly after, stationed in the main-top likewise.

On the passage out to the Pacific, and when nearly in the latitude of Cape Horn, we, that is to say, a midshipman, Old Cuff, and thirteen men, were all very comfortably asleep in the main-top, the weather being remarkably mild for that high latitude. It was the middle watch, from midnight to four in the morning; Cuff was lying athwart-ships, or cross-wise of the top, and near the fore part of it, where there were no topsail nor topmast-shrouds to prevent a fall. There was, indeed, a "life-line" from the first topmast-shroud, on each side, to the cap-shore amidships, but it was breast high, and of course afforded no security to a man who was lying down. My head was pillowed upon Old Cuff's side, the midshipman's head was on my breast, and the rest of my earthly tabernacle was occupied as a bolster by as many of the quarter watch as could get near me. About two o'clock, I was suddenly awoke by the abduction of my living pillow, and the consequent collision of my head against one of the top burton-blocks. At the same time I heard a whizzing noise, like a rope running swiftly through a block, but none of us took much notice of it; the midshipman growled some at my fidgeting about while fixing another pillow, but the absence of the captain of the top was not perceived. At seven bells, or half past three, the midshipman of the quarter deck hailed, "Main-top there! answer your musters, in the main-top."

"You had better keep awake in that main-top;" thundered the lieutenant of the deck, through his trumpet, "you have lost one of your number already by your sleeping."

All this was "Hebrew Greek" to us, but in a short time the sentry at the cabin door "reported" eight bells; the larboard watch was called, the wheel, look-outs, and tops relieved, and the mystery of the loss of "one of our number" fully explained.

"What did you heave Old Cuff out of the top for?" said the first one of the larboard watch, whose head came through the "lubber's hole."

"When did Old Cuff, fall from aloft?" said the next that ascended to the "sky-parlor."

"Old Cuff is done for," said the third that came up.

"He has broke his back-bone short off;" said a fourth, with his jacket over one shoulder.

"Yes, and four of his ribs to boot;" added a fifth, who was determined the story should not want particulars.

"The doctor says he won't live till morning," said a sixth, who had not yet hove in sight, speaking below the top, as Hamlet senior's ghost does under the stage.

By this time, the whole of the alarming intelligence was fairly expended, the remaining eight, who made up the sum total of the quarter watch, having no farther particulars of consequence to communicate, the first six who came up having already broken every bone in poor Old Cuff's body, and "abridged his doleful days" to boot. By dint of cross questioning, we made shift to ascertain, that about two o'clock, or four bells, Old Cuff had rolled away from under my head, and over the top brim. Fortunately he fell across the fore-topmast studding-sail tack, which broke two of his ribs and his fall, and thence he had gently canted over, and alighted upon the quarter-deck hammock-nettings, nearly knocked overboard the half-asleep main-topman who was perched up there as a look-out. He recovered, however, in two or three weeks, in spite of the doctor's prognostication.

Upon our arrival at Valparaiso, a similar accident happened to him, that, taken in connexion with the first, formed what newspaper folks call "a singular coincidence." A considerable portion of the town, or city, or whatever it may be, of Valparaiso, is built upon and among several high, rocky, precipitous cliffs, to which sailors, time out of mind, have given the names of fore, main, and mizen tops. It is, perhaps, another singular coincidence, that the name "main-royal," that belongs of right to the highest sail in a ship, is applied to the lowest part of said respectable sea-port. The "main-top" is the favorite resort of sailors, but I cannot say much in praise of the moral virtues of the denizens of said main-top. They do, indeed, enjoy a better prospect and a purer air than their fellow citizens, whose location is somewhat nearer the level of the sea, so that their physical elevation gives them many advantages that serve to compensate them for what they lack through moral debasement. The part of the main-top that fronts the bay, is a sheer precipice of two hundred feet; but on another part, it is simply too steep for any animal but a monkey to make a highway of. Down this part Old Cuff, who was ashore on liberty, and who likewise had his "beer aboard," contrived to trundle himself, and was picked up as dead in the street below. He, however, recovered from this tumble as speedily as he did from the other, having received but little damage, except some half dozen cuts and bruises in the countenance, which he held in but light esteem, being by no means vain of his beauty. I do not recollect that he met with any more accidents of consequence during the cruise. He returned to America in the frigate, and I have since been told that he had received a gunner's warrant, in consideration of his long, and, in his way, faithful services and many wounds; for I believe he had been wounded in almost every naval engagement during the last war.

THE RIVALS

In the neighborhood of Genoa, there lived some years since an old gardner, who, by dint of most unwearied industry and great skill in his vocation, had acquired sufficient property to enable him to purchase the farm that he had hitherto occupied as a tenant. His name was Pietro Morelli. He had no family but an only child, his daughter Bianca, at the time of our story in her nineteenth year, and who assisted her father in such branches of his occupation as were not inconsistent with her sex.

Bianca Morelli possessed all that peculiar beauty for which her countrywomen are celebrated; namely, regular Grecian features, a clear brunette complexion, a profusion of raven black tresses, and soft, languishing, and most intelligent black eyes. Her form was tall, slender, and graceful, while her disposition was amiable and gentle as her face was lovely. The beautiful Bianca was well known, and admired by most of the inhabitants of Genoa; and her sweet face and modest deportment were always, with them, irresistible inducements to purchase her fruits and flowers, when she accompanied her father to market, or visited the city alone.

It so chanced one day, that a party of Austrian officers, who had recently been quartered in Genoa, rode out to old Morelli's house, to enjoy what was to them both a luxury and a novelty;—eating fruit fresh gathered from the trees and vines.—Old Morelli was by no means ambitious of this honor; he was too firm a friend to his degraded, but still redeemable country, to desire any intimacy with the military myrmidons of her Austrian despot; so that, notwithstanding the grave and correct moral deportment which is said to be the general characteristic of the Austrian officers, and of which he was aware, he saw their approach to his humble dwelling with a vague feeling of distrust and anxiety.

Among his military visitors was General Baron Plindorf, one of those "gallant militarists" that abound in all standing armies; whose sole employment, during the "piping times of peace," and in the course of a soldier's unsettled and rambling life from quarters to quarters, seems to be, to abuse the rights of hospitality, by carrying disgrace and infamy into every domestic circle to which they can by any means obtain admittance. It ought to be a source of pride to my countrymen, that they are more of a marrying people than the English or French, and do not regard women in the same degraded light as a gambler does a pack of cards, that are to be shuffled and played with for a while, and then thrown away. Our naval and military officers are rather remarkable for their readiness to form matrimonial connexions; while on the other hand, our young men who are educated to the law, physic, or divinity, never think of "setting up for themselves," till they are "accommodated," as Bardolph says, with a wife, whom the three learned professions regard as indispensable as Starkie on Evidence to the first; a pocket case of instruments, or Dawes' Midwifery, to the second; or a Brown's Concordance, or Calmet's Dictionary, to the third.

Such characters as I have alluded to, it would seem, are extremely common in the British army; and it is to be presumed that they are not less plentiful in the armies of the European powers; though it does not appear that the community at large gain wisdom and caution from the mournful experience of their neighbors, but rather the reverse; for, if we may believe their own writers, the footsteps of a regiment, moving about through different country quarters, are marked by more incurable evils, and more true horrors, than the march of an invading army through a hostile, and resisting country. It has been said of the Turkish army, that they are far more formidable to their friends, than to their foes; if any dependence can be placed in those numerous writings, professing to be descriptions of English manners, that find their way across the Atlantic, the same may be said of that portion of the British army that is on the "home station."

Baron Plindorf was an unprincipled libertine, cold, selfish, and unfeeling. He was eminently successful too in his diabolical enterprise, although there was nothing prepossessing in his person or in his manners; but he had the reputation of being irresistible, and of course he was so; for, whatever may be the reason, it is a most lamentable fact, that to be called a professed rake, and reputed father of some half dozen illegitimate children, is a man's most irresistible passport, and powerful recommendation to the good graces and smiles of the fair sex at large; every woman is instantly eager to call into exercise that fascinating treachery that ought to doom its possessor to public infamy and detestation. The next most powerful introduction to female favor, is to be a widower or a foreigner; though the latter is almost uniformly "brought to bay," in a few months after marrying in this country, by a wife and some eight or nine children from "over the water;" the very next foreigner that comes over *alone*, is snapped up in the same way—but enough of this.

He saw and admired Bianca, as Milton's devil saw and admired Paradise, with the prospective determination of destroying its calm happiness forever.

There was one of old Morelli's visitors, how ever, upon whom the lovely Bianca's beauty, modesty and grace, had made an impression of a far different kind. This was the young Count Altenberg, acknowledged on all hands to be the most accomplished gentleman, and most amiable and estimable young man, in that division of the Grand Duke's army. Frederic Count Altenberg, was the son of Rudolf, of Altenberg, an officer of high rank, who had served his country faithfully, but ineffectually, in opposing the headlong progress of the blood-stained Corsican. The old Count had, within two years, been gathered to his fathers, and his title and estates had descended to his only son, then in his twenty-third year. At an early age Frederic had received a commission as captain of cavalry, but as every body knows that promotion is slower in the army of his Tuscan highness than in that of any other European power, he still remained a captain of cavalry, and probably would do so unto his dying day. It was his determination, as soon as he returned to Florence, to resign his commission, and retire to his paternal estates in Germany, but "diis aliter visum est," the fates had decreed otherwise. An indulgent and fond father had spared no pains nor expense in educating this his only child, and that child had amply repaid his care.

Educated most carefully in the strictest principles of the Christian religion and morality, generous, brave, and humane, he was, when he arrived to man's estate, the *beau ideal* of a man of honor, and a gentleman. By neither of these terms, do I mean that fashionable personage whose god is himself, who would seduce his friend's wife or sister, or strip him of his last farthing at a gaming table, and then shoot him through the head, by way of making amends; or who scrupulously discharges all gambling and betting debts; utterly neglecting those of the poor tradesman, or industrious mechanic, but the "justum et tenacem propositi virum," of the Roman satirist, the man of strict integrity, and immoveable principles. Frederic had long since formed a determination, that as soon as he could clear himself from the army, he would most seriously incline himself to the search of a wife. Although considered by his fair-haired countrywomen as lawful game, and moreover as one who was well worth securing, he had hitherto escaped any very serious affection of the heart. The beauty of Bianca, so unlike what he had been accustomed to, had charmed him; her unaffected modesty had commanded his respect; and when he left her father's house, he determined that it was absolutely necessary to his comfort, to see her again. Accordingly the next evening, and the next, and many succeeding evenings, saw him riding towards old Morelli's cottage; and he had long been convinced, from what he saw of Bianca, that he had at last found the woman who only of all her sex could make him happy; which is precisely what every man thinks when in love for the first time, and alters his mind in less than a twelvemonth. Nor was the gentle Bianca insensible to his evident partiality for her society; she detected herself repeatedly, without being willing to acknowledge it, wishing for evening—disappointed, if the sky was overcast, or the weather rainy—fluttering with hope, and joy, and indescribable emotion, at the sight of every distant cavalier, or at the sound of every horse's hoof upon the road towards the city. The warm blush, the speaking smile, the sparkling eyes, of both the lovely Bianca and the young soldier, would have been sufficient to convince the most casual observer that there existed the most decided case of a *serious affection of the heart*. Of course old Morelli's eyes had long before seen and made due report to his mind, as to what was the true state of his daughter's and the young nobleman's affection. Ever anxious for Bianca's happiness and welfare, and still more so now that she had attained that age when female beauty is both mature and fully developed, while at the same time it has all the freshness and rosiness of youth, he became exceedingly alarmed and agitated at the too obvious state of the lover's sentiments. He sought and soon obtained an opportunity of speaking to him, and Frederic was at that moment anxious to see the old man, and putting to him that question, which, whether addressed to the fair one in person, or to her pa and ma, is always embarrassing; always makes a man look, and feel, and act, very much like a fool; and when answered in the affirmative, is not unfrequently the forerunner of most sincere and hearty repentance. In fact, repentance being so often the consequence of marriage, (it is gravely asserted by some of the old fathers,) is in our mind reason why Catholics regard it (that is, the marriage, not the repentance) a sacrament, "because it produces repentance, which is a step towards grace." I am so far a Catholic, as to admit most cheerfully, that it is a holy state, and that there is no text in scripture more true, than that "it is not good for man to be alone;" still if I was about entering that holy state, I am sadly afraid that my feelings would be wholly uninfluenced by any hopes of approaching any nearer towards a state of grace, not even over the thorny path of the consequent repentance.

"Signior Count," began old Morelli, as soon as he had ascertained that they were alone, "you cannot suppose me ignorant of the cause of your frequent visits to my poor house, or that as a father I am so indifferent to my daughter's happiness as to see it without extreme anxiety."

"I was about speaking to you on the same subject," said Frederic, hesitatingly, "I have already told you that it is my fixed determination to leave the army, and retire to peaceful life on my own estate. But although my fortune is princely, I feel it would be valueless without your lovely daughter. Signior Morelli, I love Bianca; I have made no attempt to conceal it from you; were my intentions dishonorable, do you not think that I would endeavor to hide them from a father's eye? Do you take me for the bold, hardened libertine that would trample under foot a father's hospitality to accomplish his daughter's infamy? You wrong me, Signior, if you do; but I cannot believe that in your dislike to my country, you believe all her children base and unprincipled."

"Nay, my young friend, I believe nothing of that detestable character can be laid to your charge. But consider for a moment the immense distance between you. You are an Austrian nobleman of high rank and of ancient family, and Bianca, on the other hand, can boast of nothing but her good name and unsullied character."

"And does not virtue outweigh all worldly titles and distinctions in the estimation of every rational and virtuous mind? Your lovely daughter's virtues are far superior to my empty titles or immense wealth. In accepting me as a husband, she would confer honor, not receive it. She descends to my level; I do not and cannot rise to hers—the gain, the honor, the advantage, of such an alliance would be mine."

"You are an enthusiast, Count; your passion has gotten the better of your judgment; that you love my daughter *now* I am perfectly willing to admit, but that your affection for her will sustain the shock of the ridicule of your associates, or the contempt and neglect with which your proud and titled kindred and countrymen will treat such a wife, whom they regard so infinitely beneath them, I very much doubt. Matches between people so widely separated by difference of rank, however arbitrary and absurd those distinctions may be, can never produce aught but unhappiness."

The Count was, notwithstanding the reasonableness of old Morelli's objections, as politely obstinate as young lovers are to old fathers, when those old fathers condescend to reason with them instead of resorting to the more usual and summary process of turning them out of doors, and forbidding their daughters to hold any farther communication with the dear rejected. In a subsequent conversation with his daughter he found that both parties were nearly in the same situation; Bianca with many tears confessing her love for Count Altenberg. There seemed then but two chances to escape from this state of embarrassment, namely, either to consent to Frederic's offer of his hand, or to send his daughter to an aged relative at Padua; which last plan was liable to so many objections that, after ruminating upon it for two days, he gave it up, and permitted the lovers to enjoy each other's society, though without giving a direct consent to their union.

In the mean time the libertine Plindorf was plotting destruction to the fair Bianca. He well knew that such a woman was not to be carried by the usual attacks of flattery and money; which last, whether administered in the form of rich and dazzling presents, or simply by itself, is almost uniformly found irresistible by old and young women, according to their tastes or situations; his plan was therefore necessarily more deeply laid than any he had heretofore practised. It was accordingly with a mingled emotion of pleasure and anxiety that he watched the progress of the attachment between the two lovers. Although he feared that her attachment might prove too strong to be easily shaken, he still hoped to be able to involve them in embarrassments, and then, under the guise of friendship and pretence of assisting them, further his own unprincipled views. The impetuosity of the young nobleman, and certain circumstances that he could not foresee, brought the affair to a crisis both unexpected and disastrous.

The Baron walked out one afternoon towards old Morelli's cottage, without any fixed object, for the unequivocal dislike that Bianca always manifested towards him, had determined him to cease his visits to her father's house, and make his approaches with the utmost caution. He approached a retired spot near the house, where the lovers frequently strolled to enjoy each other's society. Bianca had also wandered there in the hope of meeting Frederic. She was occupied gathering flowers, and arranging them in a nosegay, when a rustling among the bushes attracted her attention. She hastily advanced towards the spot, exclaiming "Frederic!" when the Baron, the man whom of all others she most hated, and, for some undefinable reason or other, feared, stood before her.

"Fairest Bianca!" said Plindorf, advancing, "let me not alarm you, although I am not the person you seemed to expect; let me hope that the presence of a friend and well-wisher to both parties is not disagreeable or terrifying."

Bianca, exceedingly alarmed at the sudden apparition of one so odious to her, had sunk down upon a rude seat. The Baron approached, and taking her passive hand, seated himself by her side. Mistaking the cause of her quietness, he ventured to press her trembling hand to his lips, and attempted to pass his arm around her waist. The terrified girl suddenly sprang from him with a loud shriek, and attempted to fly; the Baron again caught her hand, and endeavored forcibly to detain her. At that moment the Count Altenberg suddenly stood before them, his eyes flashing with rage.

"Villain," he exclaimed, as soon as his passion would give him utterance, "deceitful, cowardly scoundrel! take that"—striking him a violent blow, and at the same time unsheathing his sword.

The Baron was ready in an instant, but as soon as the Count felt his weapon clashing against that of his antagonist, he became at once cool and composed. Not so Plindorf, he dashed at his more youthful opponent with a fury that had well nigh brought the combat to a speedy and fatal issue, and compelled Frederic to exert his utmost skill. The peculiar danger of his situation, and almost certain death or remediless disgrace that awaited him, even if victorious, for having struck his superior officer, were present to the mind of the young officer in gloomy and terrible colors; but it was too late to retract. The fury of the Baron threw him off his guard—he received a mortal wound, and fell dead. The unhappy survivor stood for some seconds gazing upon the inanimate form before him; and as the features, after being convulsed for a little, settled into the iron stiffness of everlasting sleep, he uttered a deep sigh, and unconsciously moved away from the spot. At this moment Bianca, recovering from the stupor into which the terrible scene had thrown her, earnestly enjoined him to fly.

"There is no time to be lost," said the agonized girl; "fly at once to the sea-side—go on board any vessel that is about sailing—in a few days, I doubt not, this unhappy business will be hushed up."

"And where shall I fly?" said the Count; "where shall I go from *him*?"—indicating the slain nobleman by a movement of his hand—"do you know what I have done? I have in one moment sentenced myself to death; or, what is worse, to disgraceful and infamous privation of all my honors and rank."

"No, no—there is yet time—go immediately on board the American man-of-war in the harbor—they dare not search for you there."

With many entreaties and tears, she prevailed upon him to take measures for his safety; and with a lightened heart saw him, from the windows of her father's house, reach the water-side uninterrupted; saw him leave the shore in a little skiff, when the intervention of other objects hid him from her sight.

The two officers were missed that evening. The dead body of the ill-fated Baron was soon discovered; for many had seen him going towards old Morelli's cottage; but no traces of Count Altenberg have ever been discovered. Morelli and his daughter underwent a rigid examination; the former could throw no light upon the mysterious disappearance of Frederic, but Bianca, the pure-minded Bianca, unreservedly related all the circumstances. The examining officers forwarded an elaborate and circumstantial report of the case to Vienna, accompanied by an earnest petition in behalf of the absent Count. The Emperor laid the affair before a select council of old and experienced officers, who, after due deliberation, and weighing the excellence of Altenberg's character against the depravity of his slain antagonist, suggested the expediency of pardoning the offender. Proclamation was accordingly made to that effect, but without success.

The unhappy Bianca lived to experience, in all its bitterness, that "hope deferred that maketh the heart sick" and eventually breaks it. She died in less than two years after the flight of Frederic, a victim to a disorder that has no place in the catalogue of nosologists, and is not recognised as a malady; though it is as incurable and consigns almost as many victims to an untimely grave as consumption, with which it is very frequently confounded—I mean a broken heart. She was buried, according to her dying request, in the little arbor that Frederic had assisted her to erect and adorn, and where she had passed those most delightful moments in human existence, the days of the first love, and first courtship, of two young, affectionate, and virtuous beings. Blessed moments! that occur but once in the dreary threescore years and ten, and fade away before we have time to enjoy them, and we only become conscious of their existence from the certainty that they are gone for ever.

Several years ago, and, if I am not much mistaken, just after the peace of 1815, an officer, in full Austrian uniform, came on board one of our frigates then lying in the harbor of Genoa. From the richness of his regimentals, and a cross and ribbon in his button-hole, it was evident that the stranger was of high ancestral and military rank.

It so happened that he came on board just at "grog time," (four o'clock) in the afternoon; and during the interesting moment that sailors are discussing their whiskey—the whole Holy Alliance, with aids and prime ministers and protocols, might come on board, and balance Europe, or upset the scales, just as unto them seemed good, expedient, or politic, without attracting any attention from these short-jacketed philosophers; unless indeed some straggler from the upper deck might come below, and casually inform his messmates, that "there was a whole raft of soger officers on the quarter-deck;" for be it known to all concerned, that the word number is seldom or never used by nautical philologists to designate things numerable, it is always "a *raft* of women," "a raft of marines," &c. I could easily go on to show that the word "raft" is a good phrase, and peculiarly applicable to women and marines; but I must resist the temptation of convincing the public, that sailors are as deeply versed in the mysteries of their mother-tongue, as many of those who stay ashore all their life-times, and make dictionaries.

The day after the arrival of this military stranger, it was ascertained by the crew, that there was a supernumerary on board by the name of Williams; for it is as impossible for the commander and officers of a man-of-war to keep a secret in the cabin, as it is for twelve "good men and true," locked up in a jury-room. The new-comer seemed to have free access to the cabin, and was treated with much respect by the officers, but it was soon observed, by the seamen, that he never went on shore. In the course of a few months, he was put on board a homeward-bound ship: and when the crew of the frigate returned to America, they saw him again in New York, abandoned to intemperance.

When on a cruise in the Pacific, the crew of one of the light vessels of the squadron were transferred to the frigate that I was on board of; their time of service having expired. Among them was Williams; and from his shipmates I learned the above particulars. In person, he was about five feet eight or nine inches high, and extremely well made. With the rest of the schooner's people, he had been on shore on liberty, where he had been continually intoxicated; his face was in consequence bloated, and his eyes bloodshot and swollen.

I further understood, that he would get drunk whenever he had an opportunity, and when intoxicated he was completely insane. He was also subject to fits of temporary derangement, independent of the insanity produced by excessive drinking, when he was both furious and dangerous; and it was always necessary, on such occasions, to confine him in irons. He was also represented as being extremely reserved, and refusing to answer any questions respecting himself, whether addressed to him by officers or seamen; that he spoke with fluency all European languages, on which account, he was extremely useful as an interpreter, both on the coast of Peru and Chili, and on that of Brazil; that he was a first rate swordsman, either with the small-sword or sabre, and a dead shot with pistol or musket.

During his short stay on board the frigate, he had one of his temporary fits of insanity, probably induced by excessive intemperance, if intemperance admits of superlatives, while on shore. He suddenly started up from a gloomy, stupid reverie, and ran about the decks like a wild beast, striking and knocking down, every one he met; then all at once plunging down the main-hatchway, he attempted to get possession of one of the boarding cutlasses, but fortunately they were well secured in the racks over the guns, to prevent them from falling down with the motion of the ship. Before he could make a second and more regular attempt, he was secured, put in irons, and placed under charge of a sentry. Had he succeeded in arming himself, he would have made bloody work on the quarter-deck, towards which it seemed evident he was steering his course; the uniforms of the officers, and marine guard, probably calling up to his diseased imagination, and memory, scenes of by-gone days connected with or the remote cause of his present insanity. The officers seemed to be so far acquainted with his history, as to feel compassion for his most wretched situation; for, as he manifested no symptoms of derangement the next morning, except his usual deep melancholy, he was discharged from confinement, to the great astonishment of the ship's company; for though the discipline on board was as mild as it could be consistent with the preservation of good order, and perfectly free from that tyranny that but too many of our navy officers think indispensable, they certainly were not accustomed to seeing such quiet jail deliveries.

Williams afterwards re-entered on board the same vessel that he came from, and I lost sight of him of course, as our frigate was on the point of quitting the station to return home. He has, in all probability, long ere this, reached the grave towards which he seemed to be hurrying, with all the speed of intemperance and insanity combined.

MORTON

CHAPTER I

Bel and the Dragon's chaplains were
More moderate than these by far:
For they, poor knaves, were glad to cheat,
To get their wives and children meat;
But these will not be fobb'd off so,
They must have wealth and power too;
Or else with blood and desolation
They'll tear it out o' th' heart o' th' nation. —

Hudibras.

Notwithstanding the success of the many daring and lawless adventurers who visited the Pacific Ocean, or "Great South Sea," as it is called in the maps and travels of the period, and who reaped many a golden harvest there, about the time of the first James and Charles of England, the coasts washed by its waves were but seldom visited, and its waters seldom ploughed by any other keels than those of discovery ships for many years. Chili, Peru, Mexico, and California, after having been definitively ceded to the Spanish crown, constituted an El Dorado, whose gates could only be opened by a formal declaration of war. Spain was generally considered by the other European powers to have a double right to South America, namely, that of discovery and conquest; and after an ineffectual struggle to wrest the golden prize from the grasp of its legitimate possessor, England, and the rest of the "high contracting powers," acquiesced in her possessing it, the more readily because they wished the same kind of title should be acknowledged in their own case. Accordingly discovery and conquest have, to this day, been considered as good and lawful titles, and a sort of deed of conveyance, on the part of the natives, to their discoverers and conquerors of all and sundry their lands and landed estates, together with their goods and chattels, when of any value.

His Most Catholic Majesty, then, finding his claim to the New World fully established, set about civilizing his new conquest in good earnest, and sending out swarms of priests, backed of course by the military portion of the secular arm, with glory to God on their lips, and hatred to his creatures in their hearts, with the sword in one hand and the crucifix in the other, soon convinced the unhappy natives of their damnable heresies. Their simple religion was destroyed, millions perished by the sword or the tender mercies of the Holy Inquisition, and as many more in the mines; and civilization and religion kissed each other, and rested from their labors of love.

This was the most received method of converting whole nations at once, then in vogue—we Protestants of the present day are far more humane; we only distribute among the newly discovered nations of the earth, rum and Calvinism, gunpowder and the venereal disease, and with these powerful agents our missionaries and merchants, have succeeded in causing Dagon to bow down before them—over all the civilized world. New Holland seems to be the only uncivilized part of this watery ball, but New Holland holds out no temptations to the missionary; the inhabitants are a little too cannibally given, and martyrdom is altogether obsolete; besides, it is doubted by our soundest theologians whether Christianity was ever intended for a people so brutal and debased.

Spain, at the time I refer to, was renowned in arts and in arms; her commerce extended from the East to the West Indies, and she was for a time one of the most powerful of the kingdoms of Europe. Her priests, finding the New World a land overflowing, not exactly with milk and honey, but with what in all ages and in all countries is considered infinitely better, gold and silver, and abounding in every thing that could pamper the pride and gratify the sense, founded churches and monasteries, while her viceroys built cities and forts, and South America became the richest jewel in the diadem of His Catholic Majesty. To secure this jewel entirely to himself seems to have been his chief anxiety, and accordingly all foreigners were rigidly excluded from its sea-ports, and although the "Assiento," or contract for supplying the colonies with African slaves, was enjoyed successively by the English and French, both of whom successively abused it by smuggling immense quantities of their respective manufactures into those colonies, the duty of supplying them with European merchandise was carried on finally solely by means of register ships, as they were called, Cadiz being the only European port where they were permitted to load and discharge.

The whaling ships were only permitted to procure supplies, or "recruit," as our unctuous brethren of Nantucket call it, at certain fixed and well-fortified ports. Still even these managed to carry on quite a respectable business in the smuggling way, especially with the ports of Mexico and California.

But a new flea was about getting into Don Diego's ear—the peace of 1783, while it added an infant giant to the catalogue of earthly "principalities and powers," also liberated from the fetters of commercial, as well as political restraints, a people active, restless, daring, prying, and enterprising to the last degree; a people whose skill in navigation and swift-sailing vessels rendered them absolutely intangible to an enemy that took occasion to chase them, while their courage, when they thought proper to "stand to it," as dame Quickly says, made them dangerous antagonists. This the reader probably "guesses" must be brother Jonathan, and he guesses about right. The same spirit of restless curiosity that prompts a cat, when she sets up her Ebenezer in a new house, to examine every portion of it, from cellar to garret, seemed to have possessed our grandpas more strongly than it does us of the present age.

This national character of ours is owing doubtless to our having been placed by the hand of Heaven in an immense unexplored region, and was no doubt much increased by the spirit-stirring scenes of the revolutionary war, which beheld our "old continentals" one day ferreting out the long-tailed Hessians from the woods of Saratoga, and another "doing battle right manfullie" on the plains of South Carolina.

While they of the land service were pushing their advanced posts to the foot of the Rocky Mountains, our seamen were carrying our striped bunting into every portion of the navigable world. Such were the people whose arrival in the Pacific the Spanish commandantes and viceroys awaited with no small fear and trembling. They knew vaguely that we had just come off victorious from a long, fierce, and bloody struggle with powerful England, and while they consigned us pell-mell to the devil, as "malditos Americanos," they doubted whether we had the additional claim to go there upon the strength of being heretics. The captains of the guarda-costas redoubled their vigilance, and sailed in chase of not a few albatrosses and whale-spouts, such was the zeal that animated them.

I should have described these redoubtable crafts, the guarda-costas, before—they were armed vessels of different classes, varying from light frigates down to mere gunboats, and were distributed along the coasts to protect trade, and prevent smuggling.

When however these formidable strangers did arrive, the readiness with which they conformed to the numerous, and in most cases vexatious, port regulations, their quiet behavior on shore, and the many novelties and luxuries that they freely distributed to the port officers, completely blinded them to the instinctive disposition to trade that characterizes my beloved countrymen, especially the New Englanders, who were the first to carry our flag into the Pacific, as they were also the first to display it in Europe.

I have made these long-winded and apparently uncalled-for remarks partly to show my learning, but chiefly in conformity with the fashion of the day, that requires that every story, long or short, should be ushered in by at least one chapter of prefatory remarks. I do not intend to be so unreasonable; but before this my first chapter is finished, shall give my readers an idea of my purposed principal scene of operations.

If then, the reader will turn to the proper map, he will find in about the latitude of twenty-one north, Cape Corrientes; and not far from this three islands, called Las Tres Marias; the Three Marys, that is, so named after the three Marys of the New Testament.

Geographers, when they make maps, seem to start with the notion that there must be a certain number of islands, &c. inserted in each map; and when they have located the larger and more important ones within fifteen or twenty degrees of latitude and longitude of their proper places, which is as near as they commonly come to the truth, they proceed to distribute the remainder according to their own taste. In compliance with this fashion of theirs, they have laid down upon all modern maps, especially those that are called the best, and in nearly the latitude that I have above mentioned, and longitude that I have not, namely, about one hundred and fifteen west from Greenwich Observatory, a little island which they call Revalligigedos. I have passed twice over the spot where this little island with the big name "stays put," in all maps by them, and have conversed with many whalemen and others, who, taken collectively, have sailed over every square inch of salt water in that place, and none of them have seen it. So too, they have studded the ocean off Cape Horn so thickly with islands, that a landsman wonders how a ship of any size can manage to squeeze through into the Pacific. I have passed that cape three times, and have been working to windward off them some weeks, but although we always kept a bright look-out for ice islands and strange vessels, we never, to use a vulgar expression, saw "hide or hair" of these supererogatory islands.

But to return; in a direction nearly east from the Three Marys, the reader will find, on most maps, a small river, called by the Spaniards, in their usual style of bombast, El Rio Grande, or the Great River; though the identical legs that I now stand upon have waded across it at low water, and, except cutting my foot with an oyster-shell, there was nothing very remarkable in the exploit. At the mouth of this mighty stream is an island on which stands the town of St. Blas.

The Spaniards, as it is well known, when they discovered America, christened every cape, bay, mountain, river, island, rock, or shoal after some saint or other, but the learned are somewhat puzzled to know who this St. Blas can be. In my poor opinion, the difficulty is easily enough got over—the word Blas is only a corruption of Blast, and accordingly we shall find that St. Blast, properly so called, is neither more nor less than our old friend Æolus, of the heathen mythology, smuggled into the calendar, who, being the god of blasts and puffs, might well be canonized under the name of St. Blast, without doing violence to the tender consciences of the good Catholics. In this way, according to Dean Swift, Jupiter became Jew Peter, and by a natural transition, *Saint* Peter. Whether he is right or not, one thing is certain, that sundry temples, of which the veritable Jupiter has been "seized in fee tail," I think lawyers call it, from time immemorial, have quietly become "St. Peter's churches," to the great edification of the Christian world, and incredible advancement of religion and piety.

The island, upon which St. Blas is perched, slopes off gradually to the eastward, but to the south and west descends in a sheer precipice of two or three hundred feet in height. The town was taken and retaken several times during the sanguinary war of the Mexican revolution. The last time it was in the hands of the royalists, they compelled all the male inhabitants, and, report says, not a few women and children besides, that they suspected of favoring the Patriot cause, to leap off this precipice. Soldiers were stationed at the foot of the cliff, to despatch those who reached the bottom with any signs of life. This piece of information I had from a widow who kept a shop in the *Plaza*, and who also told me, "with weeping tears," that her husband was one of the number who took the fearful leap.

Rather on the north-west side, the hill is surmountable by a zig-zag path, up which a loaded mule can climb with some difficulty. On the west, or seaward, side, is a strip of flat land, of considerable width, on which formerly stood the royal arsenal, rope-walks, and warehouses, the ruins of which were standing in 1822, when I visited the place. On the western extremity of this level land is a small village, called, as usual in such cases, the Porte, or landing place. The bay, which is a fine harbor, sweeps far to the eastward, when the land, trending away to the southward, with a slight inclination westerly, becomes lost in the distance. The more immediate, or inner, harbor, is formed by a point of land opposite the Porte, on the southern extremity of which is a battery, formerly of considerable dimensions, and strength, but since suffered to decay, and is much reduced in effectiveness. It was intended to command the harbor and anchorage; but with Spanish artillerymen, a mile offing, and reasonably good weather, a ship would be as safe from its fire, for three months at least, as though she was all the while in London Docks.

At the distance of two or three miles from the usual anchorage, and forming an excellent leading mark for the bay, is Pedro Blanco, or the White Rock, of two hundred feet height, perfectly precipitous and inaccessible, and resembling a huge tower, rising abruptly from the sea.

Taken altogether, the bay of St. Blas forms a very beautiful prospect, with the Andes in the back ground, which, with their

"Meteor standard to the winds unfurl'd,
Look from their throne of clouds o'er half the world;"

its white sand beach, fading gradually away to the south and east, its town roosting on its barren rock, and indistinctly seen; its low lands covered with a luxuriant growth of lime and other trees; and lastly, by way of seasoning, its moschetoes and sand-flies.

CHAPTER II

A knight he was, whose very sight would
Entitle him mirror of knighthood.

Hudibras.

Tropical climates have certainly one advantage over all others, that is not to be held in light esteem. They have rainy and dry seasons, that are exclusively rainy and dry. During six months, or nearly as long, the windows of heaven stand wide open, by night and by day, and the liquid blessing descends upon the thirsty earth beneath "in one lot," as auctioneers say; while on the other hand, the dry season has its great and manifold advantages and pleasures. With us in the temperate zone, as geographers call it, I suppose, for want of another name, a man does not think of riding twenty miles without India rubbers, a great coat, boots, and an umbrella, to say nothing of an entire change of raiment, if he is a prudent, cautious old bachelor, or widower; and even then he is as likely to get a ducking as to have fine weather.

During a tropical dry season, on the contrary, a journey of two hundred miles may be safely undertaken, without any of these encumbrances; with two or three clean shirts, a man may scamper about for months, like a Roman light-infantryman, "impedimentis relictis," unless he should be so ill advised as to carry his wife and children with him.

Throughout the rainy season, many diseases arise, and make great destruction among those who remain on the sea-coast; those who can afford it, retreat to the more salubrious mountain regions, while, as aforesaid, those who stay behind, being generally the poor, the worthless, and the useless part of the community, fall victims to the numerous diseases generated by the excessive rains, and the then swampy condition of the country. This annual purgation of society, is perhaps another blessing of a tropical country. I know of more than one community, whose moral, and in some measure physical health, would in my mere mortal and short sighted notion of the fitness of things, be vastly benefited by the visitation of an energetic, wide sweeping epidemic. Human society is very like a grate full of ignited anthracite coal, those parts of it that have lost their combustibility, and become worthless, are constantly filtering down through the bottom of the grate; and so in society, those individuals, who are daily falling from a state of grace in the eyes of their fellow-worms, either as regards fashion, or property, or reputation, go to swell the number of the outcasts from the ranks of "good society;" a convenient phrase that has recently been invented, and signifies the speaker's own particular friends and acquaintances, though he and they may be at that very moment getting out stone on Blackwell's Island. So you see, reader, that it is fore-ordained, for I am a good deal of a fatalist, that one of the ingredients of civilized society should be a certain proportion of poor miserable devils, such as you and I both know.

It was just at the close of the rainy season, when Nature looked infinitely better and fresher for having her face washed, though she had been six months about it; the air seemed purer and more healthful, and the sky looked clearer and of a richer blue, for the half year's drenching; it was at this particular time of the year, that we have thought proper to raise the curtain, and introduce the reader into the business part of the story.

It was between ten and eleven o'clock in the forenoon, the land breeze had done blowing, and the usual interregnum of calm, previous to the commencement of the sea-breeze, had taken place—the broad bay lay like a huge mirror, varied indeed by the long and regular undulations of the swell from the main ocean, which, though perhaps sufficient to discompose a landman's stomach, would not affect that of a sailor, who would probably testify under oath, that the water was "just as smooth as a mill-pond." The pelican, that grave and contemplative bird, sat on the rocks near the water's edge, with his neck coiled up and stowed away in some recess in his capacious crop, the fish forgetting, or sailed on lazy wings across the bay, to seek some sequestered spot to doze away the time, and digest his huge breakfast—the graceful white crane of Mexico was wading about, flapping her wings, to drive the small fish into shoaler water, where she might pick them up at her leisure—the gaudy Spanish ensign, resembling three flannel petticoats, two red and one yellow, hung lifeless by its staff, as though said petticoats had just got through a hard day's washing—a soldier, with a paper segar in his mouth, was lounging backwards and forwards on that part of the parapet of the battery next the sea, while another, his counterpart, was "doing military duty" in the same soldierly manner on the quay opposite.

I may as well explain to the reader now as at a future time, that every collection of houses in South America, however small, has an open space in the centre, called the Plaza; and an American Spaniard could no more conceive of a town or village without such plaza, than he could form one of Mr. Locke's abstract ideas of a horse, which ceases to be an abstract idea the moment it becomes invested with a body, head, legs, mane, tail, saddle, bridle, belly-band, or crupper.

In the plaza of the Porte before mentioned was a multifarious assemblage: the barrack for a captain's guard, with the arms of the guard piled in front of it, formed one side, and the others were bounded by the quay or different buildings; a detachment of idlers were sunning themselves, and engaged in relieving each other from certain troublesome companions, that *invariably* infest the clothes and hair of all Spaniards and Russians, from the king to the beggar; jackasses, boys, and dogs occupied the rest of the square, and were differently engaged. At this moment a sergeant ran into the square, exclaiming, "el Commandante!" The military guard fell into their ranks at the tap of the drum, the idlers and boys took up a strong position in one corner, the jackasses were cudgelled into a retreat, while the dogs, like the pigs in New York, being free of the city, provided for themselves. A moment or two elapsed after these preparations had been made, when a party of mounted officers dashed into the square at full gallop, as the South Americans always ride. The guard presented arms, the dogs barked their congratulations, and the party, having lighted fresh segars, walked down to the quay, directly opposite which lay an old dismantled Spanish frigate, and moored alongside her was a schooner, whose formidable length of main boom, and raking masts, announced her both a clipper and a Yankee. She was indeed an American schooner, that had been taken "flagrante delicto," in the very act of smuggling, for which she was condemned, and her crew sent to the mines. Such was the jealousy of the "authorities," that they unshipped the rudder, and unrove the running rigging, for fear she might go to sea of her own accord, and resume her smuggling voyage without the assistance of human agency.

The party whom we have left smoking on the wharf, consisted of the military commandant, or governor, of St. Blas, Don Gaspar de Luna, Don Diego Pinto, the commander of a guarda-costa of eighteen guns, that lay in the offing, and which, to the most unpractised eye, bore about the same resemblance to an English or American man of war of the same class, as an old, worn-out jackass does to a handsome, high spirited, well groomed race-horse. The rest of the group was made up of young officers "of no mark or likelihood," and with whom we have nothing to do, with the exception of Don Gregorio Nunez, a dashing young cavalry officer, related to the viceroy, report said his natural son, and report said too that he was soon to marry the lovely niece of the governor; but the destinies were altogether of a different way of thinking. His character may be despatched in a few words—he was a vain coxcomb, his whole soul lay in his gorgeous uniform, and he had a mortal antipathy to any thing like duty.

Don Gaspar de Luna, the redoubted governor of St. Blas and its "dependencies," bore the rank of colonel in the Spanish army. He had seen some service, having been present at the memorable siege of Gibraltar, that excited first the astonishment and then the ridicule of all Europe— astonishment at the immensity of the armament prepared, and ridicule on account of its inefficiency, in wasting years before the place without doing any thing. An advanced party commanded by Don Gaspar, then a captain, had the good fortune to get soundly thrashed by a sallying detachment from the garrison; and the king of Spain was so delighted that *something* had been done, that he promoted the fortunate captain to a colonelcy.

In early life he had been in America with his regiment, where he had married a native Peruvian woman, by whom he had two daughters. In person he was about the middling height, and so far resembled an ellipse as this, that his transverse diameter nearly equalled his conjugate, or, in plain English, he was about as broad as long. He prided himself not a little upon being a "Castiliano," or genuine old Spaniard, and professed, and probably felt, the most implacable hatred to all heretics, especially English and Americans; but it was evidently an abstract feeling, for the moment a vessel of either nation arrived, which happened very often during the dry season, and the commanders began to make those little presents that they always found it for their interest to make, his orthodox zeal began, like Bob Acres' courage, "to ooze away through his fingers."

Although in the main a kind and indulgent father, his affections were centred in his niece, of whom we shall have occasion to speak more at large, whom he preferred to his daughter, and with good reason. He was fond of punch, such as he used to find in plenty and perfection on board the strange ships, and which he could drill none of his household into the art and mystery of making, except his niece; fonder of flattery, and compliment, and salutes, from the heretical captains; and perhaps fondest of all of invitations to dine on board such ships as seemed to hold out hopes of good cheer. When a foreign vessel arrived, one would think, from his parade and flourish, that he expected an invasion; but it was all show. He was fond of telling long stories, and of sitting long over the bottle, foregoing the usual luxury of the *siesta*, or nap after dinner, to enjoy the greater one of drinking; but, although his capacious stomach would contain an incredible quantity of wine, no one could say that he had ever been seen "the worse for liquor."

The duties of his station were but trifling; for, although St. Blas was a royal naval depot, the commanders of his majesty's ships almost invariably preferred Callao, on account of its vicinity to the viceregal court at Lima. Any other person would have pined to death in such a remote and solitary corner of the earth, without society and without employment; but Don Gaspar was one of those peculiarly constituted individuals, who, having neither the faculty to communicate or receive new ideas, are as happy and contented in one place as another. He had come down to the water side at full gallop, and at the imminent risk of his neck, in consequence of a report, that a large, armed English ship, that was known to be on the coast trading, was approaching the Bay of St. Blas.

The nautical commander, Don Diego Pinto, was a man of upwards of sixty years of age, who had grown grey in the navy of Spain, without seeing any service of consequence. He had followed one of the viceroys, to whom he was recommended, to Peru, and the viceroy thought he had sufficiently done his duty to his *protégé* by appointing him to the command of a guarda-costa of eighteen guns, stationed at St. Blas, and including in her cruising ground St. Josef, Mazattan, and the entrance to the Gulf of California. His prey was good, and his duty was light; but all his hopes of promotion were cut off by being stationed at what was generally considered the "ultima Thule," the very extremity of the navigable world.

The Yankees, to be sure, scorned any such fanciful restrictions, and had long since penetrated to Nootka Sound and Behring's Straits, "the hunters of the mighty whale;" but then the Yankees were a very singular and peculiar race, and nobody in their senses cared to imitate them in their wild, and sometimes lawless, rambles over the face of the ocean—lawless, I wish to be understood, no farther than in sometimes forgetting to inquire, in a strange port, whether there was any custom-house there or not, and in most ports conceiving it to be the duty of the collectors of the customs to come on board and secure the duties, and if said collectors did not bear a hand and attend to their business, why then Jonathan, who is always in a hurry, was apt to land his cargo without the knowledge and without the leave of the custom-house officers.

Don Diego's hatred to heretics and foreigners, unlike that of the illustrious governor, was cordial and sincere, and by no means a general or abstract principle—he hated every individual as heartily as he did the whole species. He would never accept or even reply to an invitation from an English or American commander; and in the case of the American schooner already mentioned, he had treated the crew with such savage barbarity, that, but for the interference of Don Gaspar, they would have perished from starvation and ill treatment. He was by no means a favorite guest at the governor's house; the ladies of the family detested him, not so much for his cruelty, for they heard but little of that, but for his morose and churlish disposition, and, perhaps more than either, on account of the general belief that his wife, a lovely woman, and much younger than himself, had fallen a victim to his unkindness and cruelty.

Women, the dear creatures, have an infinitely larger share of *esprit du corps*, if I may so call it, or rather a community of feeling, than men. Nothing will ruin a man's character and good name among the females of his acquaintance so soon or so effectually as the reputation of ill treatment or unkindness to his wife, while the men would think but little or nothing of it. Women think, and feel, and act most correctly and justly, and in a manner that does them infinite honor, upon this subject; indeed, I am fully convinced, that on most questions of social morality, the feelings of women are more pure and right than those of men. But they have a thousand ingenious methods of making known their contempt and detestation of the cowardly scoundrel that would raise his hand against one of their sex, and every method cuts like a two-edged sword. I have known, and do at this moment know, many men who have endured the contempt and hatred of their fellow-*men* with the most stoical indifference—they went on hated and despised to the grave, but they made money at every step, and they cared for nothing else; but I never, in all my life, and in all my wanderings— and I have not travelled about this watery ball, nor so far through life, with my eyes and ears shut—I never knew a man who did not wince and writhe under the hatred and contempt of the other sex. I am not a profound believer in innate ideas, if they are such ridiculous ones as metaphysicians talk of—namely, that two and two make four, and such sort of nonsense— but I do believe in certain innate principles and feelings, that govern our thoughts and actions as powerfully and irresistibly as instinct impels the brute creation; and that one of those principles is an innate desire to please and secure the good opinion of the opposite sex, born with every man and woman, or at least developed, more or less strongly, in very early childhood, and that too without any instruction or hint from others.

While the party stood on the quay, puffing their segars with all the gravity and silence that was becoming their rank and birth as officers of his Catholic Majesty and natives of old Spain, a subaltern officer approached, and, with abundance of parade and obsequiousness, informed the governor that there was a ship in the offing, becalmed at that time, but apparently bound in. The officer proceeded to inform him farther, that there were two American ships at St. Josef, one at Monteny, and that a fourth had been seen the day before at sea, standing to the southward. His excellency, though not particularly indignant at the idea of his principality being visited by a foreign vessel, thought proper to appear "brimful of wrath" at the intelligence.

"Ah! those accursed and heretical wretches! they swarm upon this coast as thick as sand-flies."

"And should be destroyed by the same means, by fire," growled his naval associate; "they should be burnt at their anchors wherever they are found; for if they have not already been guilty of any violation of the laws, they very soon will."

"Signor Pinto," said the more humane and considerate governor, "you are to recollect that our gracious sovereign is on terms of peace and amity with this new people, who have lately come into existence, and who seem to be driven by the devils to wander abroad, instead of passing their lives peaceably at home. We cannot therefore treat them as enemies; and even when taken in violation of the laws, they must be heard in their own defence."

This grave rebuke rather mortified him of the marine department, and he was for a few minutes sulky, which the governor perceiving, and not wishing to offend him, again addressed him.

"But come, signor, cheer up. I know the sight of that schooner always makes you feel unpleasantly; you cannot forget how she misled you one dark night, and well nigh decoyed your ship ashore, by setting adrift a light in a tub."

This was but cold comfort to the redoubtable sea-officer, who was by no means fond of hearing the anecdote of the lantern in a tub repeated or alluded to; and he was about making an angry answer, when the sight of the schooner brought to his recollection that he had finally captured her, and had enjoyed the fiendish pleasure of abusing and maltreating her crew, and that, to crown his triumph, he had seen them set out for the mines. Poor man! he did not know, what indeed was a kind of state secret, that the viceroy, not wishing to embroil his sovereign in an unpleasant quarrel, or, as he was about returning to old Spain, wishing to leave behind him a character for clemency and humanity, had ordered them to be set at liberty, and they had actually embarked at Acapulco on board an English South Sea whaler. This had taken place a full year previous; and while the vindictive Spaniard was chuckling over their fancied sufferings "many a fathom deep" in the damp and unhealthy galleries of a silver mine, the objects of his hatred were jogging along comfortably towards London, with a full ship and light hearts.

In reply to the governor's "quip modest," he merely growled out something about zeal in discharging his duty, and anxiety to prevent smuggling, to which the governor replied,

"There is no danger of these foreigners smuggling, while they are so strictly watched by his majesty's ships and faithful soldiers. I wish, signor, you would go out with your ship, and bring this stranger in; I do not like to see him hovering about in this suspicious manner."

"It is impossible to go out, now that the sea-breeze is just setting in," said the naval officer, who had no more idea of working out with a head wind, than he had of flying, though the bay is open enough for the channel fleet to beat out in order of battle."

While this question was in agitation, an officer crossed in a skiff from the battery, and informed Don Gaspar that the sea-breeze had set in the offing, and that the stranger had hauled by the wind, and was standing off shore; further, that she was an American whaleman, that had probably pursued her huge prey close in shore. Don Gaspar was somewhat disappointed at this intelligence.

"I almost wish she had come in," said he, in a low tone, "for, heretics as they are, and damned to all eternity as they certainly will be, (for which blessed be the saints,) it cannot be denied that the puncho, or pontio, which they make, is most refreshing and delicious in this warm weather."

But as the Yankee manifested no symptoms of coming in to anchor, and thereby give him a chance for his glass of punch, he yielded to the suggestion of Don Gregorio, his aid-de-camp; and having lighted fresh segars, they mounted their horses, and rode back to San Blas.

CHAPTER III

A lady
So fair, and fastened to an empery,
Would make the great'st king double.

Cymbeline.

The family of Don Gaspar de Luna consisted of his wife, whom we have already noticed as a native of Mexico, and two daughters, Antonia and Carlota, who were rather pretty for Creole girls, and, like the generality of Creoles, especially when one half is Spanish, extremely ignorant and vulgar in their language and manners; the last trait being somewhat characteristic of the Spanish-American women, if we may believe travellers, to which I may add my own somewhat limited observation. They are, however, by way of amends, more civilized and sociable in their behaviour to strangers, and much more intelligent, than the men.

The lovely niece of the governor, the orphan daughter of his brother, made up the list of his family. As we have no great concern with the old lady and her two daughters, we have mentioned them first, in order to get them out of our way; but as the fair Isabella will make some figure in our pages, we can do no less than devote a chapter, or part of a chapter, to giving some account and description of her, more particularly as she differs, *toto coelo*, from her cousins, morally, and, in many respects, physically.

Isabella de Luna was the daughter of Signor Anastasio de Luna, the only brother of Don Gaspar. He was an eminent merchant of Cadiz, who, having found it necessary to go to London on business, had afterwards found it equally necessary to remain there for some time, to attend to his mercantile affairs. Here he became acquainted with a Miss Campbell, a Scotch lady of about thirty years of age, very beautiful, but poor. Her father had been taken prisoner at the defeat of the Pretender's army at Culloden, in which army he was an officer, and immediately executed without a trial, by the blood-thirsty and infamous Duke of Cumberland. Her mother died of grief a few months afterwards, leaving her an infant, and the sole surviving member of a proscribed and ruined family. She was taken, from mere compassion, by a distant relation of her father, and carefully brought up in the Protestant faith, her parents having been Catholics.

When about twenty years old, she accompanied her relation to London, and had resided there some years, when she was introduced to and captivated Signor Anastasio, and after a long courtship, and considerable reluctance on the part of the lady, because the lover was at least nominally a Catholic, she became his wife. They lived long and happily together, for whether Anastasio's religious opinions had undergone any change or not, by associating so many years with Protestants, he never interfered with his wife's religious creed or devotions, and permitted her to educate, in the Protestant faith, their only child Isabella.

I would advise all husbands to do likewise, in some measure; that is, if the wife thinks proper to perform her devotions in a Pagan temple, a Mahometan mosque, a Jewish synagogue, or a Christian church, why, let her, and welcome, unless the husband is particularly anxious to get into hot water, and commit suicide upon his domestic happiness; for nothing so effectually disturbs the tranquillity of a family, as open opposition of religious creeds. Women become religious, in the every-day acceptation of the word, from any motive rather than a conviction of the truth or reasonableness of any particular creed. It would be difficult, perhaps impossible, to define the motive that carries women into the pale of any particular church. I have heard of an old lady, who was very anxious to be permitted to carry her knitting-work to meeting, "because it was such a *steadiment* to the mind." Perhaps joining the church has the same effect upon women in general. I have seen so much discomfort in families from conflicting religious opinions, that I cannot help hoping that the destinies will so contrive it, that my wife, if they ever mean to send me one at all, shall be a member of the Episcopal church. There is about that church, what attaches to no other sect, a sort of dignified reserve, that never breaks out in four-day meetings, revivals, or any other similar ebullition of fanaticism and absurdity.

When Isabella was in her fourteenth year, her father returned to his native country, taking his family with him, having given up his mercantile business, and retiring from it very wealthy. The priests, as might have been expected, were soon around him, like sharks around a slave-ship, all eager to discover, in his conversation and manners, the contamination of heresy, with which they took it for granted he was infected, from having dwelt so long among those obstinate and perverse heretics, the English; but Anastasio was too well acquainted with human nature, and with the ways of the world, to be thrown off his guard. He gave most munificently to the church; and, in spite of all their attempts to place Isabella in a convent, as a boarder, succeeded in retaining her under the immediate care of her excellent mother.

In making this arrangement, he was much assisted by a priest, whom he had formerly been acquainted with, and whom he now took into his family, as father confessor. In short, by the judicious management of pretty large sums of money, that he was able to spare, in less than a year after his return to Spain, Anastasio de Luna obtained the character of a good Catholic, who had kept fast the integrity of his faith, during a long residence among heretics. As for Madame de Luna, after having delivered her over in trust to the devil, the clergy gave themselves little or no concern about her; though her liberal charity, and the mildness and sweetness of her disposition, made her friends of all who knew her. Many a saint, of the present day, holds his character for sanctity by as slight a tenure, as Anastasio did his as an orthodox Catholic; and many a modest, unpretending female, has been, like Madame de Luna, regarded as an infidel, and a vessel of wrath, for not sounding a trumpet before her, in the exercise of unassuming virtues.

In about three years after his return to his native country, Anastasio died, bequeathing a large sum to the church, not from any violent partiality to the Catholic faith, but in order to secure peace to his wife and daughter. His widow intended to return to England; but her health was failing rapidly, and in a little more than a year after her husband's death, she followed him to the grave, with her last breath enjoining upon her daughter never to part with the faith in which she had been educated, and never to marry a Catholic, unless she was sure of the purity and goodness of his morals. This might seem illiberal in her; but there is no accounting for the prejudices of people, especially upon religious subjects.

After her mother's death, Isabella had no alternative left, but to take refuge in the family of her uncle, Don Gaspar, who had already shown great fondness for her, and who received her with great cordiality and affection. In this family she was permitted to do much as she pleased; her gentle and amiable disposition soon won the warmest affections of her aunt and cousins, and her time passed agreeably, except that she was sometimes teased by the reverend clergy to enter a convent, and to "dedicate herself to God;" but as the young lady thought she could serve God to better purpose out of a convent than in one, she civilly declined their polite invitations to shut herself in a dungeon.

The same priest who befriended her father, extended his kindness to the daughter. He was a very influential clergyman, secretly of very liberal and enlightened views, on the subject of religion; but, not perceiving any pressing necessity for giving his body to be burnt, he had thought best to keep his religious notions to himself. He might very easily have "gained a martyr's glorious name," if he had only been one of those

"Stubborn saints, whom all men grant
To be the true church militant;"

but he was not; and, besides, martyrdom is not near so fashionable as it was during the time of the Roman emperors, when one saint insisted upon being crucified heels uppermost; and another, who was very comfortably broiling on a gridiron, sung out to be turned, when he thought he was cooked enough on one side. *Our* clergy are a grave, serious, set of men, who scorn such mad pranks; they have no idea of suffering martyrdom, or any thing else, if they can help it. I believe there have been no martyrs since the commencement of the nineteenth century, except Mr. Wolff, who was bastinadoed by the Pacha of Egypt, for interfering with what did not concern him, and some ten or a dozen missionaries, that would not do something the Cochin-Chinese bid them, and were, in consequence, made shorter by the head.

The good priest interposed his good offices, and influence, in Isabella's behalf, and gave her instructions in such branches of education as he thought were suited to her sex. But, in about a year after her mother's death, Don Gaspar received his appointment, as military commander of St. Blas, which, as I have already observed, was then a royal depot and arsenal; and, though but seldom visited by Spanish men-of-war, because there were but very few, besides guarda-costas, in the Pacific, was a place of considerable importance. Isabella cheerfully accompanied him to America; for, though neither giddy, nor thoughtless, all places were alike to her, provided she could be always surrounded with her uncle's family, with whom she enjoyed quiet happiness.

In the priests of Mexico, she saw nothing but ignorance, sensuality, bigotry, and indolence, nothing calculated to shake her faith as a Protestant, or cause her to forget her mother's first injunction; while the foppishness, frivolity, insolence, ignorance, and pride, of the men, by whom she was surrounded, most effectually protected her from the remotest thought of disobeying the second. The men, on the other hand, regarded her with the coolest indifference; accustomed to admire the black eyes, and hair, and colorless complexions of the Spanish and native, or Creole, women, varying from a sort of dirty cream color, to a deep and beautiful copper, Isabella's rather lightish brown hair, blue eyes, fair complexion, and cheeks rosy with health and cheerfulness, had no charms for them; and, while her cousins had lovers, or danglers, by the dozen, Isabella found herself, to her infinite satisfaction, completely deserted and neglected, by all the starched and pompous fools that visited her uncle, during a stay of some months in the city of Mexico.

She had, on the arrival of the family at St. Blas, contrived to employ her time in cultivating such female accomplishments as her mother had instructed her in, and was, at the time we introduce her to the reader's notice, in her twentieth year. In person, she was about the medium height of women, or, perhaps, a little below it; and would be called, in New England, rather a small woman. Her form was exceedingly well-proportioned and beautiful, although, what may seem incredible, it had never been cramped, crushed, and distorted, by tight lacing, of which her mother had a very reasonable horror; and, in consequence, her movements were free, graceful, and unconfined.

I know very well that the idea of a lady's form being beautiful, unless moulded by corsets into the form of a ship's half-minute glass, will be scouted as absurd and impossible; but to the ridicule that such a proposition must necessarily excite, I can oppose my own observation, leaving antiquity, with its faultless statues and sculptures, to shift for itself. The Hindoo women, of whom I have seen hundreds at once bathing in the Hoogly, of all ages, from childhood to decrepitude, have extremely fine forms, when young, that is from twelve to twenty-two or three, at which period they have all the marks of old age. As they bathe with only a single thin cotton garment, which, when wet, sticks close to their bodies, and developes their forms most completely, any body that visits Calcutta can satisfy himself of the correctness of this fact, and yet they tolerate no sort of confinement whatever about the person.

Isabella's face was of an oval form, with an exquisitely delicate and fair complexion; when her features were at rest, the expression was quiet and serious, rather bordering upon the pensive, a cast of countenance that she inherited from her mother; but her smile was exceedingly attractive, with an air of frankness and innocence attending it, that made it perfectly fascinating. Her eyes were of a deep blue, that, in conversation or when any emotion agitated the tranquillity of their owner, were extremely lively, animated, and sparkling. Her eyebrows were very delicately traced, slightly curved but not arched, as poets and others rave about—I never saw a pair that were, on forehead male or female, except among the Chinese, and *they*, in consequence, looked like—no matter who—nor can I imagine how arched brows can be beautiful.

It was not the fashion, forty years since, for girls to cut off their hair and sell it to a barber for fifty cents, and then give ten dollars for a set of artificial curls, nor was it fashionable in Mexico to wear false hair; if it had been, nature had been so bountiful to Isabella in that beautiful ornament and pride (it ought to be) of a woman, that she could save the expense by the arrangement of her own luxuriant tresses.

Her temper was mild, and by no means easily ruffled; her disposition was gentle, humane, amiable, and cheerful, though seldom or never breaking out into extravagant gaiety. Like all young ladies of her age, who have much unemployed time on their hands, and I believe the same remark will apply to young men similarly situated, she had experienced a void, a want of something in the heart, that she felt acutely enough, but could neither describe nor account for; that peculiar feeling that certainly is not love, but a symptom of the wish to love and be beloved; it is that state of the heart when the affections go forth, like Noah's dove, and finding no object on which to repose, return weary and dejected to their lonely prison.

It is an old adage, that "when the devil finds a man idle, he sets him to work;" when love finds a heart unoccupied, he soon finds it a tenant, for it always has been, is now, and always will be true, that

"Love is a fire that burns and sparkles,
In men as nat'rally as in charcoals."

Isabella, almost without knowing it, and without the faintest suspicion of the real state of the case, gradually neglected and ceased to take pleasure in her usual occupations; her books, her music, her needle, and her flowers, all seemed to be equally tiresome and unpleasant. While in this unhappy state of ennui and loneliness of feeling, peculiar to the youthful days, or some portion of them, of both sexes, when the mind, like Hudibras' sword,

"Eats into itself, for lack
Of somebody to hew and hack,"

she was thrown into unspeakable grief and consternation, by her uncle one day proposing to her to receive and encourage the addresses of Don Gregorio, as her future husband.

To her passionate tears and entreaties to be spared such a dreadful calamity, that she declared was infinitely worse than death, the old Don replied, that it was natural for a girl to be frightened at the idea of leaving a comfortable home, to become the mistress of a family; that he only wished to provide for her, and see her well settled in life, that the proposed husband was handsome, rich, and connected by blood with the viceroy; and also urged many other reasons "too numerous to mention." To all which, the weeping and agonized girl replied, as soon as her uncle was out of breath, and she had an opportunity of speaking, "But, my dear uncle, you know his character, and why, oh! why, will you sacrifice me, whom you have always treated with so much affection and kindness, to one whom every one knows to be a fool and a coward?"

The Don was somewhat startled by this appeal. He was certainly aware that Isabella was perfectly right in so calling her proposed lover, who he knew was both a silly coxcomb and a despicable coward, but it was altogether past his comprehension how his modest, retiring, gentle niece, had found out two such very important points in the character of a man, whom he had noticed she seemed to avoid more than any one who visited his house. But after a few days, seeing that her dejection was extreme, that her appetite and animation had failed, and she was sinking under the weight of her grief, and being likewise severely rated by the wife of his bosom, in a curtain lecture, he relented, and calling Isabella to him one morning, with many expressions of fondness, bade her cheer up, for though he wished to see her well married, he would by no means force her inclinations, and she should please herself in the article of matrimony.

This intelligence soothed and consoled her, and the rosy hue of health once more revisited her sweet countenance; her eyes once more sparkled with much of her wonted animation and cheerfulness, but still there was a shade upon her mind amounting almost to sadness; her uncle had unmasked his battery, and she felt that she was doomed to much persecution, on what, under existing circumstances, was to her a most painful subject. But the destinies, that manage matrimonial affairs infinitely better than free agents, were busy on her behalf.

CHAPTER IV

"Why," said the knight, "did you not tell me, that this
water was from the well of your blessed patron, St.
Dunstan?"

"Ay, truly," said the hermit, "and many a hundred pagans
did he baptize there; but I never heard that he drank any of
it. Every thing should be put to its proper use in this world.
St. Dunstan knew, as well as any one, the prerogatives of a
jovial friar."

Ivanhoe.

It was nearly six months after the warlike and portentous visit of
the puissant governor to the Porte, when he was roused one morning by
intelligence, that an American whale-ship had arrived in the night, and was
then at anchor just within Pedro Blanco. He immediately commenced, in his
usual style of vaporing and flourish, as though this Yankee ship, arriving
without his knowledge and consent, had compromised the welfare of the
Spanish monarchy. Before his zeal had half done effervescing, a sergeant
brought word that the captain and first officer were at his usual place of
transacting business, or *bureau d'office*, and wished to see him. This piece of
information had by no means a sedative effect. Here was a heretic, not only
stealing into the bay, like a thief in the night, but carrying his impudence
still farther, by insisting upon an interview, and that too out of business
hours, with the representative of His Most Catholic Majesty, by the grace of
God, King of Two Spains and the Indies.

However, he very graciously sent word, that he would attend to them
in a few minutes; and having drank his chocolate, he proceeded to his office,
where he found waiting for him a grave elderly man, and a handsome
young one. The American captain could speak no Spanish, but the young
man could fluently, and he immediately proceeded to inform his excellency,
that the parties who had ventured to intrude upon his valuable time, were
Captain Hazard, commander of the American whaling ship Orion, and
himself, Charles Morton, first officer of that ship; that the ship was filled
with oil, and bound home; that they were out of wood, short of water,
and desirous of obtaining fruit, vegetables, fresh and salt provisions, and

live stock, previous to their commencing their long and tedious passage towards home; and, finally, that trusting to the well-known kindness and humanity of his Excellency General de Luna, they had presumed to anchor in the outer harbor, till they had obtained his permission to move further in shore, and to purchase their supplies.

The old hero of Gibraltar was delighted: he had heard himself called general, and "vuestra excellencia" half a dozen times at least; and that too by a gentleman, whose modest deportment and language convinced him of his seriousness. He instantly acceded to their request, and would, at that moment perhaps, have given them his house, if he thought they could store it away on deck, or get it down the main hatchway. Still it seemed as if there was something lacking on their part; and he was soon set at ease. The two Americans communicated for a moment, when the young man, in polite and set phrase, gave the wished-for, and expected, invitation to the governor and his family to visit and dine on board the Orion, the next day at twelve o'clock; for sailors, and some others, stick to the primitive and convenient habit of dining in the middle of the day—fashionable people, I believe, don't dine till to-morrow morning.

The parties then separated, mutually pleased with each other; the Americans at having their request so easily and cheerfully granted, and the old Castilian in high glee with the prospect before him, of a good dinner, plenty of punch, and plenty of wine. Being gifted with olfactory powers equal to Job's war-horse, he smelled, not a battle, but a dinner, afar off, or within thirty divisions of "old Time, the clock-setter's" dial.

The Orion was indeed the American whaleman in sight when the governor visited the water-side, and was then coming in, but just as the sea-breeze commenced, the look-out at the masthead reported a large school of sperm whales in the offing. Although the want of vegetables and fresh provisions did grieve him sore, yet want of oil did grieve him more; and accordingly, Captain Hazard, whose ship was but little more than half full, commenced beating out towards his huge game, which led him away from the land and to the northward; where, in a little more than five months, he had made up his quantum of oil; and preferring St. Blas to Monterey, or St. Josef, he made the best of his way thither.

The governor, having notified his womankind of the whale-catching captain's invitation, proceeded to hold grave and high communication with Father Josef, his ghostly counsellor, and the keeper of his conscience.

Father Josef was a priest, turned of fifty; and, like most of the Spanish American clergy, who are turned of fifty, and are of any thing like fair standing for sanctity, was somewhat rotund about the abdominal regions, and of an apoplectic appearance; that is, his head was firmly plunged down, and imbedded between his shoulders, without being plagued with the intervening isthmus of neck, which is so expensive to modern fashionable ladies and gentlemen, being considered by one sex as a part of the body expressly created to hang neck-laces, gold chains, and lace pelerines upon; and by the other, as intended merely as a place of lodgment for the stock and shirt-collar. This priest's nose and cheeks bore a large and bountiful crop of, what are sometimes called, "the fruits of good living;" indeed, his parochial duties were not of a kind calculated to mortify the flesh; and as his church was well endowed, and he received many presents from the wealthy members of his flock, it was not a matter of wonder, that he enjoyed such creature-comforts as lay in his way; and the Catholic clergy are generally possessed of a sufficient degree of modest asurance in taking possession of them. In disposition he was mild, and good-natured, (fat people generally are;) was much attached to the governor's family, and possessed great influence over him. He was, over and above all, a man of considerable learning and intelligence: spoke English quite passably; and, as a proof of good taste, we add, that he was the only masculine biped, who visited Don Gaspar's house, who really understood, and rightly appreciated, Isabella's beauty of person, and intellectual character. As it was well known that the governor placed great confidence in him, all who had a suit to the civil or rather military potentate, in the first place made interest with the ecclesiastical one; and this was soon perceived and imitated by the commanders of foreign vessels, from whom he received many presents. This was the clergyman whom the governor now summoned to a council.

"Father," said he, when the priest made his appearance and bestowed his benediction, "you are doubtless aware of the arrival of an American ship in this harbor, and that I and my family have been invited on board to-morrow."

Father Josef bowed in the affirmative.

"I am not sure that I am doing right," resumed the Don, "in accepting such invitations, as it throws me into the society of heretics so often; and you know we cannot touch pitch without defilement."

"We cannot indeed handle pitch without being defiled, but in the line of duty."

"But duty does not call me there."

"Nay, but hear me, my son; duty requires that you should see that his majesty's laws against unlawful trading are not violated."

"That is very true."

"And there can be no better opportunity of ascertaining the real character of these foreigners than by a personal visit."

"A most just observation, father."

"Therefore, make yourself easy on the score of its sinfulness, for there is none in it."

"I don't see how there can be," said his excellency, who was thinking of the future punch and dinner.

"If I can assist you farther—"

"Oh, true! you will accompany us to-morrow?"

"Most cheerfully."

"And now, father, I wish to consult you upon another subject. You know that it is my wish to marry my niece to Don Gregorio Nunez."

"You have said something of this before."

"And she is most obstinately opposed to such a union."

"I can easily conceive it," said the priest drily.

"He is rich and well connected."

"Riches and rank do not charm all women."

"It is my wish to see her well married."

"The woman that marries Don Gregorio is not necessarily well married; besides, I believe you know his character."

"I think I do."

"That he is a fool."

"He is certainly rather weak in intellect."

"And a coward."

"I cannot deny it."

"And a coxcomb."

"He is certainly very vain of his high birth and of his rank in the army: young men are apt to be in such cases."

"You would not consent to his marrying one of your daughters?"

"No; I have other views for them."

"And yet you profess to love your niece as affectionately as your daughters."

"You know I do, father."

"And loving her as you profess, you are striving to render that niece miserable for life by uniting her with one whom you admit to be a fool, a coward, and a vain fop."

The old Don, whose intellectuals were none of the brightest, had got himself, without perceiving it, completely into a *premunire*, by the Socratic mode of reasoning adopted by his more skilful antagonist, who at parting once more addressed him:—

"Take my advice, Signor de Luna, and leave your niece to herself on this subject: a young female heart cannot be made, like one of your soldiers, to march and countermarch at the word of command; it is, besides, of very frail materials, and, when once injured or broken, can never be repaired. The happiness of one so dear to you as your niece, may be destroyed forever, by forcing her into a match she detests; but it will then be too late to repair your fault, and it will always be to you a subject of the bitterest regret and unavailing remorse."

With these words he departed. But the governor, although convinced by the priest's arguments, and set into profound meditation by his last words, was one of those people, of whom we see so many at every step we take through life, who ask advice when they need it, are convinced of its soundness when given, and yet, though their natural good sense assents to dispassionate reasoning, return to their old, foolish, absurd, and ruinous opinions and intentions.

Don Gaspar, therefore, although convinced that he was a fool, and an unfeeling relation in attempting to force his niece into a marriage with such a worthless puppy as he readily admitted the proposed lover was in every respect, continued to adhere to his original intention, which he thought best, however, to defer for a time.

CHAPTER V

There is as weighty reason
For secresy in love, as treason.
Love is a burglarer, a felon,
That at the window-eye doth steal in
To rob the heart, and with his prey
Steals out again a closer way.

Hudibras.

The morning of the day appointed for the visit to the ship Orion rose as pure, and clear, and beautiful, as though no party of pleasure was intended, but not more pure, and clear, and beautiful, than the weather always is during the dry season of tropical climates, which, with the cool and refreshing sea-breeze, is one of the delights of those climates that I forgot to particularise in its proper place. With us of the temperate section of this round world the case is altogether different—the day appointed a week beforehand for a party of pleasure being almost invariably rainy, blowy, haily, snowy, drizzly, foggy, cold, uncomfortable, villainous weather; or else so hot that the mere act of breathing is too much for feeble human nature—and this, too, whether the party is made for sailing, riding, rambling about in the woods, or even for dancing, or tea-drinking, or whist-playing in a warm, comfortable room. This is, perhaps, one reason why geographers call our part of the globe the temperate zone; because all our proposed and anticipated pleasures, that depend in the slightest possible degree upon the weather, are sure to be tempered and qualified by some unexpected botheration on the part of the weather.

The party from the shore accordingly arrived alongside the Orion about eleven o'clock in the forenoon, without accident by sea or land. The governor was in high spirits and full regimentals; Madame Governor was as stately, dignified, and bejewelled, as became a lady of her station and rank; the two daughters sparkled with gems and fluttered with silks, thinking of the impression they were to make upon the officers of the strange ship; the priest, in sacerdotal dignity, and with his weight giving the boat three streaks heel to starboard, sat hoping some contingency might take place that would elicit a present from the Yankee commander; the young officers, but three in number, including, of course, the military aspirant to the fair

Isabella's hand and fortune, thought of but little or nothing except their pretty persons and dashing regimentals.

Isabella, who expected no pleasure from this party of pleasure, but the reverse, as it would compel her to be for some hours in the company of a man she had so much reason to detest, sat in the stern sheets, with the fat clergyman directly in front, and forming an impenetrable rampart against the impertinent gallantries of the coxcomb Gregorio. She wore no jewels or ornaments, and from her pensive and serious expression of countenance, might have passed for an Athenian tribute-maiden whom the annual ship was about to carry to the den of the Minotaur.

An arm-chair of capacious and old-fashioned dimensions, its ponderous wood-work carefully hidden by the American ensign, the *fly* of which was to serve as an envelope for the feet and ancles of the ladies, was strongly slung and lowered into the stern sheets of the governor's state barge, a *craft* containing nearly as much timber as a fishing schooner, and about as burdensome. Mr. Morton, the first officer of the ship, and a remarkably handsome man, now came over the side into the barge, to arrange the ladies for their aeronautic excursion, safer than Durant's, for their car was slung with strong hemp not dependent upon a bag of inflammable gas. As a matter of course, he tendered his services to the old lady first, who, though she had been *whipped* in and out of as many ships as any English dragoon-horse during the war of the Peninsula, thought proper to curvet and prance, and show as much skittishness as a mule embarking at Hartford, or Weathersfield, or Middletown, for a tour of duty at Surinam or Demerara. She was, however, hoisted in without accident, and received on deck by Captain Hazard and Mr. Coffin, the second officer, with much politeness. The two young ladies were the next in order, and accomplished their flight successfully. Isabella lastly took her seat in the chair without trepidation or affectation of alarm. Morton's eyes had already done hommage to her superior beauty; but he was too busy with the other ladies to notice her any farther than as the most lovely of the female visitors. He now remarked the pensive expression of her lovely countenance, and it excited in his heart an undefinable and uncontrollable interest. We have already said that Isabella inherited her mother's beauty, which had not one of the usual characteristics of a Spanish female countenance; and it was this peculiarity that struck the young seaman forcibly, and probably increased the interest he felt towards her, and the curiosity to know something more of her history, as he had only understood vaguely that she was Don Gaspar's niece.

There is a peculiar phrase, or rather word, that I have left unexplained, and concerning which I will now proceed to enlighten the terrestrial and unenlightened reader. I spoke of whipping the ladies into the ship. The whip, then, consists of a tail-block on the main yard-arm, with a sufficient rope rove through it, and a similar purchase on the collar of the main-stay. One end of each of these ropes is made fast to a stout arm-chair, covered generally with the ship's ensign, with the loose part of which the lady wraps her feet. The other ends are in the hands of careful, steady seamen. The lady, being arranged and fixed in the chair, with a "breast-rope" from arm to arm, (of the chair, not of the lady,) is hoisted up by the yard-whip till she has approached the zenith sufficiently to go clear of the waist hammock-nettings, when the stay-whip is hauled upon, carrying her in a horizontal direction over the gangway, when both whips being lowered, she is disentangled of her "wrappers and twine," and received in the arms of a lover, a husband, or a brother, as the case may be. Ladies and gentlemen, whose curiosity on the subject of whips is still unsatisfied, will find their theory demonstrated and illustrated by a diagram in "Enfield's Natural Philosophy."

I have known the somewhat startling nautical command, "Get the whip ready for the ladies," blanch many a fair cheek with sudden and most causeless alarm. It cannot be denied that we "gentlemen of the ocean" have singular names for things; but every thing at sea must have a name, or there would be no getting along.

I have only farther to remark on this subject, that horses are infinitely more tractable in taking on board a ship, than ladies; for the moment the horse perceives his feet are clear of the ground, he becomes perfectly quiet and passive; whereas, the lady is always quiet while a handsome young officer is arranging the flags, &c. about her feet; but as soon as she is fairly in the air, she begins to scream, and kick, and bounce about, to the imminent risk of her bones; and just at the time when common sense and instinct teach the quadruped to keep perfectly still, women, who have but little common sense in such cases, and no instinct at all, are the most intractable and restless.

Morton followed the last lady, namely, Isabella, and, as he stepped over the gangway, was accosted by his brother officer.

"What a thundering pretty girl that last one is!"

"She is the governor's niece," said Morton.

"You may tell that to the marines," said Coffin; "I'll be shot if there's as much Spanish blood in her veins as would grease the point of a sail-needle."

"They say so ashore," said Morton.

"I don't care what they say; I'll believe my eyes before the best Spaniard among them."

"Who knows," said Morton, "but that infernal soldier, that's buzzing about her, may one day be the husband of that sweet girl?"

"There's no knowing," said Coffin, yawning; "but you and I, Charlie, can't marry all the pretty girls that are like to have fools for husbands."

As this conversation went on, the mates had walked aft, and were close behind Isabella, who stood by the companion-way, while the governor, and his lady, who was not far behind him in corporeal dimensions, were accomplishing their descent into the lower regions.

"That rascally soldier," said Morton, "wants nothing but a tail to make him a full-rigged monkey, and that lovely girl is about to be sacrificed to him."

"Poor girl!" said Coffin; "it's bad enough to marry a sojer, any how; but to marry such a critter as that is going it a little too fine."

Poor Isabella, who had heard and properly understood every syllable of their conversation, was exceedingly affected. She had heard a person, whose appearance and manners approached her *beau ideal* of a gentleman, expressing, in warm and energetic language, the liveliest compassion for her, and guessing (for she could not imagine how he could know with certainty) her exact situation, and manifesting an apparently sincere and hearty interest towards her. Although her uncle had forborne to trouble her upon that hateful subject, after he had first proposed it, she knew his disposition too well to regard the reprieve as an abandonment of his original design.

As she turned away to conceal her emotion from her cousins, her streaming eyes encountered those of Morton. The young seaman was shocked and alarmed at her tears, though he had not the most distant suspicion that she had understood a word that had been said. Her beauty had first attracted his notice—it was so un-Spanish, and so nearly resembling that of New England ladies; the pensive expression of her countenance had excited a lively interest and curiosity towards her; but her tears, the evidence of that "secret grief" that the heart, and only the heart, knoweth, had called up all the sympathies of his heart.

I believe there are few men, who deserve the name, that are proof against a woman's tears, and there are few such men, who, when they perceive a woman, especially a young and beautiful one, oppressed with grief, anxiety, or distress, do not feel an irresistible impulse to assist and relieve her.

It may be objected that I have made my hero fall in love at first sight. To this I answer that I cannot spare time to lead him step by step through all the crooks and turns of the bewitching passion; secondly, love is *not* like the consumption; people do not go gradually into it by a beaten road, every foot of which is marked and designated by its appropriate and peculiar symptoms. "Nemo est repente vitiosus," says Juvenal—nobody becomes completely depraved all at once; very true, but folks certainly do, to my certain knowledge, fall in love all at once, and that is doubtless the reason why they are said to *fall* in love. Love is like the Asiatic cholera; a man is suddenly laid flat on his back, with all the marked and violent symptoms, when he thought all the while he was in perfect health. "Love," says Corporal Trim, "is exactly like war in this, that a soldier, though he has escaped three weeks complete o' Saturday night, may nevertheless be shot through the heart on Sunday morning." In the third place, a man, who for two or three years has seen nothing in the female form more attractive than the copper-colored beauties of Asia, the South Sea Islands, and the whole western coast of America, or the ebony *fair* ones of Africa, is most astonishingly susceptible when once more restored to the society of ladies of his own complexion, and of more refinement than those we have mentioned. I have had the ineffable pleasure of testing the truth of this theory more than a dozen times in my own person. If any gentleman doubts the fact, I can only advise him to banish himself from female society, in a man-of-war or whaleman, for three or four years. If he does not fall in love fifty times a month, when he returns, he is either more or less than human, and, in either case, I should wish to remain a stranger to him.

The whole party were now "under hatches," and examining the wonders of a whaleman's cabin. Morton had attached himself to Isabella, and, as he spoke the Spanish language fluently, and, what was more to the purpose, was impelled by an irresistible feeling to entertain and amuse her, soon drew her into conversation, and was astonished and delighted with her good sense. He had visited different parts of South America before, and had seen enough of the women to perceive that they were excessively ignorant, superstitious, and vulgar. He was therefore not a little surprised to perceive in Isabella's conversation marks of a cultivated and polished understanding.

The rest of the party had gone into the steerage to examine some of those curious specimens of whalebone work, in the fabrication of which whalemen employ so much patience and time, during their long and often unsuccessful voyages. As Isabella and Morton stood together by the cabin table, the lady opened a bible that was lying there, and seemed for a moment or two engaged in reading it.

"Do you understand that?" said the seaman, still speaking Spanish.

"Yes," she replied, in English, "my mother was a Scotchwoman, and a Protestant."

"Good heavens! then I am afraid—I am sure—that—in short, I believe that something was said before you came below, that must have been unpleasant—that, indeed, could not but hurt your feelings."

Isabella was extremely agitated, and turned away her head.

"What would I not give," continued he, in a low voice, "what would I not sacrifice, to be able—to be permitted, to assist you in any way."

He stopped, scarcely knowing what he said, or hardly knowing whether he had spoken at all. The poor girl raised her swimming eyes in supplication.

"For heaven's sake! drop this subject; if my uncle knew that you had spoken thus to me, he would carry me back immediately."

"But tell me, dearest lady, tell me, is there no way in which I can be of service to you?"

"No, no, no, leave me; if you have any regard for me, leave me. I thank you for the interest you have shown for me; but it will avail nothing."

The tone of extreme dejection, and melancholy, in which she pronounced these last words, almost drove Morton beside himself. He was completely bewildered with conflicting emotions—a young and beautiful woman, lovely in person and in mind, and, what made her irresistible to an unsophisticated, warm, generous, and feeling heart, in affliction—affliction that seemed more remediless, because not understood by one, nor communicated by the other.

From this situation of mutual embarrassment, they were relieved by the entrance of one of the young ladies, who came to call her cousin into the steerage, to see the wonders already alluded to. Luckily, Carlota, although a good-natured girl, and fond of her cousin Isabella, was not remarkably keen-sighted, or she must have noticed the agitation and embarrassment of both parties.

In the meantime, Mr. Coffin, who had a large share of a particular kind of shrewdness, had noticed that his friend seemed inclined to enjoy the society of Isabella uninterrupted; and, to assist that manœuvre as much as possible, engaged the young officers with some tremendous tough fish stories, in which he was ably supported by one of the boat-steerers, a Portuguese, who spoke Spanish, as a matter of course, and helped out his officer, when his imperfect knowledge of the language brought him to a stand still. So he managed to hold them, as jackasses are held,—by the ears,—till he saw his companion and the young lady come into the steerage, when he broke off somewhat abruptly, in the middle of a very tough yarn, leaving the gentlemen of the sword to guess at the catastrophe.

As the party stood around a chest, upon which these whalebone toys, and other curiosities, were displayed, Antonia dropt a bouquet from her bosom. As Morton picked it up, and returned it to its fair owner, he made some remark upon the beauty, and fragrance, of the flowers.

"Are you fond of flowers?" said the young lady.

"Yes, very."

"That I can answer for," said Coffin; "he is always, when on shore for wood, water, or pleasure, in search of rare flowers, and shells. It is well there are no such things at sea, or we should never have taken a single whale—and then he paints those he finds so beautifully."

"What! *he* paint flowers! a *man* paint flowers! Santa Maria! who ever heard of such a thing!" echoed the two young ladies.

"And why not, my children," said the fat priest, laughing; "do you ladies think you have an exclusive title, and right, to all the elegant accomplishments?"

"I do not doubt," said Coffin, "that Signor Morton would be proud to show the ladies his drawings. Come, Charlie," he continued, in English, "you shall not keep your candle under a bushel any longer—you see you're in for it, and you may as well submit with a good grace."

So saying, he led the way to the cabin, where the drawings were paraded upon the table. They were certainly very beautiful; for to a fondness for the "serene and silent art," Morton added a natural taste for it, which he had ample leisure to cultivate, during his long voyages. After admiring them for some time, Madame de Luna gave the artist a cordial invitation to visit their house, and garden, a mile or two beyond the town; in the latter, she assured him, he would find some rare and beautiful subjects for his pencil. Morton was exceedingly gratified by this kindness, and said, in a low voice, and in English, to Isabella, but without looking at, or apparently addressing, her, as she stood next him, "Then I shall have the happiness of seeing you once more."

CHAPTER VI

Love's power's too great to be withstood
By feeble human flesh and blood.
'Twas he that brought upon his knees
The hect'ring kil-cow Hercules;
Transform'd his leaguer-lion's skin
T' a petticoat, and made him spin;
Seiz'd on his club, and made it dwindle
T' a feeble distaff and a spindle.

Hudibras.

The dinner on board the Orion, which was not served up till one o'clock, by the way, as Captain Hazard wished to be more than usually genteel, was excellent, and was preceded, and followed, by copious libations of punch; after which the wine was set on table, and the veterans, that is, the military, the nautical, and ecclesiastical, part of the company, proceeded to discuss it, "in manner and form." The governor, as was his custom on such occasions, told interminable stories of the siege of Gibraltar, during which, his hopeful nephew elect enjoyed a very comfortable nap, and even Father Josef nodded occasionally.

The ladies had made their escape, as soon us dinner was finished; and Morton, on the watch, like a cat to steal cream, was on the alert, as soon as he perceived their intentions, and accompanied them on deck. To his great satisfaction, none of the Spanish officers made any attempt to leave the table; for, as the old Don had just got fairly under weigh with one of his campaigning stories, they were afraid to treat him with so much disrespect, and, of course, hazard their hopes of being invited to attend him again upon a similar party. Accordingly, Morton had the pleasure of enjoying the society of the ladies, without interruption, and found many opportunities of saying a few words to Isabella. In this, he was again much beholden to the skilful manœuvring of his messmate, Coffin, who was already higher in the good graces of the mother and daughters than Morton, who, though a handsome man, had not so much of that dashing, off-hand, sort of gallantry as the other; and which goes an incredible way with most ladies.

Morton had seen more of the polite world, and was better educated, and more refined in his manners, than Coffin; but, besides being, at that time, wholly engrossed and engaged by a particular object, he had that peculiar kind of modesty, or diffidence, that does a man so much injury with the other sex; who, though they pretend to prize modesty so highly among themselves, abominate it as unnatural, absurd, and affected, in men; while the pert and obsequious fluttering of a fashionable water-fly, which is always received with a smile, is generally more prized, and rewarded more bountifully still. There is, however, some consolation in the thought, that repentance always overtakes, and punishes, the silly woman who has allowed herself to be so fatally "pleased with a rattle;" she perceives, after marriage, that she has given herself irrevocably to a thing "of shreds and patches."

There is a certain sort of little attentions, that ladies generally expect from our sex, and a skill and adroitness in showing which makes no inconsiderable part of a modern gentleman's education. I have known many young men, who could not write two consecutive sentences, without coming to an open rupture with orthography, grammar, or common sense, or all three, if it was to save their well-*stocked* necks from the halter, or their souls, (what of that commodity they have,) from Satan's grip, but who stood very high, and, doubtless, deservedly so, in the estimation of the fair sex, simply from their skill and precision in going through a certain routine of little trifling acts of politeness.

As far as ladies are concerned, politeness appears to consist chiefly in a man's putting himself to more or less inconvenience, or exposing himself to danger, on their account. With regard to the last, I do not know but I could acquit myself to advantage, partly from the peculiar recklessness that is acquired at sea; and partly because facing danger, in the protection of the weaker sex, is both the duty of the stronger, and the stronger generally can do it with less embarrassment, than perform those innumerable, nameless, attentions, already alluded to. I cannot say, however, that when walking out with ladies, I have felt peculiarly desirous of the apparition of a mad bull, a ghost, or the devil, to give me an opportunity to show my courage; but I think it is certainly easier to most men to expose themselves to danger, in the service of a lady, than to perform acceptably, and without awkwardness, those little acts of politeness, that, in the present state of society, ladies are somewhat rigorous in exacting. I have passed the very cream and flower of my life at sea, that is, from nineteen to thirty-two, and now, "in these latter days," begin to feel myself very much like a fish out of water. How often have I "sailed into the northward" of a fair lady's displeasure, for neglecting to assist her into, or out of, a carriage! never dreaming, "poor ignorant sinner" that I am! that the ascent up the steps of a coach was attended with any more perils, than that of the stairs that lead to her bed-room; or that a girl, perhaps twenty years my junior, glowing in the full bloom of youth, health, and sprightliness, and with a step as light and elastic as Virgil's Camilla, required the assistance of such an old weather-beaten beau as myself. How often have I been pouted at by the ripest, rosiest, lips in the world, for omitting to wait upon their owner home, on a dark, stormy, evening, and half a mile out of my way, simply because I preferred the company I was with, to the half-mile *heat*! I do not know that I have ever felt very desirous of living my life over again; but I confess I should like to go back, say, to the age of three or four and twenty, merely to take a few lessons in the graces, and then "jump the life to come," as far as where I am now, namely, *thirty or forty.*

By Mr. Coffin's management, Morton and Isabella were much of the time together, and both instinctively avoided any allusion to painful subjects. He described to her the various implements used in the whale-fishery, gave her a short account of the voyage, and of the different parts of America, and of the islands in the Pacific, that he had visited; and, in short, exerted himself to please and entertain her, and was successful.

When in the society of those we love, and from whom we are soon to separate, perhaps forever, how much we can manage to say in a little time! how earnestly do we strive to render delightful those moments, perhaps the last that we are ever to pass with those friends! Dr. Johnson says, the approach of death wonderfully concentrates one's ideas; so does the approach of the hour of parting.

Isabella heard herself, for the first time, for many years, addressed in the language of respectful politeness, and unassuming common sense; the pictures of refined, polished, and enlightened, society, drawn in the few excellent English authors her mother had left her, seemed realized and presented to her eyes, in all the richness of life. She did not stop to analyse, or try to explain to herself the peculiarly delightful feelings that occupied her mind; though if she had been left alone for five minutes, her own good sense would have told her it was love: that pure, unalloyed, unreflecting, ardent, *first* love, that, like the whooping-cough and the measles, we never have but once; though some patients have it earlier in life, and more severely, than others.

Ladies will never admit, and never have admitted, from the time the stone-masons and hod-carriers struck work upon the tower of Babel, (for want of a circulating medium of speech, that would be taken at par by all hands, down to the present Anno Domini, 1834, and twenty-second of

October,) that any of their sisterhood ever fell in love "at sight," as brokers call it, or that her eyes influenced her heart. With regard to the female, who, in early life, takes up the "trade and mystery" of a fashionable belle, *ex officio* a coquet and a flirt, this is in some measure true; for I have observed, that very beautiful women of that description, who have had at their feet wealth, and talent, and eloquence, and virtue, generally "close their concerns" by marrying sots, fools, gamblers, rakes, or brutes; they seem to choose their husbands as old maiden ladies do their lap-dogs; which are invariably the most cross, ugly, ill-tempered, filthy, noisy, little scoundrels, that the entire canine family can muster. But their practice is at variance with their profession. It is physically and morally impossible that women, whose chief strength consists in external appearance and show, should hold in light esteem external appearance and show in our sex; and, if they are not guided by their eyes in the choice of their lovers, I should like to know what the d—l they are guided by; for in a company of feather-pated girls, the chief object of ridicule is the personal defects of their male acquaintance.

Time, that stands still with married men, and sometimes with old bachelors, flies with lovers; and the sun's "lower limb" was dipping in the haze, that skirted the western horizon, when the steward came on deck, and informed the ladies and gentlemen that coffee was ready, and, accordingly, they descended into the cabin. After this refreshment, preparations were made for going ashore. Morton and Coffin ran on deck, to get the whips ready; and the former, calling his own boat's crew aft, had his boat lowered down from the quarter-davits, and brought to the gangway, while the governor's bargemen were lighting fresh segars. With a few words of explanation to the second officer, Morton sprang into his boat, and, in a few minutes, Isabella and her two cousins were safely stowed in the stern-sheets. The bowman obeyed the command, "shove off;" the swift boat, impelled by five strong-limbed seamen, flew like a swallow across the bay, and reached the landing-place at least ten minutes before the cumbrous barge of his excellency bounced her broad nose against the side of the quay, and recoiled, like a battering-ram.

Morton improved the time he was on the shore with the ladies, by paying more attention to the governor's daughters than he had done heretofore, and easily succeeded in entertaining them. They repeated their mother's invitation to the young seaman to visit their house, declaring they had never seen any foreign gentleman that spoke such pure Spanish; that the Americans were much more polite, and respectful, and hospitable, and obliging, than the English; and concluded, by wondering why, if the United States were so near Mexico, it should take six months to go from St. Blas there. To all which Morton made the appropriate replies; and, when the rest of the party were assembled, assisted the ladies to their horses, renewing to Isabella, as he adjusted her in the saddle, his promise to call at her uncle's house the next day. As this promise did not cause the young lady to "jump out her skin" or saddle, it is highly probable that she did not perceive any great harm in it; nor did it occur to her then, or when consulting her pillow at night, that she violated female propriety, by answering, simply, and somewhat emphatically, "I hope you will."

On their ride homeward, the party were loud in their praises of the entertainment of the day, their eulogies being directed to different parts of the entertainment according to the different tastes of the individuals performing the concert; for instance, the young ladies made honorable mention of the politeness and attention of the "dos pelotos hermosos," the two handsome mates; the old lady chanted the praises of the china ware, and table linen, and the knives and forks—all of them luxuries at that time in South America; the governor eulogized the punch, and Father Josef the dinner; the young officers were in raptures with the wine, in which they were joined by the civil and ecclesiastical dignitaries in grand chorus. Perhaps there never was a party of visitors that left their entertainer's house, whether riding at anchor in port, or standing on hammered granite "underpinning" on shore, better pleased with what they had had, or in better humor or spirits.

CHAPTER VII

Farewell! God knows when we shall meet again.
I have a faint cold fear thrills through my veins,
That almost freezes up the heat of life.

Romeo and Juliet.

Isabella arose at her usual hour the next morning, and after breakfast walked into the garden, from a sort of unacknowledged hope and wish that she might soon be joined by the young American, who had occupied her thoughts, both sleeping and waking, since she had parted with him on the beach the evening previous. At the sound of every horse's feet she started, and her heart beat quicker. But he came not that day, and as evening approached, her disappointment became almost insupportable; she tried to frame excuses for him; he had never been to the house; perhaps he had, by a very natural mistake, gone to her uncle's house in town, instead of that where she now was, and which was rather more than a mile from St. Blas, and whither the family came regularly to lodge, though they spent most of the time at their town residence; perhaps he was detained on board by his duties; or he might be sick.

"And why," said the weeping girl to herself, "why should I wish to see him again? Alas! I have already seen him too often, for my future peace of mind. He is going home to his parents, his relatives, his friends, his home, and perhaps to his wife;" and this last thought crossed her mind with a feeling of peculiar anguish; "but no, when he spoke of his friends and parents, he said nothing of his wife; but he is going, and in a few short months he will forget that he has ever seen me, or that such an unhappy being has ever existed."

With these painful and self-tormenting reflections she passed the evening, and much of the night; but youthful hope, that cheers the heart with flattering and deceitful promises, never sufficiently well defined to resemble certainty, but always brilliant; hope, whose elasticity raises the sinking heart, soothed and composed her spirits, and she sank into sound and refreshing slumbers, to wake to a brighter and more flattering day; but at the same time, to sink deeper and more irrevocably into that bewitching, bewildering passion, whose existence she could not now avoid acknowledging.

As she was sitting in the garden the next day, she was suddenly startled by the approach of her two cousins in full chat, and close behind them, Morton. Isabella seemed rooted to her seat, the light swam before her eyes, her tongue was paralyzed, and her limbs were unable to raise or support her. The young seaman approached, and in broken, incoherent, and unintelligible accents, attempted to express the delight he felt at once more seeing her. Perhaps, if the two cousins had been out of the way; he would have acquitted himself better, perhaps not so well. "Iron sharpeneth iron," saith Solomon; "so doth a man the countenance of his friend." It may be so in some cases, but I doubt whether any man can make love so glibly, so off hand, before half a dozen spectators, especially females, as he can "all alone by himself;" on the other hand, there is something absolutely awful in being alone with a pretty and modest woman, and being compelled to "look one another in the face," like the two bullying kings of Judah and Jerusalem. It is much like "watching with a corpse," a ceremony derived, I believe, from the orientals, and still prevalent in good old New England.

The parties were soon relieved from their embarrassment; the two cousins, after asking a thousand questions, and only waiting to hear two hundred and fifty of the answers, bounced off into the house, leaving the two lovers, for such they were now most decidedly, to the luxury of their own thoughts and conversation. We have no time, inclination, nor ability, to describe the steps by which they advanced from mere acquaintance to the can't-live-without-each-other and hopeless state of deep and incurable love.

Perhaps Morton was not grieved or angry when it was declared, after a thorough survey by Captain Hazard, Coffin, and himself, to be absolutely necessary to procure a new foremast and bowsprit for the ship before she sailed—the first being rotten, and the other badly sprung. As Captain Hazard placed the most implicit confidence in Morton's capacity to purchase and superintend the making of the requisite spars, the latter, to his great joy, was requested to take charge of the shore department. By this arrangement his opportunities of seeing his beloved Isabella occurred several times each day.

Though there had been no formal declaration of love between them, they were each conscious that they loved and were beloved in return; the most unreserved confidence existed between them, and Morton, who felt most keenly for Isabella's unpleasant situation, had repeatedly hinted at the happiness she was sure to enjoy in a more favored country, if she would leave her uncle's house, and take passage in the Orion for New England. She affected, at first, not to understand him; but when it became impossible to avoid perceiving his meaning, she only answered, "No, no—I cannot—I dare not;" but the answer was always accompanied with a sigh and a tear;

and as from day to day he informed her of the progress the ship made in her repairs, her negative became fainter and less resolutely expressed.

Owing to the necessity of making some repairs in his country residence, the governor and his family had latterly resided altogether in St. Blas; and as the puppy Don Gregorio watched with a suspicious and malignant eye, the frequent visits of Morton, the lovers had generally met at the house of Dame Juanita, the front of which was occupied as a shop, with a little parlor back of it, to which Isabella had access by passing out of the gate in the rear of her uncle's house, without going through the street.

With all the glowing eloquence of young love, and hope, and confidence, Morton detailed to her the thousand and one schemes that his fertile imagination suggested; Isabella could see but one hideous feature in them all—the dreadful fate that awaited him if unsuccessful.

"Listen to me," said he one day to her, as she had been urging to him the terrible risk he encountered—for she seemed to have no eyes for the certain immuring in a convent that awaited *her*—"listen to me, dearest Isabella; the ship is now nearly ready; she will sail in three or four days at farthest, and will sail at ten or eleven o'clock at night, to take advantage of the land-breeze. I will have my boat at the quay, and horses here in town; in the dusk of evening, and with a little disguise, you will not be recognised; there is no guarda-costa here now, and before the sun rises we shall be out of sight of land, and beyond the reach of pursuit."

She made no reply, but sat pale as marble; the images of her kind and affectionate aunt and cousins, and even of her much-feared but still much-loved uncle, floated before her eyes, and seemed reproaching her with unkindness and ingratitude; while, on the other hand, her fancy painted her the wife of the man she loved, and without whom she felt life would be wretched: she saw herself surrounded by enlightened and polished society, such as her sainted mother had graced before her; she saw herself moving in a new sphere, and fulfilling new duties: then imagination placed before her bewildered mind the sinfulness of deserting the station in which Heaven had placed her. She sighed deeply as she almost determined to refuse, when a glimpse of her abhorred lover, Don Gregorio, caused a sudden and violent revulsion of feeling, and to Morton's repeated entreaties, "speak to me, dear Isabella; say yes, love," she at length murmured a scarcely audible or articulate consent. The delighted seaman caught her in his arms, and pressed kiss after kiss upon the lips of the struggling, blushing girl.

"Remember, love," said he, as they parted, "be punctual here three nights hence. I will have horses ready at the end of the street, and before day dawns you shall be safe."

There was still one thing to be done, and that was to obtain the consent of Captain Hazard, who, though an excellent, kind-hearted man in the main, had some rather old-fashioned notions of propriety, especially in outward form, and would, as Morton knew full well, have very serious objections to advance against such a mad scrape; but he trusted to the fondness of the good old seaman towards him, and his own upright and honorable intentions, to overthrow all the veteran's scruples.

CHAPTER VIII

On the morning of the day that the above arrangement was made by the parties concerned, Captain Hazard observed that Morton had despatched his breakfast very hastily, and was on deck, waiting for his boat's crew to finish their meal, long before the Captain and Mr. Coffin had shown any symptoms of pausing in their discussion of salt beef, coffee, and pilot bread.

"What can be the matter with Mr. Morton lately?" said the old seaman to his second officer; "he was never so fond of going ashore anywhere else, and now here he's off and into his boat, like a struck black-fish."

"Why, I some expect," said Coffin, "there's a petticoat in the wind."

"The devil! who?"

"Well, I rather guess it's that pretty blue-eyed, English-looking girl, that came on board with old Don Blow-me-down, when he first came in here."

"Ah! I recollect her. I thought Morton seemed to take a shine to her."

"They say she's Don Strombolo's niece."

"They may tell that to the marines; she don't look no more like the rest on 'em than the devil looks like a parson."

"I don't know" said Coffin gravely, "how the devil looks; but they say he can put on the appearance of an angel of light, and I don't see why 'taint jist as easy for him to put on a black coat, and come the parson over us poor sinners."

"Well, well; she's a sweet pretty girl, and looks kind o' as though she wasn't over and above in good spirits."

"Well, now; I some guess I know a little something about that."

"Why how the d — — did *you* come to make yourself busy?"

"Why, you see, there's an old woman keeps a *pulparia* [3] close to the old Don's rookery."

"Hum! so, Mr. Sam Coffin, when you're cruising for information, you overhaul the women's papers first and foremost."

"Why you see, Captain Hazard, if you ask one of these men here a civil question, all you can get out of the critter is that d—d 'quien sabe,' and blast the any thing else."

"Can sarvy! why that sounds like Chinaman's talk; what does it mean?"

"It means 'who knows,' and that's the way they answer pretty much all questions."

"Well, what was't you was going to say about the girl?"

"Well, the old woman told me the girl's mother was an Englishwoman."

"I told you she wasn't clear Spanish—and being a girl, so, why she takes altogether after the mother."

"And the old woman said furdermore, that her mother wasn't a Catholic; she was a what-d'ye-call-'em."

"A Protestant, I s'pose you mean."

"Yes, yes, a Protestant—that's it. Well, you see, her mother did not die till this girl, her darter, was nigh upon sixteen years old, and it's like the old lady eddicated her arter the same religion she was brought up in herself."

"Aye, now I begin to see into it all."

"Well, so you see, as nigh as I can make out, for the old woman wouldn't talk right out—only kept hinting along like."

"Hum! a woman generally can *hint* a d—d sight more than when she speaks right out."

"Well, so it seems this Isabella, being half English and whole Protestant, won't exactly steer by their compass in religious matters."

"Poor girl! poor innocent little creature!"

"Well, I got a talking 'long with the old woman, and, arter a good deal of trouble, I got hold of pretty much the whole history about this 'ere girl. So she told me, amongst other things, that the girl's uncle wanted her to marry one of them officers that was aboard that day."

"Which of them?"

"That thundering cockroach-legged thief, that was copper-fastened with gold lace and brass buttons chock up to his ears, with a thundering great broadsword triced up to his larboard quarter and slung with brass chains."

"Ah! I recollect him."

"And so do I, blast his profile. He cut more capers than the third mate of a Guineaman over a dead nigger, and went skylarking about decks like a monkey in a china-shop."

"I took notice that he looked marline-spikes at Mr. Morton for paying so much attention to the girl."

"Aye, that he did; but I worked him a traverse in middle latitude, sailing on that tack. I got him and the rest on 'em into the steerage, and Mr. Morton and the girl had a good half hour's discourse to themselves in the cabin."

"I should be sorry to have Mr. Morton try to engage the poor girl's affections; and if I thought he had any improper intentions towards her, I would go ashore immediately, and speak to the old governor about it."

"Well now, Captain Hazard, I guess there isn't no danger on that tack. Mr. Morton may go adrift now and then among the girls, and where's the man that doesn't? No, no; Charlie Morton isn't none of them sort that would gain a poor girl's affections only to ruin her. No no; he's too honorable and noble-spirited for such a rascally action as that."

"Well, I am of your opinion. So now, Mr. Coffin, we'll set up our fore-rigging for a full do; for we must sail Wednesday evening, right or wrong."

"Ay, ay, sir."

When Morton returned to the ship at night, he hastened to lay before Captain Hazard the history of his love, and his plans for bringing it to a successful crisis, declaring that his intentions were strictly honorable, and that the lady might easily pass upon the crew as a passenger. The old seaman heard him to an end, as he urged his request with all the fervor of youthful eloquence and love; and, having scratched his head for a while, as if to rouse himself, and be convinced that he was awake, replied:

"A queer sort of business this altogether, my son; I don't exactly know what to make of it—what will your father say to your bringing home a young cow-whale, in addition to your share of the oil?"

"Make yourself easy on that score, my dear sir; I know my father wishes to have me quit going to sea, and marry."

"Yes, but is not a wife, brought into your family in this way, liable to be looked upon as a sort of contraband article—run goods like?

"I am not much afraid of that, on my father's part," said Morton; "and if," he continued, laughing, "if the grave old ladies of my acquaintance find fault, I can quiet them in a moment, by quoting the conduct of the tribe of Benjamin, in a similar situation, by way of precedent."

"Ah, Charlie! your scheme, I am afraid, is all top-hamper, and no ballast; wont the enemy give chase? I am sure that Don—Don—what's his name, that young officer, more than suspects your good standing in the young lady's affections: wont he alarm the coast, and put the old folks up to rowing guard round her, so that you can't communicate? Ay, that he will."

"Trust me for that, sir; if I cannot weather upon any Spaniard that ever went unhanged, either Creole or old Castilian, I'll agree to go to the mines for life."

"Don't be too rash, my dear boy; though the Spaniards are only courageous behind shot-proof walls, and when they number three to one, they are deceitful as well as cruel; and, if their suspicions are once excited, they will murder you at once, and her too, poor girl! and think they are doing God service, because you are both Protestants."

"I can only repeat, trust to my prudence and management; I have too much at stake to hazard it lightly."

"Then remember, Charles, we sail Wednesday evening: it will be starlight, but not too dark to see your way. I will defer sailing till eleven o'clock, if that will suit your schemes."

"It will exactly; or if you sail the moment I return, so much the better."

With these words, they separated—Morton, overjoyed at the completion of his preliminary arrangements, all night, like Peter Pindar's dog,

> "lay winking,
> And couldn't sleep for thinking."

The appointed day at length arrived; but the destinies, who had hitherto spun the thread of the two lovers' fate as smooth and even as a whale-line yarn, now began to fill it full of *kinks*. Well did the ancients represent them as three haggard, blear-eyed, wrinkled, spiteful, old maids, who would not allow any poor mortal to live or die comfortably, and who took a malicious pleasure in disturbing "the course of true love." The inexorable Atropos brandished her scissors, and at one snip severed the thread asunder.

Daring the night there had been a tremendous thunder-squall, and the morning showed huge "double-headed" clouds, mustering in different parts of the horizon, and, apparently, waiting some signal to bid them commence operations; others, dark and suspicious looking, but of a less dense consistence, were seen scampering across the firmament in all directions, like aids-de-camp before a general engagement; the land-breeze had been interrupted by the night-squall, and the wind, what little there was, blew from every point of the compass but the usual one; the shags, that tenanted the top of Pedro Blanco, seemed unusually busy, as if anticipating a change of weather; and, in short, every thing announced that the delightful, salubrious, dry season had come to an end, and the empire of continual rain, and drizzle, and cloud, and mud, and putrid fevers, and rheumatism, and every thing disagreeable, had commenced. Still the day was delightful after ten o'clock, and the weather as clear as ever.

Morton had seen these indications of the approach of wet weather with no small anxiety; he knew full well that the governor and his family would pass the rainy season at Tepic, a city about ninety miles from the coast, or at some of the other large towns, in the more elevated and healthy regions inland. With Captain Hazard's permission, he hastened to the town, and to Juanita's house, but Isabella was not to be seen. After waiting for some time, a little girl brought him a short note, simply saying that she would see him in the evening, but could not before. With this promise he was obliged to content himself, and rode slowly back to the Porte. He was punctually on shore again at sunset, and once more hastened to town, having hired another horse, and directed his boat's crew not to go away from the quay. Having secured his horses at a certain place near the zig-zag descent towards the harbor already mentioned, he passed into the plaza, and was struck with consternation and despair, at seeing assembled before Don Gaspar's door, horses and mules in abundance, caparisoned for a journey. In fact, there was indisputable proof that the family were, in military parlance, on the route.

He hastened to the good dame Juanita's, and, in a few minutes, Isabella entered the room, and, throwing off, in her distress, all unnecessary reserve, threw herself weeping into his arms.

"All is over, dear Charles, all is lost—I set out to-night for Tepic, and we shall never meet again but in heaven."

"All is *not* lost, my own Isabella; every thing is in readiness—fly then with me—while your family are in confusion you will not immediately be missed, and, before an hour passes, you shall be safe on board."

"No, no; I dare not, I cannot."

To all his entreaties she seemed deaf, positively refusing to consent to escape with him; but whether from fear of being overtaken, or from maidenly timidity, it would be, perhaps, difficult to decide. At last, Morton, who was nearly beside himself with disappointment and vexation, relapsed into a short and stupified silence.

"Isabella," said he, at length, and with composure that startled her, "reflect for one moment upon your situation; you know your uncle's temper;

you know he is not a man that will easily give up any of his plans—this is your only chance for escape from the fate you dread; do not then reject it."

She only answered with tears, and continued to repeat, as if mechanically, "I dare not; no, no, I cannot." Morton was silent a few moments, when a sudden ray of hope enlivened his gloomy reverie.

"Hear me, dearest; there is one, and only one, chance left yet. If your uncle urges you to marry, entreat him for one year's delay. Before that time expires, I trust to be here again. Vessels are constantly fitting out from the United States to this part of the world—if such a thing can be effected by mere human agency, I will be on board one of them, if not, I both can and will purchase and fit out a vessel myself. Promise me then, my love, that you will use all possible means to defer any matrimonial schemes your uncle may form for at least two years. But I trust, if my life and health are spared, that, before half that time has expired, I shall be here, to claim your first promise."

"I will, I will, dear Charles; I will not deceive you. I know my uncle loves me, and will grant me that delay. And now we must part; I shall be missed, and I dare not stay a moment longer. For heaven's sake, keep out of sight of—you can guess who I mean."

A parting scene between two lovers had always better be left to the imagination of the readers; because the author, unless he is gifted with the power of a Scott, a James, an Edgeworth, or a Sedgwick, is sure to disappoint the reader, and himself besides. My reader must therefore draw the picture, and color it, to his or her own peculiar taste, and fancy an interchange of kisses, locks of hair, rings, crooked sixpences, garters, or any thing else that constitutes circulating medium or *stock* in Love's exchange market.

The Orion had dropped out to the roads, and, with her anchor a short stay-peak, her topsails sheeted home but not hoisted, and her whole crew on deck, waited only for her first officer. Between nine and ten o'clock the sound of approaching oars was heard, but in a moment the practised ears of Captain Hazard and his second officer perceived that the advancing boat pulled very leisurely.

"Poor Charlie is coming off empty-handed," said Coffin.

"Yes, I was afraid the bird had flown, or the enemy was alarmed. I am sorry for it from my very heart, for he will be low spirited all the passage home."

"Well, I aint so sure about that—I've always found salt water a sartain cure for love."

"I dare say you have, Mr. Coffin; but love is like strong grog, it operates differently upon different constitutions and dispositions."

"Well, I s'pose that's pretty nigh the case. A good, stiff glass of grog, in a cold, rainy night, makes me feel as bright as a new dollar for a while, but then it soon passes off."

"I am afraid poor Morton's love is too deep-seated to be worked off by salt water or absence. But here comes the boat—hail her, Mr. Coffin."

"Boat ahoy!"

"O-ri-on."

"Are you alone, Mr. Morton?" said the captain in a low voice, as that gentleman came over the side.

"Yes, sir, but not without hopes another time."

The two officers then descended to the cabin, and Morton explained the cause of his failure, and expressed his determination to make another attempt as soon as possible after his arrival in New England. Captain Hazard insisted upon his turning in immediately, to recover from the fatigue and anxiety he had undergone during the day, and to his remonstrances laughingly observed that he was not in a proper state of mind to be trusted with the charge of a night-watch, and that Robinson, the oldest boat-steerer, should take his place. Coffin earnestly recommended a glass of hot punch, as "composing to the nerves;" but the patient declined, though he permitted Captain Hazard to qualify a tumbler of warm wine and water with thirty drops of laudanum.

The topsails were now hoisted aloft, the topgallant-sails set, and the anchor weighed; and, with a fresh breeze off the land, the first officer sound asleep and dreaming of "the girl he left behind him," a press of sail, and the starboard watch under the charge of Mr. Coffin, spinning tough yarns on the forecastle and calculating the probable amount of their voyage, the stout Orion left the Bay of St. Blas at the rate of eleven geographical miles per hour.

[3] Pulparia, a small shop, generally pronounced *pulparee.*— *Diabolus Typographicus.*

CHAPTER VIII

Alexander. —They say he is a very man *per se,* And stands alone.

Cressida. —So do all men, unless they are drunk, sick, or have no legs.

Troilus and Cressida.

Charles Morton, whom we have somewhat abruptly introduced to our readers, and exhibited for two or three chapters, without much explanation, was the only surviving child of a wealthy merchant in one of the sea-ports in the southern part of Massachusetts. He had received a liberal education, as a collegiate course of studies is at present, and in many instances most absurdly, called. Morton could, however, lay a just claim to be called liberally educated. He went to college without contemplating to pursue either of the three learned professions, but merely to acquire a more intimate acquaintance with the classics, history, belles lettres, and mathematics, than it was then supposed he could obtain elsewhere. People begin to think differently at the present period, and have a faint sort of notion that a boy can become qualified for the every day duties of life, or for practice in the three professions, without having received a diploma from a college, exclusively controlled in all its attitudes and relations by one particular sect of religion, or passing four years of "toil and trouble" in another university, where he is kept wallowing and smothering in the darkness of metaphysics or the more abstruse and *higher!* branches of mathematics; both sciences as utterly useless to him in any situation of life as a knowledge of the precise language that the devil tempted Eve in, and which some ecclesiastical writers have laboured to prove was High Dutch. I have been several times to different parts of the East Indies, and on more than one voyage have kept a reckoning out and home, assisted in taking lunar observations and those for determining the time and variation of the compass, and without knowing any more of algebra, fluxions, or conic sections, than a dog knows about his father.

After Morton had had the sacred A. B. "tailed on" to his name at a grand sanhedrim of solemn blacked-gowned fools, sagely called a *commencement,* because a youngster there *finishes* his studies, he felt a strong desire to visit "the round world and them that dwell therein," and, like many New England youth, not only then but within my own observation and time, and before the signature of the august "præses" was dry on his sheep-skin diploma, was entered as an under graduate in a college of a somewhat different description—the forecastle of a large brig bound on a trading voyage up the Mediterranean—a school not one whit inferior to old Harvard itself for morality, and one where a man, with his eyes and ears open, might acquire information fifty times more valuable than any that could be drilled into him at any learned seminary whatever—a knowledge, namely, of the world and of human nature.

This habit, if it can be called one, of exchanging the quiet of a college room for the bustle and privations of a sea-life, is not near so prevalent now as it was several years since; and yet I have known many instances, and have repeatedly met, in merchantmen and men of war, men who have received a collegiate education, and have known one case, on board of an English line-of-battle ship, the Superb, of a dissenting minister, a foretopman, who could clear away a foul topsail-clewline, or explain an obscure passage in Scripture, with equal facility and address, and was both a smart seaman and a smart preacher:

"As some rats, of amphibious nature,
Are either for the land or water."

It is a pity our professional men do not travel more, especially clergymen, who, though generally learned men, are not deep in the knowledge of their own species. Of course I do not apply this remark to the Methodist clergy; as their vagabond life makes them but too well acquainted with the weaknesses of one portion of the human race, while the alarming and arbitrary dominion they thereby acquire over the minds, bodies, and estates of both sexes, is beautifully illustrated in the trial, not many years since, of a reverend gentleman of oil of tansy and hay-stack celebrity.

Morton's first voyage was rather a long one, but it introduced him to the most interesting portion of the world, the nations bordering upon the Mediterranean, while his knowledge of the Latin language was of no small advantage to him in acquiring a knowledge of the Spanish and Italian— an advantage that he certainly did not think of, when he was plodding through Virgil and Horace, Cicero and Tacitus. He returned from his first voyage a thorough practical seaman, and more than tolerably acquainted with European languages. He rose in his profession, and might at the time we introduced him have commanded a ship; but a sudden desire to go at least one whaling voyage seized him, and a whaling he accordingly went. In person Morton was above the middling height, some inches above it, in short he had attained the altitude of five feet eight inches—my own height to a fraction. Like most young men born in New England, and who choose a seafaring life, his frame had acquired a robustness and solidity, his countenance a healthy brown, his chest a depth, and his shoulders a breadth, that are each and all considered—and with justice—by the present generation, as irrefragable proofs and marks of vulgarity. But folks thought otherwise thirty years since, and, however incredible it may appear, there are actually now in existence a great many painters, sculptors, anatomists, and perhaps as many as a dozen women, who persist in thinking that a human being looks much better as God made him, after his own image, than as the tailor makes him, after no image in heaven above, or in the earth beneath, or in the waters under the earth. Forty years since, ladies did not by tight lacing crush and obliterate all symptoms of fulness in the front of the bust, nor did gentlemen stuff and pad their clothes till they resemble so many wet-nurses in coats and breeches.

It was the established rule with novel-writers, and that until very lately, to represent their heroes as tall grenadier-looking fellows, never *under* six feet, and as much above as they dared to go, and keep within credible bounds. "Tall and slightly but elegantly formed," was the only approved recipe for making a hero. So that a black snake walking erect upon his tail, provided he had two of them, or an old-fashioned pair of kitchen tongs, with a face hammered out upon the knob by the blacksmith, would convey a tolerably correct idea of the proportions of the Beverleys, and Mortimers, and Hargraves, of a certain class of novels. Sir Walter Scott, Mr. James, and most of the best writers, have disbanded this formidable regiment of thread-paper giants, and we now see courage, manly beauty, talents, wit, and eloquence, reduced to a peace-establishment size, instead of those long-splice scoundrels, that used to go striding about our imaginations, like Jack the giant-killer in his seven-league boots, kicking the shins and treading on the toes of every common sized idea that came in their way.

It was also considered indispensably necessary, that the heroine should be "as long as the moral law," and accordingly we heard of nothing but "her tall and graceful figure," "her majestic and commanding height," &c. &c. Let those who prefer tall women take them; for my part, I wish to have nothing to say to such Anakim in petticoats: conceive the embarrassment and confusion of a common sized bridegroom compelled, before a room-full of company, to request his Titan of a bride to be seated, that he might greet her with the holy kiss of wedded love! On the other hand, it was by no means unusual to represent the heroine as a mere pigmy; so that the lovers whose destinies we were interested in, might be represented by the following lines from an old sea-song, which, for the benefit of musical readers I beg leave to observe, is generally "said or sung" to the tune of "The Bold Dragoons:"

> "He looked like a pole-topgallant-mast,
> She like a holy-stone."

Thank Heaven! the taste for this species of writing has "had its day," and we have something better in the place of it. Bulwer has indeed tried very hard to compel the public to admire murderers and highwaymen, and our own dear, darling Cooper, the American Walter Scott, has held up for admiration and imitation sundry cut-throats, hangmen, pirates, thieves, squatters, and other scoundrels of different degrees, showing his partiality and fellow-feeling for the kennel; and, if he had not at last, as we say at sea, "blown his blast, and given the devil his horn," would have managed to set the whole female portion of the romance-reading community to whimpering and blowing their noses over the sorrows of Tardee and Gibbs—the wholesale pirates and murderers, the loves of Mina—the poisoner, the *trials* of Malbone Briggs—the counterfeiter, or the buffetings in the flesh that Satan was permitted to bestow upon the old Adam of that god-fearing saint, Ephraim K. Avery.

The hero of a novel of the by-gone class was always and *ex officio* a duellist; and though the best English writers err against morality and religion in following this absurd track, it may be urged in extenuation of their offence, that duelling is generally considered in Europe as part of a gentleman's education and accomplishments, and in this country to refuse a challenge brands a man with everlasting infamy, though the crime is held in the most profound speculative abhorrence, and every state has a whole host of theoretical punishments, never inflicted, for the violation of its equally theoretical laws, that are daily evaded, outquibbled, or broken, with impunity.

Morton's countenance we have taken the liberty to describe elsewhere. His disposition was naturally cheerful and mild, his temper even, and not easily provoked. Although somewhat inclined to taciturnity, yet when drawn out to converse upon any subject he was acquainted with, he was naturally fluent, and in his language pure and correct. He was a universal favorite with the youth of both sexes in his native town, and, during the intervals between his voyages, was always in demand when a Thanksgiving ball was contemplated, or a sleigh-ride, or a "frolic," as all such parties of pleasure were and still are called in New England. At sea he was always beloved, by both officers and seamen, for his nautical skill and good-nature. Notwithstanding the confinement that his duties made unavoidable, he had managed to make himself acquainted with men and manners, and, during the many leisure hours that those engaged in the whale-fishery always find, he had amused himself with drawing—for which he possessed a natural talent, reading, and keeping a sort of memorandum of different occurrences and his reflections upon the habits of the different nations he visited,—and was, in short, one of those somewhat rare but still existing prodigies, a well educated, well informed gentleman with a hard hand and short jacket, many individuals of which nearly extinct species of animals I have had the singular good fortune to fall in with during my voyage through life.

CHAPTER IX

Here comes Romeo, here comes Romeo—without his roe,
like a dried herring. O flesh, flesh! how art thou fishified!

Romeo and Juliet.

Upon his return to his dear native town, Morton was received by his father with his usual quiet affection; for old Mr. Morton was one of that nearly obsolete school of parents, husbands, and members of society, that do not think their duties in either relation require any sounding of trumpets, and who are of opinion that those who feel most deeply and sincerely religion, Christian charity, or human affections, are generally people who seldom make any parade of either. This sect seems to be very nearly extinct, or at least their leading principles, I have been told, are exploded from the creeds of modern saints; but as my acquaintance with modern saints is, thank God, very limited, I cannot vouch for the fact.

It was not long after Morton's return, when the young people of his own age and standing began to perceive an alteration in his manners, and that he, who was a leader in their gay parties, was now a moping, stupid, silent, dull creature, without any of his former animation and gaiety. The young ladies took it for granted that he was in love; and as it was evident that he was not in love with any of them, why of course some nymph in the Pacific had stolen his heart; and as, moreover, they had no idea of the existence in that remote and unknown quarter of creation of any females more fascinating than the amphibious and lascivious damsels of the Sandwich Islands, (to convert whom from the error of their ways, more missionaries have been sent out, or volunteered their services, than to all the rest of the "poor ignorant heathen" put together,) or the ladies of the North West Coast, who smell too strong of train-oil to comprehend the truths of Christianity, or rather of Calvanism, which is altogether another affair, and who are in consequence left in their original and antediluvian darkness.

Impressed with this idea, and feeling both grieved and mortified that so excellent a young gentleman as Charles Morton should give himself up to such an absurd and, in their estimation, unnatural passion, the young ladies of New Bedford determined to tease him out of it; much upon the same principle as the Roman emperors endeavored to suppress the Christian religion by exposing its professors to wild beasts: the wild beasts grew fat upon Christians, and Christianity grew fat and strong upon persecution. Perhaps if the diademed tyrants had treated it with indifference, the effects would have been otherwise.

Whenever poor Morton was met in company, he was always the object of ridicule to these lively and well-meaning young ladies.

"Pray, Charles, do tell us something about this lady-love of yours; what's her complexion?"

"How much train-oil does she drink in the course of a day?" said another.

"Or how much raw shark serves her for a meal?" asked a third.

"Does she wear a spritsail-yard through the gristle of her nose?" said a fourth.

"Or a brass ring in her under lip?" said a fifth.

"Is she tattooed on both cheeks, or only on one?" said a sixth.

Such was the peculiar style of banter to which he was sure to be subjected, whenever he went into company; and in a short time he abstained from visits, and devoted his time to perfecting himself in his nautical studies, and making diligent inquiries after vessels bound round Cape Horn. If ever you noticed it, madam, a man in love does not relish jokes at the expense of his idol. "Ne lude cum sacris," ecclesiastically rendered, signifies, do not make fun of the clergy; but among lovers it means, do not speak of my love with levity or contempt. I remember when I was in love for the third or fourth time—I was then studying trigonometry and navigation—my passion being unable to expend itself in sonnets to my mistress's eyebrow, I gave way to geometrical flights of fancy, and took the altitude of every apple-tree and well-pole in the neighborhood, and made my advances to *her* upon the principles of traverse sailing.

Nor was old Mr. Morton unconscious of the great alteration in his son's behaviour while at home, so unlike any thing he had ever observed before in him, and he saw the change with no small pain.

"The poor boy cannot have fallen in love," said the senior to himself; "there is nothing more amiable than a copper-colored squaw, beyond Cape Horn."

One Saturday evening, the old man, being comfortably installed in his leather-cushioned arm-chair, with his pipe and pitcher of cider (for merchants, forty years since, drank cider at a dollar the barrel, instead of London particular Madeira at five dollars the gallon, and the consequences were—no matter what), commenced the conversation:

"Ahem! well, Charles, my son, do you intend going to sea again, or would you prefer commencing business ashore? You are now at the age when most young men think of settling down for life. Let's see—you are five-and-twenty, are you not?"

"Five-and-twenty next month, father."

"Aye, true; well, it's strange, now I can never recollect your age without looking into the bible there. I recollect, now, it was so stormy that we did not dare to carry you to the meeting-house, and so Parson Fales christened you in this very room."

"I wish," said Charles, speaking with difficulty, "I wish, my dear sir, to make one more voyage round the Cape as soon as possible, and then I don't care if I never see a ship again."

"Well, that's strange enough; why, what have you seen in that part of the world so very enticing?"

"Enticing, indeed!" said the young man, springing from his chair, and hurrying across the room in agitation; "something that I must possess, or die!"

"Why, what a plague—why, what's got into the boy?" said the old gentleman, dashing down his pipe; "you haven't got be-devilled after those island girls, like a young fellow that I knew from Boston, who got so bewitched after the copper-skinned, amphibious jades, that his father was finally obliged to locate him there, as a sort of agent."

"O! no, no, no! she is as white as my own mother, well born, well educated, and a Protestant," said the son, hurrying his words upon each other; for he felt that the ice was broken, and saw the old gentleman's countenance lengthening fast; "oh, father, if you could but see her—if you but knew her—"

"Hum," quoth pa, "I dare say that sixty and twenty-five would agree to a charm on such a subject; but pray, how the deuce came this well born, well educated, white, protestant damsel in the Pacific, where the devil himself would never dream of looking for such a phenomenon?"

"It is a long story," said Charles.

"If that's the case," said the senior Mr. Morton, "you had better step down cellar, and draw another mug of cider."

So saying, he replenished his pipe, and disposed himself in an attitude of calm resignation. As our readers are already acquainted with the history of the rise and progress of young Morton's love, we shall say no more of his narrative than that towards the close of it, his father was surprised out of his gravity, and ejaculated the word "d—nation!" with great emphasis, at the same time, flinging his pipe into the fire, and exclaiming by way of sermon to his short and pithy text,

"Why the d—l didn't you bring her with you, you foolish boy? Why, you have no more spunk than a hooked cod-fish! You'll never see her again, if you make fifty voyages round the cape; she's in a nunnery by this time, or, what is more likely, married to that Don What-d'ye-call-him."

Charles could only repeat his conviction that neither event had taken place, and his firm reliance upon Isabella's constancy.

"Fiddle-de-dee! A woman's constancy! I would as soon take Continental money at par!" was his father's reply.

Their conversation on this interesting topic was protracted to a late hour, when they retired, the old gentleman to—sleep as sound as usual, and Charles to yield himself most unreservedly to the illusions of sanguine, youthful hope and love—that love that one never has *very* severely but once in his life; for love is like a squall at sea; the inexperienced landsman sees nothing alarming in the aspect of the heavens, and is both astonished and vexed at the bustle and hurry, the "thunder of the captain and the shouting;" but when it comes "butt-eend foremost," he suffers a thousand times more from his fears than the oldest sailors. After one has become acquainted with the disorder, he can distinguish its premonitory symptoms, and crush it in the bud, or let it run on to a matrimonial crisis. For my own part, I can always ascertain, at its first accession, whether it is about to assume a chronic form, or pass off with a few acute attacks.

CHAPTER X

O for a horse with wings!

Cymbeline.

Morton's low spirits and anxiety, on his return home, arose entirely from his having ascertained that there was no vessel then fitting out for the Pacific, except whalemen; and as their route always depends upon circumstances, and can never be calculated beforehand with any degree of certainty, he declined several advantageous offers in them. A few days after the eclaircissement with his father, he learned to his inexpressible joy, that there was a ship fitting out at Salem for what was in those days somewhat facetiously denominated a "trading voyage;" that is, an exclusively smuggling one.

To Salem, then, he hastened, furnished with most ample and satisfactory letters of introduction and recommendation. He waited upon the owners of the ship, and was by them referred to Captain Slowly, then on board. At the very first glimpse of this gentleman, he felt convinced that there was no chance for a situation on board. Captain Slowly was one of those mahogany-faced, moderate, slow-moving, slow-speaking, slow-eating people, that one occasionally meets with in New England, who are the very reverse of Yankee inquisitiveness, and never answer the most ordinary question, not even "What o'clock is it?" in less than half an hour; men who, in short, as they never ask any questions themselves, think it not worth their while to answer any. We have been several times horrified by such people, and our fingers have always itched to knock them down.

"Good morning, Captain Slowly," said our friend Morton.

The captain, hearing himself addressed, went on very deliberately with the examination of a jib-sheet block that he held in his hand, turning it over and over, and spinning the sheave round with his finger, much after the manner of a monkey, with any object he does not understand—as, for instance, a nut that he cannot crack—and at last replied,

"Morning."

"I understand," said Morton, almost mad with impatience, "that you are in want of a first officer; or at least, so says Mr. — —."

Captain Slowly, having cast the stops off a coil of running rigging, the main-top-gallant clewline, that lay at his feet, and fathomed it from one end to the other, examining all the chafed places with great attention, answered with, "Was you wanting to go out in the ship?"

"Yes sir," said Morton, who saw what kind of a dead-and-alive animal he had to deal with, and was determined to have an answer from him, if he beat it out with his fists; and though his heart revolted at the bare thoughts of passing at least a year in the same ship with such a stupid creature, yet it seemed to be his only chance for reaching the coast of Mexico in season; "yes sir, and the owners have directed me to you; they know that I am very desirous of going out in the ship, and they approve very much of my recommendations and certificates. My name is Charles Morton; I am the son of old General Jonathan Morton, of New Bedford; I was out last voyage with Captain Isaiah Hazard, of Nantucket, in the whaling ship Orion; I am perfectly well acquainted with the west coast of South America, from Baldivia to St. Joseph, and up the Gulf of California; I am about five-and-twenty years of age, and have been three voyages as mate of a vessel; for further particulars, I beg leave to refer you to the papers in my pockets; I am somewhat in a hurry, and should feel very much obliged if you would let me have your answer as speedily as possible."

Captain Slowly, who had never heard an oration of one quarter part the length addressed to himself before, seemed for a few minutes completely bewildered. At last, after drawing a prodigious long breath, he ejaculated, "Well, I declare, I never."

Morton, having waited a reasonable time to give the man a chance to recover his scattered faculties, at last asked, "Well, Captain Slowly, what do you think of it? shall we make a bargain?"

The captain was now completely startled out of his half existent state, and began to talk and act like a man of middle earth; that is, he began to ask questions.

"Well, let's see; you say you was 'long of old Captain Isaiah Hazard?"

"Yes; are you acquainted with him?"

"I've heard tell on him. Let's see, where do you belong?"

"To New Bedford; are you much acquainted down that way?"

"Some."

"Perhaps, then, you may know my father, old General Morton?"

"I've heard tell on him" — — A pause, during which Captain Slowly took a fresh chew of tobacco, and Morton looked at his watch with great impatience——"Well, let's see; what kind of a time did you have on't 'long with old Captain Hazard?"

"Very good."

"Make a pretty good v'y'ge?"

"Middling: thirty-two hundred barrels."

"Well, I declare"—another pause—"well, let's see. Calculate to go round that way again?"

"Yes; and that's what I have called to see you about: the owners approve of me, and have sent me down to you, and I wish you would give me an answer."

"Well, I expect I'm supplied with both my officers."

"I thought that was what you was coming to. Good morning, sir."

"Won't you step down below, and take a little so'thing?"

"No, I thank you;" and Morton walked away, cursing him by all his gods.

After satisfying himself that there was no chance for him in Salem, he returned to Boston. Lounging about the wharves the next day, he was attracted towards a fine, large, new ship that was setting up her lower rigging. He drew near, to examine her more closely. Her guns were lying on the wharf, as were also her boats and spare spars. From the number of men employed, and the activity with which their operations were carried on, it was evident that the ship was to be off as soon as possible. Morton stepped on her deck: an elderly man, with a fine, open, manly countenance, expressive of great kindness of disposition and goodness of heart, was superintending the duty. Morton was about to address him, thinking to himself, "This is no Captain Slowly," when the senior gave him a nod, accompanied by that peculiar half audible greeting that passes between two strangers.

"You have a noble ship here, sir," said Charles, by way of starting the conversation.

"Yes, she is—so, nipper all that; Mr. Walker, you're getting that mainmast all over to starboard—yes, yes; she's a fine ship, that's certain. Your countenance seems familiar to me, and yet I can't tell where 'tis I've seen you."

"I belong to New Bedford; my name is Morton."

"Morton! what, old Jonathan Morton's son?"

"The same, sir."

"Why, d—n it, man, your father and I were old schoolfellows—and are you old Jonathan Morton's son?"

"Yes, sir; I have followed the sea ever since I left college, and am now looking for a voyage."

"Well, perhaps we can suit you; times are pretty brisk just now, and you will not be obliged to look long or far—and are you Jonathan Morton's son?"

After a short explanatory conversation, a bargain was made.

"And when will you be ready to commence duty?"

"I am ready this moment," was the answer of the impetuous young man.

"No you are not. Don't be in too big a hurry; take your own time;" and they parted, mutually pleased with each other; Morton treading upon air, and very much disposed to build castles and other edifices in that unquiet element.

Reader, if thou art a sailor, thou canst understand and appreciate the pleasure mixed with pain that fills and agitates the heart when thou hast unexpectedly obtained a voyage to thy liking. It is then that ideas come thick and fast into the mind, treading upon each other's heels, and climbing over one another's shoulders; the parting with much-loved friends; the anticipated delights of the voyage, seen through that bewitching, multiplying, magnifying glass, the imagination; the pride and delight that fills a seaman's breast as his eyes run over the beautiful proportions and lofty spars of his future home; all these feelings are worth, while they last, an imperial crown. But soon comes the reality, like Beatrice's "Repentance with his bad legs:" bad provisions, bad water, and not half enough of either; ignorant and tyrannical officers; a leaky, bad-steering, dull-sailing ship; the vexatious and harrassing duty of a merchantman, where the men are deprived of sufficient sleep, for fear that they should "earn their wages in idleness," and of a sufficient supply of wholesome food, lest they should "grow fat and lazy." Such is the theory and practice of most New-England merchants: it was different forty years since, and the outfit of the good ship Albatross had an eye to the comforts of the crew as well as the profits of the owners; for merchants then thought that the two were inseparable—the march of intellect has proved the reverse.

Although, as I have already taken occasion to observe, Fortune is peculiarly hostile to lovers, yet she is sometimes "a good wench," and so she proved herself, at least for a time. The passage of the Albatross from the cradle of liberty and aristocracy to Valparaiso was unusually short, considering that vessels outward bound at that period made a regular practice of stopping at Rio Janeiro, whether in want of supplies or not. She was singularly fortunate, likewise, in crossing the "horse latitudes," not being becalmed there much over a week, a period hardly long enough to call into proper exercise the Christian virtues of patience and resignation.

Her passage into the Pacific was shortened by another fortunate circumstance: Captain Williams was an adventurous as well as a skillful seaman, and having a steady breeze from the north-east, he ran boldly through the Straits of Le Maire, and thus shortened his passage perhaps by a month; for ships have been known to be four months off Cape Horn beating to the westward, and after all obliged to bear up and run for Buenos Ayres for supplies.

CHAPTER XI

BeholdThe strong-ribb'd bark through liquid mountains cut,
Bounding between the two moist elements,
Like Perseus' horse.

Troilus and Cressida.

It was on a fine Sunday morning, in the month of December, 179-, that the oblique beams of the sun were reflected back by the snow white canvass of a stately ship of about six hundred tons, that with a fair wind, a good breeze, and all sail set, was steadily pursuing her course, somewhat east of north. She was in, or about, the latitude of eighteen north, and one hundred and fifteen degrees west of Greenwich; consequently, she was in the Pacific Ocean, and not far from the west coast of Mexico. The north-east trade-wind, which is generally almost due east, was sufficiently *free* to allow her to carry her starboard studding-sails, under which she flew gracefully and swiftly on her appointed course.

The weather, as usual within the limits of either trade-wind, was extremely beautiful and mild; the heat, that on shore in the same latitude would have been excessive, was moderated by the refreshing breeze. Indeed, it has never been my lot to find such lovely weather in any other part of this round world, as we meet with through the whole course of the trade winds. The long, regular swell, so peculiar to that part of the ocean, gave the noble ship a peculiarly easy, rolling motion, extremely grateful to a seaman, as the regularity and length of the swell is a certain indication of a continuance of good weather. As she lifted her huge bows above the foaming, sparkling wave, her bright copper, polished by dashing so long and so fast through the water, flashed in the sunbeams like burnished gold; at the same time, her temporary and partial elevation above the surface, revealed a sharpness of model below the water's edge, that at once accounted for the graceful and majestic swiftness of her motion. The whiteness of her canvass, and her bright-varnished sides, sufficiently indicated her to be a Yankee, without the trouble of hoisting the "gridiron."

Her stern "flared" a great deal; that is, its outline formed a very acute angle with the horizon, which was the fashion of building ships forty years since. It was ornamented with a great profusion of carved work, some of which was hieroglyphical, to a degree that would have puzzled

Champollion; but over the centre were two figures in bas-relief, that could not well be mistaken, inasmuch as the sword and scales plainly indicated that the one on the starboard side was Justice, while the cap on the point of a lance "seemed to fructify" that her companion was no other than Miss Liberty.

Liberty goes bare-headed now—our rulers, wisely reflecting that she is upwards of fifty years old, and has arrived at years of discretion, have ordered her to leave off her child's cap. There are among us those who think that the stripping will go further, and that, in a short time, she will be as bare as Eve.

The noses of both goddesses had been knocked off shortly after they condescended to mount guard on the stern of the good ship Albatross, in consequence of coming into frequent collision with the gunwale of the jolly-boat, as she ascended and descended to and from her station at the stern davits. At her quarter davits, on each side, hung one of those light, swift, and somewhat singularly shaped boats, called whale-boats. Eight iron nine-pounders on each side, thrust their black muzzles through their respective ports, and gave her, in spite of her bright-varnished sides, a warlike appearance.

The upper part of her cut-water was fashioned into a scroll, like the volute of an Ionic pillar, forming what is called, by naval architects, a "billet head;" and which, for its neatness and beauty, is very generally adopted, both in national vessels and merchantmen. Nor was the bow without its share of hieroglyphics; on one side were displayed a bee-hive, a bale of cotton, and a crate of crockery; and on the other, a globe, an anchor, a quadrant, and a chart partly unrolled.

Her royals were set flying, a technicality that I shall not attempt to explain; she had no flying-jib, nor any of those pipe-stem spars that are got aloft only in port, to make a ship look more like the devil than she otherwise would, and are always sent down and stored away when she goes to sea. Ships, forty years since, carried no spars aloft but such as were stout enough to carry sail upon, in fair weather or foul—sliding-gunter sky-sail masts, and other useless sticks, were as much unknown to ship-builders and riggers, as railroads and steam-boats.

Sitting upon the weather hen-coop, attached to the companion, or entrance to the cabin, with spectacles on nose, and a well-worn bible on his knees, sat an elderly man, the commander of the ship. He was tall, and very strongly built; long exposure to the weather, in every variety of climate, had bronzed his countenance, and given him an older look than his real years would have done under other circumstances; but at the same time, long exposure to the weather had hardened his frame, and strengthened his constitution, points of some importance forty years since; so that his chances for a long life were much better than those of a man of forty, especially one of modern date, who had never allowed "the winds of heaven to visit his face too roughly." His age was, in short, about sixty. His countenance, notwithstanding the rude and ungenteel manner with which the winds and the weather had treated it, was indicative of much good-nature and benevolence of disposition. He raised his head from time to time, looked aloft at the sails, occasionally addressed a word or two to the mate of the watch, who was walking fore and aft the quarter-deck, and then resumed his reading.

In the weather mizen-shrouds was a remarkably handsome young man, of four or five and twenty, busily engaged in hanging out to air his "go-ashore" clothes; a very common Sunday morning occupation at sea, when the weather is fine. Apparently the sight of his gay garments had called up a train of ideas of a very varied and checkered hue, to judge from the different expressions that flitted across his fine manly countenance, at one moment shaded with anxiety and doubt, at another bright with hope and joy. In height he was about five feet eight or nine inches, strongly and compactly built, but far too stout and athletic, too broad-shouldered and thin-flanked, to pass muster as an exquisite in Broadway; as his form, though anatomically perfect, a model for a statuary, and considered very fine by the ladies of his acquaintance forty years since, would be altogether out of date at the present day. His countenance, of an oval form, and shaded by rich, curling, chesnut hair, from exposure to the weather, had acquired that healthy brown that ladies do not dislike in a young man's face, though they carefully eschew any thing that will in reality or imagination produce it in their own lovely physiognomies.

It may be a mere old bachelor's whim of mine, but it always has appeared to me that ladies who have had the advantage of mixing much in society, and seeing something of human nature, are *not* peculiarly partial to that effeminate fairness of complexion that many fashionable gentlemen are so careful to preserve, when they have it by nature, or, when nature has been unkind, to obtain by artificial means; so that Dogberry's axiom, that "to be a well-favored man is the gift of fortune," is not altogether absurd. At any rate, I have seen many a "cherry ripe" lip curled with an expression of irrepressible scorn when the owner of the lip was accosted by one of these very fair, delicate-skinned gentlemen. Girls just let out of a boarding-school generally run mad after these animals; but ladies who have gone through one or two husband-hunting campaigns, are not to be taken in by such painted butterflies: they very wisely conclude that a man who takes such a reverend care of his complexion worships none but himself, and of course he will have no devotion to spare to his wife.

But to return to the gentleman we have left dangling in the starboard mizzen-rigging of the ship Albatross: his countenance was indeed somewhat tanned, but his forehead was as clear and white as ivory; its breadth and openness gave an expression of frankness and candor to his face,—so that, taken altogether, his physiognomy, though not regularly perfect, was exceedingly prepossessing.

The second officer, who was walking the deck, being the officer of the watch, was also a very good-looking young man, with large black whiskers, and was two or three years younger than his messmate in the rigging. His frequent stoppages at the caboose-house, to confer with the cooks, indicated the second mate, who is always, for some reason or other, a sort of "Betty," or "cot-quean," as Shakspeare calls it, continually quiddling about the galley, to the annoyance of the doctor, as the ship's cook is generally called.

About the after-hatchway were seated the gunner and sailmaker, both engaged patching old clothes,—while the old carpenter, like the captain, was reading the bible,—and the armorer was lying flat on his back, and singing. A very pretty boy of fourteen, an apprentice to the captain, was playing, or in sea language "skylarking," with a huge Newfoundland dog. I might as well complete the *rôle d'équipage* of the good ship Albatross, by observing that Mr. Jonathan Bolton, M.D., the surgeon of the ship, and Mr. Elnathan Bangs, the supercargo, were neither of them on deck. Perhaps they were engaged with their breakfasts, or their toilets, or their devotions, or their studies, or—in short they were below.

Just forward of the mainmast were what a painter would call the deeper shades of the picture, for there the black cook and his equally sable adjunct, the cook's mate, held their vaporous and dish-washing levee; while forth from the cloudy sanctuary occasionally pealed a burst of obstreporous laughter, that the most unpractised hearer might swear came from the lungs of a negro, without the trouble of invading their premises for further evidence. Upon either of these culinary worthies, to use the somewhat hyperbolical language of sailors, "lampblack would make a white mark."

I cannot avoid taking occasion to remark here, that sailors, like the orientals, are exceedingly addicted to the use of tropes and figures of speech, to similes and metaphors. In fact, if any gentleman was about compiling a treatise on elocution, I would recommend to him to pass a year or two on board one of our men of war, where he would daily hear specimens of eloquence, known and unknown to exclusively terrestrial orators, whether in the halls of Congress, at a public dinner-table, or on a stump. There is the *narratio*, or anecdote, or sometimes the *long yarn*; the *aprosiopesis*, or sudden pause, very powerful when in good hands; the *apostrophe*, or addressing an absent person as though he was present; the *obtestatio* and *invocatio*, two different modes of invoking the gods celestial or infernal; and lastly, the *simile*, or comparison, in which sailors are a thousand times more fruitful than Homer himself. The steward—who came up with the breakfast-dishes, &c., or "dog-basket," as it is called by them of the forecastle—was a thought lighter skinned than the cooks.

The crew were lounging about the forecastle and weather gangway; some walking fore and aft, with their hands in their jacket pockets, some washing or mending their clothes, and some stretched out in the sun, chatting and laughing in utter disregard and carelessness of what tomorrow might bring forth, and most literally obeying the divine command, to "take no thought of what they should eat, or what they should drink, or wherewithal they should be clothed."

The crew mustered forty-four in number; for forty years since, ships that traded to the coast of California, or any part of His Catholic Majesty's American possessions, or to the North West Coast, calculated upon a brush, either with the guarda-costas or the savages, before their voyage was up, and accordingly went well manned and armed.

A group of ten or a dozen were collected around the fore-hatch, where one of their number sat reading to them the twenty-seventh and twenty-eighth chapters of Acts—two favorite chapters with seamen generally, not that they contain any peculiarly glad tidings of great joy, but because they give a sort of log-book account of almost the only nautical transactions of moment recorded in holy writ.

The reader, like all who are so unfortunate as to be persuaded to read to a company, was perpetually interrupted by some one of his auditors to ask a question, or make a comment. He had, however, this advantage over the ill-starred wight who essays to read to a party of ladies, that he stopped and asked as many questions, and made as many remarks and comments, as any of his auditors.

The reader, after a few verses, describing St. Paul's voyage, came to the eighth verse of the twenty-seventh chapter: "And hardly passing it, came unto a place which is called the Fair Havens," &c.; when old Tom Jones, the boatswain, an old English man-of-war's man, who was lying on his breast across the weather end of the windlass, interrupted:

"Now, as to all them places you've been reading about, I never heard of none on 'em before, except Cyprus, and I've been cruising off there in a frigate; but your Sea lashes and Pump fill ye (Cilicia and Pamphylia), I never heard on in all my born days; and as for Fairhaven, why every body knows that's right acrost the river from New Bedford; though how the d—l they got there so soon I don't see, unless so be Paul worked a marricle, and it's like enough he did, to let the rest on 'em know what kind of a chap they'd got for a shipmate."

"Nevertheless," continued the reader, at the eleventh verse, "the centurion believed the master and owner of the ship more than those things that were spoken by Paul."

"Well, now I don't see no great harm in that," said one of the audience; "Paul was nothing but a kind of Methodist parson, goin' about and preachin' for his vittles and drink, and whatever folks was a mind to give him; so 'taint likely he knowed any more about a ship than any other minister."

"Yes, but you know he was a saint," said the reader, "and could foretell the weather, aye, a year aforehand."

"Could he, faith?" said another, "then I wonder he did not make his eternal fortin making almanacs."

"But what is a centurion?" asked a third.

"Centurion?" said old Jones, "why she's a sixty-four gun ship; I've seen her often enough at Spithead, but I forget now whether she was in the first of June[4] or not."

"Then I 'spose she was convoying the craft that Paul was in," observed another blue-jacket.

This knotty point being satisfactorily cleared up, the reader proceeded: "And when the south wind blew softly, supposing they had obtained their purpose, loosing thence, they sailed close by Crete."

"Now you see," said the boatswain, "just so sure as you have gentle breezes from the south'ard, you'll have a thundering Levanter at the back of 'em."

"Yes, yes," said a tar, "I know that to my sorrow. I was up the Straits last v'y'ge, 'way up to Smyrna and Zante, arter reasons,[5] and we ketch'd one of these thundering Levanters, and was druv 'way to h—ll, away up the Gulf of Venus (Venice); yes, I've been boxing about the Arch of the Billy Goat[6] 'most too long, not to know a little so'thin' about the weather there."

The reader continued: "But not long after, there arose against it a tempestuous wind."

"There," said Jones, "didn't I tell you so? I knowed you'd have a real sneezer in a varse or two."

"Called Euroclydon," continued the reader, finishing the verse.

"What! avast there! overhaul that last word again."

"A tempestuous wind called Euroclydon," repeated the reader.

"Well, you may call it a Rock-me-down, but I say the regular-built name on't is Levanter; but then I s'pose them thunderin' printers puts in any thing they're a mind to."

The reading proceeded without much more interruption, except that the honest tars, who had been up the Mediterranean, were not a little puzzled by the strange names of places, and could not imagine what part of the world the saint had got into.

"About midnight the shipmen deemed that they drew near to some country; and sounded, and found it twenty fathoms; and when they had gone a little further, they sounded again, and found it fifteen fathoms."

"Egad, I should think they was drawin' nigh to some country pretty thunderin' fast too, when they shoalened their water so quick, from twenty to fifteen faddom."

"Then fearing lest they should have fallen upon rocks, they cast four anchors out of the stern, and wished for day."

"Four anchors out of the starn!" shouted the boatswain, "what the h—was that for?"

"Why, you see," said the reader, "they used to bring up by the head or starn in them days—it didn't make a ropeyarn's odds which—they didn't know no better."

"But four anchors out of the starn," continued the man-of-war's man, "why, d—it, the very first sea would onhung the rudder, if she was pitching into it, and knock the whole thunderin' starn-frame into *smithareens* in a quarter less no time."

"Now you see," said one of the audience, "I've a notion that the craft in them days was built with goose starns, like a Dutch galliot."

"May be," said another, "she had all her anchors stowed aft, to bring her down by the starn."

"But four anchors out of the starn!" murmured the still perplexed Tom Pipes, "I wonder what old Lord Howe, or Admiral Duncan, would have said, if they'd heard a first leftenant give out such orders in a gale of wind."

"Why, there couldn't have been no sailors aboard the hooker, or they would have let go one anchor first, and if that didn't bring her up, then another, and so on; but letting all four anchors go at once right under foot, is what I call a d—d lubberly piece of business, let who will do it, whether St. Paul or St. Devil, and I don't believe they could get insurance on the craft in any insurance office in the United States."

"Yes they could, and I'll tell you why; if a ship goes ashore with an anchor on her bows, the owners can't recover no insurance; but if the skipper will swear that all his anchors were down, and good cables clinched to 'em, he can get his insurance."

"Yes, but there's a thunderin' sight of odds betwixt letting go your anchors in a ship-shape, sea-man-like manner, and bundling 'em all overboard at once in such a lubberly way as that you was readin' about."

The reading proceeded, leaving the law question respecting insurance "open for discussion" at some more appropriate season. Much indignation was expressed by the round-jacketed audience at the thirty-second verse: "Then the soldiers cut off the ropes of the boat, and let her fall off." A vast deal of satire was expended upon "the thunderin' troops," of all classes, periods, and nations, the whole clinched and concluded by a remark from the boatswain:

"Aye, sojers, and pigs, and women, is always in the way, or else always in mischief, aboard a ship, more 'specially in bad weather."

The reading afterwards progressed without much interruption, except at the fortieth verse: "They—hoised up the mainsail to the wind, and made toward shore," and then only to remark, "Aye, she was a schooner, or else a morfredite brig, and they was goin' to beach her; she'd steered better if they'd sot the foresail too."

The eleventh verse of the twenty-eighth chapter gave occasion for question and explanation.

"And after three months we departed in a ship of Alexandria, which had wintered in the isle, whose sign was Castor and Pollux."

"Sign!" said Tom Pipes, "what does that mean?"

"Why, her figure-head, I s'pose," said the *questionee*.

"Yes, but, d—n my buttons, there's two on 'em."

"Well, I s'pose they fixed 'em as the Dutchmen does De Ruyter and Von Tromp, put one on the knight-heads and t'other on the rudder-head."

"Ay, that indeed."

The reader went on to the fifteenth verse:

"And from thence, when the brethren heard of us, they came to meet us as far as Appii-forum, and The Three Taverns; whom when Paul saw, he thanked God, and took courage."

"Took courage?" said old Tom; "I don't know who the d—l wouldn't take courage with three taverns all in sight at once. I wouldn't wish a better land-fall if I'd been cast away."

"That there Happy afore 'em must have been a jovious kind of a place," observed a seaman, "to judge by the name on't; and then them three taverns so handy—a fellow might shake a foot, and have a comfortable glass of somethin' whenever he took a notion."

All further reading and commentary was suddenly put a stop to, by one of those occurrences that frequently take place at sea, and cause so much bustle and hurry as is very apt to frighten passengers. The good ship Albatross was neither thrown on her beam-ends by a sudden squall, for squalls are not fashionable in the trade-winds, nor did she strike upon a rock, for there was none sufficiently near the surface; but still, for a few minutes every thing seemed to be uppermost, and nothing at hand, like the contents of a lady's travelling trunk.

One of the crew, who had been for some time lying on his breast on the weather cat-head, crooning over some interminable "love-song about murder," suddenly surceased his singing, raised himself up, and cast an eager and hurried glance ahead of the ship, shouted "Fish ho!" at the very top of his lungs, sprang from the cat-head, and ran down the fore-scuttle. In an instant all was commotion and hurry. Captain Williams threw down his bible with most anti-christian and unorthodox carelessness, and hurried to the forecastle, shouting, "A bottle of rum for the first fish;" the premium always offered formerly, though I believe it is getting out of date now, and not only the first fish, but all the fish caught, are seized and confiscated "for the benefit of those whom it may hereafter concern," namely, the "cabin gentry;" the claims of the captors being waived, set aside, and overruled. The two mates soon followed their commander, "armed and equipped," the one with the graves, (a sort of harpoon for taking smaller fish,) and the other with a large reel of fish-line and hooks, baited with salt pork—the commentators on the two last chapters of Acts broke up their conference, leaving St. Paul and the centurion in comfortable quarters at The Three

Taverns; their reader carefully stowing away his bible in the bows of the long-boat before he joined the groups of fishermen on and about the bows—the great dog Pomp, so named after the illustrious Roman, Pompey the Great, and not after the allegorical personage to whom Will Shakspeare so earnestly recommends physic, came galloping forward and ascended the heel of the bowsprit, where he stood whining, and yelping, and wagging his tail, exceedingly delighted with the animation and excitement of the scene; and looking up, from time to time, in the faces of those nearest him, with an expression that said, as plain as mere expression can speak, "Why the plague don't you catch some of them?" Even those two privileged idlers, the doctor and supercargo, made shift to get on deck, yawning and stretching themselves.

In the mean time, one of the most active seamen, who was perched upon the jib-boom end, fishing with a bait made of a piece of white duck cut into a "swallow-tail," hauled up a huge albicore, whose struggles had well nigh thrown him overboard; but a dozen pair of eager hands were ready, the fish was safely deposited in a bag, and passed on board, and the bottle of rum was secured to the legal claimant. The sprit-sail yard, bowsprit, and cat-heads were crowded with fishermen, and in half an hour there were nearly seventy fine, large fish flouncing and fluttering their last on the forecastle of the Albatross.

The cooks at the galley, who had quietly prepared the usual Sunday dinner, which, forty years since, was generally the same for cabin or forecastle, namely, flour pudding, called at sea, "duff," and salt beef; the cooks did by no means contemplate this addition to the ship's bill of fare with complacency or delight. They foresaw that there would be fried fish, and broiled fish, and boiled fish, and fish stews, and fish chowders, and fish sea-pies; in short, there would be no end to the cooking of fish, till the fish were all eat up. They were not long kept in suspense on that subject. Mr. Walker, the second officer, approached their smoky temple—

"Doctor, is the beef for the people in the coppers?"

"Yes, sar, I put 'em in at three bell."

"Well, take and out with it, and get your coppers ready to make a chowder for all hands; and you, Peter, come down in the steerage with me, and I'll give you some pepper and onions, and the rest of the combustibles."

"Yes, Massa Walker, I come ereckly. Dam fish! I wish all fish in 'a world dead; den 'spose 'a want fish, let 'em eat cod-fish and tatoe."

With this pious ejaculation, which he took care not to give utterance to till Mr. Walker was out of hearing, he followed that officer down the after hatchway, while his helpmate, grasping his tormentors, proceeded to transfer the half-boiled "salt junk" from the coppers to a tub, and make preparations for a dinner of a more savory and agreeable description.

[4] June 1st, 1794, Lord Howe's victory over the French fleet, off Ushant.

[5] *Quasi* raisins.—*Printer's Devil.*

[6] The sailor probably meant the Ionian _Archipelago_; they generally mistake the word as it stands in the text.—*P. D.*

CHAPTER XII

All hands! bring ship to anchor, ahoy!

Boatswain's Mate.

In the meantime Isabella had suffered her full share of persecution. Shortly after the family had retired from the coast to the vicinity of the city of Tepic, where Don Gaspar had an estate, he had urged her to accept Don Gregorio before their return to St. Blas. The tears and entreaties of the unhappy girl had, however, so far mollified him that he consented to put it off some time longer. A severe fit of the gout, during which Isabella attended him with the most assiduous and unremitting affection, had also operated as a powerful auxiliary to her wishes. Pressing her affectionately to his bosom one day, the old governor declared his unwillingness to part with her; and, "upon this hint she spake," and easily obtained from him a promise not to trouble her with any matrimonial schemes till she had completed her twenty-second year, and even then, if she felt disinclined to the holy state, she should be at liberty to retire to a convent. As she was not yet twenty-one, she regarded this reprieve as equivalent to a full release, and awaited anxiously the return of the dry season. It came at last, and the family returned to St. Blas.

Several American ships, whalemen and others, visited the port for supplies, and for the purpose of a little private speculation, with which the custom-house was not troubled. Dame Juanita's shop, being rather the largest in St. Blas, and possessing, moreover, the additional attraction of her own buxom countenance, and that of a pretty daughter behind the counter, was visited daily by the mates and crews of these ships; and of them she inquired, by direction of Isabella, concerning the officers of the Orion, without success for a long time, till at last the mate of a trader declared that he knew Mr. Morton very well; that when he saw him last he was engaged fitting out a ship bound round Cape Horn; and that she was, in all probability, on the coast at that moment, and would most probably soon visit San Blas.

This intelligence operated like a cordial upon Isabella's spirits; her eyes were constantly directed towards the western horizon; every sail that appeared, caused the utmost trepidation and eager hope; and when the distant sail proved to be some coasting vessel, or the guarda-costa, that was prowling about continually, her disappointment was keen and painful. Her cousins laughed at the perseverance with which she watched the harbor; and, fearful of exciting suspicions, she afterwards only looked out upon the blue expanse of ocean when alone.

At last, one lovely morning, just after the sea-breeze had commenced blowing, a white speck was seen in the horizon, that rapidly increased in size, till in two hours it was plain to all eyes that it was a large ship, and many thought a man of war. Various were the speculations as to her object, and still more so as to her nation; for coming directly before the wind, her colors could not be seen.

As she approached the anchorage, her light sails were taken in and furled, with a despatch very unlike the manœuvres of a merchantman, and which confirmed the opinion of her being a man-of-war. Presently a flash of red flame and cloud of thick, white smoke issued from her starboard bow, followed by a corresponding one from the other side, and repeated alternately, to the number of twenty-one; but the fourth flash was distinctly visible to those on shore, before the roar of the first gun came booming over the water, awakening the thousand echoes that slumbered in the hills and woods about the city.

The ship, having now reached her intended berth, slowly emerged from her "sulphurous canopy," that the light breeze had kept wrapped around her, like a veil; and, clewing up her topsails, gracefully swept round towards the westward, as if intending to go out to sea again; and, in the evolution, a large, bright-colored, new American ensign floated upon the gentle breeze from her mizen gaff. She remained stationary for an instant, when the anchor was dropped, and the sails furled; and the machine, that but half an hour before,

"Walked the waters like a thing of life,"

now lay upon their bosom a dark, motionless, inanimate mass.

CHAPTER XIII

As an owl that in a barn
Sees a mouse creeping in the corn,
Sits still, and shuts his round blue eyes,
As if he slept, until he spies
The little beast within his reach;
Then starts and seizes on the wretch.

Hudibras.

The salute of the Albatross was duly returned from the battery, and the entire *posse* of idlers in the port, or little village at the landing-place, which is rather more than two miles from the town of St. Blas, were collected at the pier to see what manner of men her whale-boat contained, as she pulled swiftly in towards the shore. About half way between the ship and the shore the whale boat was met by that of the harbor-master; the crew of the former tossed their oars out of the water, and held them upright in token of respect, while, at the same time, the officer in the stern-sheets arose and raised his hat. This respectful behavior was by no means lost upon the military dignitary, who listened with great affability to the stranger's account of himself—namely, that he was first officer of the ship Albatross, of Boston, commanded by Captain Israel Williams; that she had put in for supplies of wood, water, and fresh provisions; that she was bound to Canton, and sundry other particulars of minor consequence; Mr. Morton not deeming himself bound in honor or honesty to inform said harbor-master that it was the intention of the captain and officers to smuggle certain cases of silks, cloths, and linen on shore without his, the said harbor-master's, privity or consent.

As soon as the strange ship had anchored, Don Gaspar mounted his horse and galloped through the plaza towards the landing-place, at the imminent risk of his own neck, and compromising the sublunary welfare of a swarm of children that were basking in the hot sand in utter defiance of parental authority and of all passengers, bipedal or quadrupedal. Not long after he had gone, Isabella threw her veil over her head, and tripped, with a palpitating heart, towards Dame Juanita's house, which she entered by a back passage well known to herself, and sat down in the little room behind the shop. In a moment the good dame made her appearance, her face literally shining with pleasure.

"I have seen him, senorita! I have seen him and spoken with him."

"Seen him! seen whom?" gasped Isabella, but blushing rosy red at the same time.

"Ah, senorita, you know whom," said Juanita, "that handsome American that you used to meet here a year ago nearly."

As the young lady sat with her back towards the shop-door, and was besides eagerly drinking in all Juanita's news, she did not perceive that a man had entered the room. A gentle voice that thrilled to her heart pronounced her name; she turned, uttered a shriek, and fell fainting into the arms of Morton.

Excessive joy did, in ancient times and in one or two instances, prove fatal; but I suspect that the world has grown more wicked, or the human heart less susceptible, for I doubt whether there is any body now alive who has ever experienced a sufficient degree of pleasure at once to do more than agitate the nerves for a few minutes.

Isabella soon recovered her senses, partly from the effects of cold water sprinkled upon her face by the tender-hearted Juanita, and perhaps there might be something reviving in a soft kiss that the young seaman could not avoid dropping upon her lips as he supported her in his arms. I have already intimated my incompetency to describe a parting scene between two lovers, for reasons then specified: a tender meeting is liable to the same objections. Such things should always be left to the reader's imagination; for it is ten chances to one if the author's description pleases any body, not even himself.

After the first emotions of meeting had subsided, Isabella informed her lover of her uncle's promise, and that she was free from all persecution with regard to Don Gregorio. Morton, on the other hand, communicated to her all that had passed between his father and himself. "So that you see, dearest Isabella, if you had consented to go home with me as I urged, we might at this moment be comfortably seated at my father's fire-side. In the mean time, Captain Williams knows how I am situated, and will give the most effective assistance to my plans. We shall probably be detained here for two or three weeks, and I shall have daily opportunities of seeing you."

Time flies with lovers, and they had been nearly an hour in conversation, when Juanita put them in mind of its lapse, and urged the danger of Isabella's staying away from her uncle's house any longer. They separated with a thousand promises to meet again.

In a day or two, Captain Williams had made arrangements for disposing of the remnant of his cargo, in a quiet way, to certain merchants who are always and every where to be found, ready and willing to evade the exactions of the custom-house.

One branch of the river empties into the north-eastern, part of the bay, from which the slope up to the plaza on the summit of the hill is gradual. The point formed by this branch and the bay is covered with a thick growth of limes and other trees, through which winds a scrambling sort of path, passable by mules, and but very seldom used. After winding through the trees and bushes, and up a steep hill, that farther to the left, or westward, becomes an abrupt precipice of two hundred feet in height; it emerges in an obscure and narrow street on the eastern side of the town.

The Albatross's launch was sent every night, under the command of one or other of the mates, with a cargo of goods, which were landed near the termination of the above-mentioned winding path, and loaded upon mules that were always ready, concealed among the bushes, to be brought out at an appointed signal from the boat. It would be difficult to select a place better adapted for the peculiar purpose; unguarded and unsuspected, nobody had ever dreamed of any smuggling attempt being made there.

This plan of landing cargo had been carried on with equal secrecy and success for many nights, till nearly all was discharged. In the mean time, information had been conveyed to the commandant, by some person who had accidentally seen the boat one night engaged in discharging her precious freight, and the mules loading on the beach. In consequence of this intelligence, orders had been issued to the officer commanding the troops at San Blas, to march a strong party to the place, and secure all merchandize and persons found there. Part of this behest was executed to the letter; the remainder Jupiter dispersed into thin air.

Mr. Morton, with six hands in the jolly-boat, came on shore at the usual time, bringing all the remainder of the cargo, which was hardly enough to load two mules. Every thing was landed and loaded upon the mules without interruption, excepting a small package containing silk handkerchiefs, when suddenly a low whistle was heard in the bushes.

"What is that?" said Morton, who held the aforesaid package in his hands.

"Santa Maria!" exclaimed the muleteers, springing upon their horses, and putting them and the mules into rapid motion; "vienen los soldados malditos," the d—d soldiers are coming; the signal was repeated, and in an instant soldiers rushed from different parts of the adjacent bushes, and surrounded the whole party. So sudden and complete was the surprise, that the seamen, though standing in the edge of the water, were intercepted and made prisoners. Morton, as soon as he perceived that flight and resistance were equally out of the question, hailed the two men in the boat that was lying a few yards from the shore, and ordered them to make the best of their way to the ship—an order that was acknowledged by the customary "ay, ay, sir," and obeyed by hoisting their lug-sail, which, filled by a fresh land-breeze, soon carried them out of danger. He, with the remaining four men, were made prisoners. Whether the soldiers were not used to acting against cavalry, or thought the prisoners of more consequence than the merchandise, is doubtful; the mules and their drivers got off safe, although several shots were fired at them as soon as their retreat was perceived.

Ascertaining that there was nothing more to be got on the field of battle; for it was indeed one, as one of the sailors, feeling somewhat restive under the tight grasp that the corporal laid upon his collar, had bestowed upon that humble candidate for military honors a slap in the face, that caused him, in the Nantucket dialect, to "blow blood;" the guard took up their line of march through the wood with their five prisoners. On their melancholy route towards the town, the commanding officer of the party, mindful of the politeness and attention with which he had been treated by Mr. Morton, behaved to his prisoners with great kindness, and endeavored to console this officer by representing that nothing had been found that would or could be deemed sufficient to convict them of any attempt to violate the laws of the province; that the escape of the mules was a favorable circumstance, as they had carried off whatever might have otherwise appeared as evidence against them, whether merchandise or men; which last, with the treachery peculiar to Spaniards, and more universally inherent in the mixed breed of the colonies, would compound for their own safety by implicating their employers; that the governor was a gentleman, and a man of kindly feelings, and that he would undoubtedly pass over what had occurred that night without the exercise of any greater severity than perhaps the imposition of a moderate fine; with sundry other and similar topics of consolation, suggested by kindness and sympathy. But Morton's mind was too confused and agitated by the events of the evening, to allow him to make much reply or to pay much attention to the consolations of the officer; he longed to reach the guard-house, where, in the solitude and silence of the prison, he might have time and opportunity to arrange his ideas, and reflect upon his melancholy and apparently hopeless situation, and correspond, if permitted, with his commander, and with one other.

"But no," he thought, after the lovely image of Isabella had presented itself to his mind, "no, she will not dare to visit me, or exert herself in my behalf—and why should she? it would but expose her to suspicion, and me and these poor fellows to greater rigor."

He knew but little of the strength of woman's love—her devotedness, her acuteness, and energy and activity, in contriving and executing plans for the relief or comfort of her loved one in affliction. His four companions in misfortune, with all that philosophical indifference to calamity and danger that characterizes seamen, after expending an incredible number of strange curses and sea jokes upon their captors, stretched themselves upon the stone floor of the "caliboza," or prison, and were soon sound asleep; and Morton himself, fatigued in body and harrassed and bewildered in mind, soon lost all consciousness of his unhappy situation in deep and prolonged slumber.

Having lodged his prisoners in the guard-house and given orders that they should be treated with all kindness, the officer waited upon the governor, and reported the proceedings of the night. His excellency looked rather blank at learning that none of the goods had been secured; but having complimented the officer upon his vigilance and zeal, he retired to rest, feeling all the pride and self-gratulation of a little mind, after having done a very little action. He did indeed feel somewhat anxious as to the effect the intelligence might have upon the ladies of his household, who had been projecting another visit to the American ship, being the fourth that had already taken place; but he finally determined, as the only course left him, to ensconce himself behind the intrenchments of his dignity, and to merge the urbane feelings of the hospitable gentleman in the awful gravity of the dog in office. Besides, he hoped that his vigilance and severity on the present occasion would be a sweet savor in the nostrils of his august monarch, and that promotion would follow as an affair of course; and he dropped asleep, fancying himself Lieutenant-General Don Gaspar de Luna, Knight of the most noble order of St. Jago de Compostella, and Governor-General of the island of Cuba or St. Domingo.

CHAPTER XIV

I'll follow him no more with bootless prayers.

Merchant of Venice.

The old Don, on rising the next morning, found all his womankind "overwhelmed with grief" in consequence of the news of the capture and imprisonment of the American seamen, and prepared to assail him with prayers, petitions, and tears, as soon as he made his appearance. In vain he tried to assume the governor, and to look and act dignified; he had not, either in appearance or manner, or even language, so "much of the Roman" in him, as a certain other potentate who shall be nameless; the persevering ladies followed him, and gave him no rest; and perhaps, by their pertinacity, drove him to declare, in his vexation, that it was his fixed and settled resolve to inflict upon his prisoners the extremity of the law's indignation. In fact, the tribulation caused in the governor's family by the unhappy events of the past night, had reached to an extravagant and general height; for even the wife of his bosom remonstrated in no very gentle terms against her lord's severity; so that his poor excellency found the gubernatorial chair as uncomfortable a seat as though its cushion had been stuffed with pins. He made good his retreat as quick as possible to his usual place of official business, or *bureau d'office*, but there new trials awaited him; for the very first person he saw there, and evidently waiting for him, was Captain Williams.

Isabella, in the mean time, had not yet risen; her sleeping thoughts had been too delightfully occupied with visions of happiness, and her waking reveries had so engaged her with day-dreams of prospective felicity, that she was not conscious of the lapse of time. She had just commenced dressing, with the assistance of a favorite servant, a native Mexican girl, when her weeping cousins rushed into the chamber in an agony of grief. With voices choked and interrupted by sobs and tears, it was some minutes before they could make their poor cousin comprehend the melancholy truth, with the gratuitous addition that the prisoners were to be shot the next morning in the plaza, and directly in front of the house. Having communicated all they knew, and all they had invented, they retired to spread the intelligence, to collect more, and to remove the furniture in the front chamber, for the more convenient witnessing the execution of the next morning.

Isabella, when left to herself, neither screamed, nor went into hysterics or tears; she sat still and motionless in the chair, into which she had sunk when the dreadful truth was made known to her; she became deadly pale, her temples throbbed, her breathing seemed oppressed, the light swam before her eyes, she uttered a convulsive sob, and, to the terror of her faithful and sympathising attendant, fell senseless upon the floor. The Indian girl, with great presence of mind, though sorely frightened, dashed water in her face, loosened her clothes, and practised all those modes of relief, better understood by ladies than described by me. The unhappy young lady at length recovered, and, with the assistance of her attendant, threw herself upon the bed, and gave way to a flood of tears, to the relief caused by which, and her subsequent repose, we must for a time leave her.

Captain Williams saluted the governor, as they met, with a countenance partaking of anger as well as sorrow; and, without much circumlocution, proceeded to state his business, and interceded most warmly in behalf of his men in confinement. But the old Don, before whose mind visions of promotion and honors were floating, was in no humor to grant petitions of any kind, much less one, the acceding to which would overthrow all his air-built castles; and he steadily refused to listen to the warm-hearted old seaman's arguments, urged with all the fervency of almost paternal affection for both Mr. Morton and his seamen. Unable to oppose or refute the arguments of Captain Williams, proving the innocence of the prisoners, or, at least, the veniality of their offence, if guilty, and the unreasonable disproportion between the crime and the punishment;wearied by the perseverance of the petitioner, and convinced, though unwilling to own it, by his arguments;—convinced, too, that he was making a very ridiculous figure in the eyes of his officers and several merchants who were present, he did, as all obstinate and pig-headed people do when they find themselves in the wrong, and see that they are making themselves contemptible: that is, he plunged still deeper into the wrong, by giving the good old seaman a harsh refusal to his prayer.

At this unexpected and ungentlemanly rebuff, Captain Williams suddenly became calm and silent, and, a moment after, left the office. Those who were present thought they saw in the stern, determined expression of his countenance grounds for apprehension and alarm; having the most extravagant opinion of the desperate and daring courage of the Americans, they looked to see the ensuing night signalized by some desperate attempt on the part of the seaman, to release his companions from imprisonment. Their apprehensions were confirmed in a space of time that seemed impossible to have enabled Captain Williams to reach his ship, by seeing the Albatross, under jib and spanker, slowly standing to the westward, and again anchoring full half a mile farther out to sea than before; not, to be sure, out of reach of the guns of the battery, but at such a distance as to render it extremely problematical whether *Spanish* artillerymen would be able to throw a shot within half a mile of her, especially in a star-light night.

This movement of the ship alarmed the governor not a little; for he knew that the guarda-costa was absent on a cruize, and it was doubtful when she would return, and that there were but thirty soldiers on duty at the barracks, the rest having recently been drafted into the interior, to wage war against certain straggling, light-fingered gentry, known in that part of the world by the general title of "monteneros," or highlanders, being analogous in their habits and manners, and confused ideas of *meum* and *tuum*, to the highland cattle-stealers of Scotland. In this dilemma, the governor's heart began to relent—he thought that he was carrying his severity too far.

On retiring to his house to dinner, he was met by a message from his niece, requesting to see him in her chamber, being too unwell to meet the family at noon. Thither his Excellency ascended with reluctant steps and slow, like a child called from his play to be whipped and sent to bed. He found his niece reclining upon a sofa, pale, languid, and evidently much agitated. She rose to receive him with her accustomed affection, and the old Don seated himself by her side.

"Isabella, my love, you appear to be distressed; what is the matter, child?"

"Dear uncle, my cousin Antonia tells me dreadful news."

"Dreadful news! what is it, dearest?" "She tells me," said Isabella, shuddering and gasping for breath, "that these unfortunate Americans are to be put to death to-morrow morning."

"Poh, poh! what nonsense! you know as well as I do that the law gives me no such power."

"But, dearest uncle, why should they be punished at all? nothing is proved against them, nothing is found about them that indicates guilty intentions," for, notwithstanding her indisposition, she had learned all the facts of the case from her gossip, Juanita, and the officers that had called in the course of the forenoon, "I have heard all the particulars, and confess that I see no reason why they deserve punishment at all."

"You know nothing at all about the matter, child. They have been seen, at other times than last night, landing boxes and bales at the same place."

"Are you quite sure that it was not some other persons?"

The governor paid no attention to this question, which he had never dreamt of asking his informer.

"Besides, if these are pardoned, other offenders will plead their innocence, and refer to the case of these men as a precedent. No, Isabella, I cannot, I dare not do it; they must abide by the consequences."

"Then if their lives are to be spared, what is to be done with them?"

"I shall write to the Viceroy, and keep them confined till I receive his instructions as to their future destiny."

"And that," said the young lady, in a faint voice, "will be worse than death! O think of it, dear, dear uncle."

"You take too gloomy a view of the case," said Don Gaspar, kissing the forehead of the lovely suppliant; "the Viceroy may pardon them, but I dare not—You plead in vain," continued he, as he saw she was about to speak; "were they my own sons, they should undergo the sentence of the law for their misconduct."

Fearing to excite her uncle's suspicions by too great urgency, Isabella changed her battery—

"At least, let them be used kindly—let them have plenty of good food and wine."

"Certainly, dearest little niece," said the governor, delighted to find the most formidable and irresistible of his female assailants so lukewarm in the cause of the prisoners, "and you shall be their provider."

"Me, uncle? well, I own I should wish to visit the prison occasionally, to see that they are comfortable."

"You shall whenever you please," said the Don, rising, and going to Isabella's writing desk; "there, there is an order, signed by my own hand, that will admit you whenever you please." So saying, he retired.

CHAPTER XV

I know that a woman is a dish for the gods, if the devil
dress her not.

Antony and Cleopatra.

A writer, evidently a Frenchman, in the British or some other
Encyclopædia, under the article "Man," draws a very ingenious contrast
between the two sexes, which is correct enough in its general principles,
but exceedingly erroneous in many very important points. Speaking of
the different behavior of men and women, under the pressure of grief or
calamity, he says, "Woman weeps—man remains silent—woman is in
agony when man weeps—she is in despair when man is in agony."

Mr. Philosopher, you are a goose. It is obvious that you have drawn
your conclusions from your observations of Frenchmen exclusively, who
are theatrical and affected from the cradle to the grave.

"Woman weeps while man remains silent."—True; she gives vent to
her feelings by weeping, and her full heart is tranquillized by her tears,
which seem not only to relieve and refresh the swollen and burning eyes
of the body, but to render those of the mind more clear and penetrating.
What, for instance, was the language and sentiment of Mary Queen of Scots,
when Rizzio was murdered in her presence? "I will dry up my tears," said
the high-spirited descendant of the Stuarts, "and think of revenge." Man's
remaining silent is not always an evidence of fortitude or resignation; it may
be stupidity and want of feeling, or gloom and sulkiness; a disposition to
find fault with Divine Providence for visiting him with affliction.

"Woman is in agony when man weeps." Absurd! her tears have relieved
her agony. Like the elastic and pliable willow, she has yielded to the storm
of grief, and her buoyant spirit rises comparatively uninjured from the
conflict.

"Woman is in despair when man is in agony." It is said that the
difference between a fool and a madman is, that the fool draws wrong
conclusions from correct principles, and the madman correct conclusions
from erroneous principles. I leave my readers to judge under which
denomination the author quoted comes. There is but one step in his climax
that approaches the truth, and he has drawn a series of wrong conclusions

from that. The concurrent testimony of a host of writers, both moralists and historians, goes to establish the fact, that, under the pressure of remediable misfortunes, women have infinitely greater acuteness and quickness of perception of means of relief—more promptness, energy, and courage in carrying them into execution, than men. "Hope the deceiver" retains possession of the heart of woman long, long after man has hanged, shot, or drowned himself in despair.

Isabella was certainly almost overcome by the melancholy intelligence, when first communicated; but weeping and the repose of the morning had tranquillized her, and the facts that she had ascertained had given her fresh courage and hopes. Not daring, however, to urge her uncle too far at that time, as she saw he was out of humor, she was still determined not by any means to regard one, nor two, nor twenty refusals as decisive; but, if he could not be "carried by boarding," to blockade him into compliance. Her uncle's order for her admittance to the prison, she determined only to use occasionally, and as circumstances pointed out, for fear of exciting suspicion; but to reserve it as a sort of sheet anchor for the perfection of a half-formed scheme that was already agitating her brain.

Under pretence of merely ascertaining that the prisoners were supplied with all the comfort that their situation would admit, but in reality to communicate with her lover, she visited the prison that very day. She found the prisoner, who was already heart-sick of the confinement, independently of its probable termination, walking listlessly up and down the passage leading to the inner prison, which was both spacious and airy; for, as before observed, his excellency had so far relented as to direct that the prisoners, during the day, should be permitted to enjoy the air. His surprise at seeing her was extreme—not that he doubted she would make an attempt to see him, but he considered it a hopeless one. She met him with tranquillity, almost cheerfulness.

"Thank heaven!" he exclaimed mentally, "there is some hope of once more snuffing fresh air; that sweet girl would never be so composed unless she had some plan in her mind for my delivery. Isabella, dearest Isabella, tell me, for heaven's sake, how have you managed to get into this place, that every one else is so anxious to keep out of? Has the old Don dismounted from his high horse? He has been polite enough to make me a morning call, but I am afraid he does not intend to allow me to return it. However, as long as he permits you to follow his example, I hope that I shall be enabled to bear the disappointment with becoming resignation."

"Hush, hush! how can you talk so giddily, when you know not what may be your fate?"

"Why, hanging is not a favorite Spanish punishment, so I suppose he will honor me so far as to expend a little powder and shot upon me."

"O, Charles! Charles! be quiet, for heaven's sake. Tell me, what did my uncle say?"

"Say? why, he scolded a good deal, said that I had heretofore behaved very decently, and that he was very sorry to see me here."

"He has written to the viceroy, to know what he is to do with you. My uncle, with all his faults, is an angel of mercy, compared with that cold-blooded, bigoted, cruel man. I have read somewhere that it is written over the gates of the infernal regions 'Let all who enter here leave hope behind.' Let all who fall into the hands of that haughty nobleman, whether innocent or guilty, leave hope behind too. He is governed entirely by his priests, and the very circumstance of your being a Protestant, however harmless, and found in his dominions, would be sufficient to make you an object of hatred and vengeance."

"Well, all that may be; but recollect my country will not tamely permit her sons to be dragged to foreign prisons, without knowing wherefore."

"You cannot suppose that your country will plunge into a war for your sakes?"

"No, no, my love; she would be a fool if she did; but there is a set of fellows called ambassadors, that often do more with their tongues than ten thousand good fellows can with their bayonets. But tell me, if you know, where is the ship? what says the good old Captain Williams to the scrape?"

"The ship has moved farther out, and he has been on shore twice to-day to intercede for you, but without effect, though my uncle has so far relented as to order you all the comforts that you wish."

"I should be obliged to him, then, for the comfort of walking out of prison."

"When the ship moved out of gunshot," continued Isabella, without noticing what she thought his artificial gaiety, "there was some apprehension that Captain Williams intended to make some desperate attempt to release you; but he has been on shore since, and had an interview with my uncle, and the alarm has subsided."

"Well done! that is the best thing I have heard this long time—a whole garrisoned Spanish town thrown into consternation by a single Yankee merchantman! upon my word, I shall entertain a more exalted opinion than ever of Spanish courage."

Isabella permitted him to indulge his national vanity, when she again urged that his situation was but little short of desperate, unless he was speedily relieved from it.

"I know, I know that my head is in the lion's mouth, and how it is to be got out I know not. If I could see Captain Williams—perhaps a good round fine paid to his high mightiness might open these doors."

"I will write to Captain Williams myself," said the young lady, "perhaps something of that kind might be done. In the mean time, whenever you have any wine or other provisions, of which I will see that there shall be no lack, make a point of sharing it with the guard; and, by all means," she added, in a lower tone, "see that the sentry is never forgotten."

"Ha! oho! I see the whole affair—there are never but five men on duty here at night." "Rash, hot-headed creature! there will be no occasion for such madness. Even if you should escape from prison, and reach your ship in safety, which would be next to impossible——"

"Well, what?" said Morton, observing that she was silent. She raised her eyes, swimming in tears.

"I understand you—dear, dear Isabella, do you think I would leave this country without you? No, never."

"Then remain perfectly quiet, attempt nothing, do nothing of yourself. In the mean time," continued she, rising, "do not abandon yourself either to hope or despair."

With these words she left the prison.

CHAPTER XVI

As cannons shoot the higher pitches
The lower we let down their breeches,
I'll make this low, dejected fate
Advance me to a greater height.

Hudibras.

Captain Williams, immediately upon his landing on the morning after the events related in the last chapter had taken place, was met at the Port by a woman of rather ordinary appearance, who put a letter into his hands, and retired without speaking. The letter was written in a woman's hand, but without signature, and was as follows:

> "Sir:—A friend of Mr. Morton is making every possible exertion to deliver him and his companions from imprisonment. That friend entreats that you would do nothing rashly, or that may give cause of alarm or suspicion to the governor or garrison, or to any of the inhabitants. If you will call this evening at the shop of dame Juanita Gomez, in the plaza of San Blas, a person will meet you there, and explain more fully the friendly intentions of the writer."

The honest seaman, after mature deliberation, came to the conclusion that the writer of this anonymous epistle could be no other than the fair Isabella, of whom he had heard Morton speak so often; and he resolved to attend to its directions most strictly. Accordingly, as a preliminary step, he thought best to reconnoitre the plaza as soon as possible, that he might make no unpleasant mistakes in the dusk of evening.

While at St. Blas, he had another interview with the governor, and endeavored to ascertain the intentions of that dignitary with regard to the destination of his prisoners. The governor, however, seemed to regard that as a state secret, and declined making any but a very evasive answer. As some amends for his severity, he condescended to give Captain Williams full permission to visit the prisoners, of which the veteran immediately availed himself. The kind-hearted old seaman was deeply affected, as he held Morton in his arms with all the affection of a fond father—

"That ever I should live to see my old school-fellow Jonathan Morton's son in such a situation, and not be able to help him," —were the first words he was able to articulate. Morton endeavored to calm him, by repeated assurances that he felt no apprehension; that he had no doubt that a certain friend was busy in projecting a plan for their deliverance. It was some time before he was sufficiently composed to converse.

"Have you tried the old Don with a few doubloons?" asked Morton.

"No, d—n him, I never thought of that; I can't get a word of common sense or common civility out of the old mule."

"I believe if he had taken the boat-load of goods when he took us, that he would have been more willing to listen to you."

"Ah, very like; the old fox missed the goose, and he is venting his malice upon you in stead. But, my dear boy, I don't exactly know how to go to work to offer a bribe. Damme, I could land thirty men this blessed night, and pull this old rookery down, and get you all out that way; but as for bribery, it is a devilish dirty piece of business, to make the best of it; besides, I tell you, I don't know how; if I did, I would try it, as dirty as I think it."

Morton, could not forbear smiling at the old man's unwillingness to employ a piece of machinery, at the present day so indispensable in our government throughout all its branches; he assured him that nothing was more simple; it was only to wait upon the Don in private, and request his acceptance of either cash or certain valuable merchandize, that would be attractive in the sight of the governor. "There are my silver-mounted pistols, and curious East India dagger, and my rifle, that all might be thrown out as baits to begin with;" —it was all in vain; the blunt old seaman still persisted that bribery, or any thing that approximated it, was but a dirty affair after all; and that, although he would leave no plan untried to effect the liberation of the prisoners, there was a moral contamination attached to the mode proposed that he neither could nor would submit to.

True to his appointment, Captain Williams, soon after sunset, repaired to dame Juanita's shop, with the location of which he had previously made himself acquainted. He was introduced by that worthy old lady into her back parlor, if a little apartment ten feet square, with a clay floor and no windows, deserves so dignified, or rather so *comfortable* a title; and in half an hour a female, closely veiled, entered the room. Notwithstanding her disguise, the old seaman had tact enough to perceive that his companion was young and graceful, or in more modern language, genteel, while the silvery music of her voice, as she addressed him, convinced him that she could be no otherwise than beautiful.

"Are you," said the lady, in a hesitating, tremulous voice, "are you the commander of the American ship in the bay?"

"I am; and you, senorita, are the lady who wrote me the note that I received this morning?"

"Yes, I—that is, I sent you a note requesting to see you."

"And you are the generous, devoted, and true friend that takes such a lively interest in the fate of my friend and officer, and his companions in prison and misfortune?"

"I am—I am," replied the lady hurriedly.

"And you are, in short," continued the commander, rising and respectfully offering his hand, "you are the lady Isabella de Luna?"

"I cannot deny it," said she in a faint voice.

"Then, madam, you see before you one who is acquainted with your story. Nay, never hang your head for shame; Charles Morton is worth any woman's love. I am here ready with hand, heart, and head, to second any and every plan that you may propose, to effect his escape."

The lady remained silent for a few moments, then placing her small hand in the broad, hard palm of the old seaman, replied, "I know that I can put the most implicit confidence in you. I have heard from others—why should I deny it? Mr. Morton has told me often, that, next to his father, he regards you with affection and esteem as his dearest and truest friend."

"And he shall never be deceived in old Israel Williams, I can tell him that, nor shall you, my dear young lady."

"I have but little time to spare," said the young lady, with increasing trepidation, "and my communication must be brief, as my plan is simple. To-morrow night, at ten o'clock, Captain Williams, let your swiftest boat be at the place where Mr. Morton and his companions were taken, and let her wait there until day-break. It may not be in my power to effect my object to-morrow night; but let not one nor two disappointments deter you from repeating the experiment. In the mean time, be on shore to-morrow as though nothing was in agitation; avoid exciting any suspicions by either words, looks, or actions; and be assured, that, if the plan for the rescue of the prisoners fails, it must be from some accident that can neither be foreseen nor prevented."

The commander of the Albatross having promised to follow all these directions to the letter, they separated; he to return to his ship with a joyful heart, and Isabella to reconnoitre the prison previous to retiring to her uncle's house.

She passed the guard-house at a slow pace and at such distance as to avoid observation, but sufficiently near to ascertain that all the guard, four in number besides the corporal, were wrapped up in their cloaks and stretched out sound asleep upon the stone floor of the guard-room, which was lighted by a large clumsy lamp sufficiently to allow her to see its interior. The sentry at the door, who was slowly pacing backwards and forwards with a paper segar in his mouth, was the only one awake.

As she bent her steps homeward, she perceived some one approaching her, in the very direction that she was going, with an uncertain, faltering footstep that denoted considerable intoxication. To avoid him she turned to the right with the purpose of making a circuit; but, before she had gone ten yards with that intention, she perceived that the stranger had quickened his pace and changed his direction, coming directly towards her. Exceedingly alarmed, she turned short round and ran, and in a moment perceived that her pursuer was likewise running, and rapidly gaining upon her. Fear lent her speed, and with the swiftness of a hunted deer she flew across the plaza towards an open space, terminated at its further extremity by the precipitous cliff that the town is built upon, and which we have mentioned more than once. Her intention was to turn quickly round the corner of a house that stood within four feet of the edge of the cliff, and gain another street; or, if there were no other means of escape, to take refuge in the house of a poor widow, one of her pensioners, and obtain a guide and protector to her uncle's house.

Her pursuer was no other than her self-constituted lover, Don Gregorio. He had dined that day with a party of officers, and had dipped rather deeper into the bottle than, to tell the truth, he was often guilty of doing. He suspected that Isabella was in the habit of visiting the prison; but as she was generally accompanied, in all her rambles, by one or both her cousins, he had thought nothing more of the circumstance. But now he was convinced that she was just returning from, or going to, a nocturnal appointment with the prisoner Morton, who had always been an object of his hatred, and in an instant his jealousy was in full operation.

The cliff, towards which he was now approaching, was undefended by wall, fence, or barrier of any kind. My readers have doubtless seen something similar in their lives; that is, a nuisance that has acquired such a venerable character from its antiquity, that it seems a species of sacrilege, a sort of violation of municipal privileges, to remove or repair it. Such, for instance, in city or country, is a gap in the street or road, large enough to swallow a brace of elephants at once: the inhabitants become acquainted with its localities; and, wisely considering that, as it is *every* body's business, of course it is *nobody's* business, to repair it, leave it "open for the inspection of the public" for a twelvemonth at least; and if any unfortunate stranger tumbles in and breaks his neck, on a dark night, it is ten chances to one that the jury of inquest return for a verdict, that "the deceased came to his death in consequence of intoxication," although he may be the most abstemious water-drinker that ever the sun shone upon. Such was, ten or eleven years ago, to my certain knowledge, the cliff of San Blas.

Maddened with jealousy, and rendered incapable of commanding his movements by intoxication, the unhappy Don Gregorio was whirled, by the impetuosity of his own motion, far over the brow of the hideous precipice. One dismal yell of mortal agony broke the stillness of night, and the next moment his body was heard far below, crashing among the bushes and loose stones at the foot of the cliff. Fainting with horror at the dreadful sight, though ignorant of the person of the victim, Isabella sank upon the ground, and it was some minutes before she recovered sufficiently to rise. When, at length, she was somewhat restored, she turned towards her uncle's house with feeble steps and slow, frequently stopping to lean against the walls of the houses; she tottered into the room where the family were assembled, and sank senseless upon the floor. Her relatives, exceedingly terrified, administered restoratives, and conveyed her to her own chamber, where, when she was somewhat composed, she informed her anxious friends that she had been pursued by an intoxicated person, and was extremely terrified, and begged to be left to her repose, which she assured them was all she required. Having obtained all the information they were likely to, her kind and inquisitive cousins left her, after compelling her to swallow a composing medicine. She awoke in the morning perfectly refreshed; the horrid scene that she had witnessed the night before seeming rather like a terrifying dream than a mournful reality.

Before she left her chamber, a man, with his jaws standing ajar with horror, called upon the governor, and requested to speak with him in private. He then informed his excellency, that as he was rambling through the woods at the foot of the precipice, he had found the dead body of an officer, who had evidently fallen from the cliff above; that it was so frightfully mangled by the fall, that no vestiges of humanity were recognizable in the countenance, or in the body; but that, from the peculiar fashion of the regimentals, he was almost sure that it was his excellency's aid-du-camp, Don Gregorio Nunez. Alarmed by this intelligence, the governor despatched a servant to that officer's quarters, who soon returned with the intelligence that he had not been there since the morning of the preceding day. Further inquiry among his brother officers informed him that he had left their company the evening before about ten o'clock: that he had been drinking freely, rather more freely than usual; and that they had not seen him since.

Having commanded the attendance of two or three officers and as many soldiers, the commandante proceeded to the spot, guided by his first informant, and was convinced, as soon as he saw the crushed and mutilated mass, that it was no other than his unhappy officer. Having given orders for transporting the body to town, he returned to his family, who, although aware, from his abstracted and pensive manner, that something had happened to discompose him, forbore to ask any questions—a line of conduct which, by the way, we would most earnestly recommend to all wives and daughters. Isabella's mind was too much occupied with her own thoughts to notice the silence and melancholy of her uncle; she ate nothing, but her aunt and cousins attributed her want of appetite to the fright of the preceding evening; as her eyes met their kind and anxious looks, and she thought of her determination to quit them forever, she could not restrain her tears; but rising hastily from the table, she took shelter from observation and questioning in her own chamber.

CHAPTER XVII

— — I did compound
A certain stuff, which, being ta'en, would cease
The present powers of life; but in short time,
All offices of nature should again
Do their due functions.

Cymbeline.

Shortly after the sea-breeze had set in—that is, between eleven and twelve o'clock—a sail was discovered in the western horizon, standing in for the land; which sail the commander of the Albatross, in a short time, made out, with the help of his glass, to be the guarda-costa, to his no small vexation and disappointment. She stood in, however; but instead of anchoring as usual, in what may be called the outer harbor, she ran close in to the landing-place, furled her sails, and then, to Captain Williams's great relief, sent down her fore-yard, stripped it of the sail and rigging, and launched it overboard. Two boats, full of men, were soon seen towing it ashore, the spar having been "sprung" in one of those sudden and violent "flaws" of wind so peculiar to high and mountainous coasts.

All this was extremely gratifying to the commander of the American ship; in the first place the Venganza (for that was the warlike name of this redoubtable man-of-war), by lying so far up the harbor, was out of the line between the Albatross and the point where it was intended to send a boat that night; and secondly, the absence of so indispensable a spar as the fore-yard would render pursuit impossible.

Captain Williams went on shore in the afternoon, and met the old Don, who treated him with great condescension, and even hinted at the probability of his making another visit to the Albatross, to which hint the seaman replied as politely as could be expected. It was nearly night when he once more entered dame Juanita's shop, from which he took the liberty to despatch a message to Isabella. She appeared in a few minutes, and hastily assured him that the prospect of success was bright, and that nothing existed at that time that threatened to defeat their plans.

As soon as he returned to his ship, he made preparations for getting under way as speedily as possible; the bower anchor was hove up, and the ship rode by a light kedge, there being then but little wind or tide; the gaskets were cast off the topsails, and their places supplied with ropeyarns, which would break as soon as the "bunts," or middle of the sails, were let fall; the chewlines and other running-rigging were overhauled; and every other plan for making sail upon the ship as expeditiously and as silently as possible, was adopted. The crew of the Albatross performed all these different acts of duty with silence and alacrity. Although their commander had not communicated his plan to them, they knew by instinct that something bold and daring was to be attempted that night for the rescue of their favorite officer, and their four messmates; and their hopes of a brush with the "Don Degos" were most keenly excited. They were assembled on the forecastle, holding "high dispute" and conjecture upon the course about to be pursued.

"Now if I was the old man," said one of the younger seamen, "I tell you what I would do. I would jest land as many of us as could be spared, with cutlasses and boarding-pikes" —

"And pistols," interrupted another.

"No; d—n your pistols; they make too much noise; they're all talk and no cider; besides, they miss fire half the time; and before you get ready for another shot, Don Dego has his thundering baggonet right in your g—ts; and then where are you?"

"Now you may all of you," said an old seaman, "you may all of you just pipe belay with your jaw-tackle-falls. Captain Williams knows what he's about, and you'll know before morning what he's up to. You'd better take a fool's advice, and catch a cat-nap before you're called away. The boats a'n't histed up, and when did you ever know 'em in the water after dark since we've been lying here?" So saying, the veteran disappeared down the fore-ladder.

"There goes old Jemmy Bush, starn foremost down the fore-scuttle, like a land-bear going into his hole."

"Well," said another smart, active young seaman, the favorite of the crew; "I shall take old Jemmy's advice, and go and get forty winks in my hammock. If there's more or less of us sent on this expedition, we sha'n't be called away till ten or eleven o'clock, when all the Degos are asleep, and there's nothing awake in the town but fleas and cats."

The proposition for sleeping prevailed, and the groups on the forecastle began to disappear, when the voice of the second mate was heard:

"For'ard there!"

"Sir, sir," answered half a dozen eager voices at once.

"Who has the anchor watch?"

"Bill Thompson and Sam Hughes, sir."

"Go in the boats alongside, and see that they have their full complement of oars; and see, too, that the masts and sails are on board all of them."

"Ay, ay, sir."

"Do you hear that, my sons of brass?" said old Jones, the boatswain, "that looks as if there was going to be wigs on the green before morning."

We must now leave the marine department for awhile, in order to attend to exclusively terrene concerns. As night closed, Morton could not avoid feeling extreme anxiety; Isabella had not visited the prison since the day previous, nor had she sent any message. Doubts the most annoying possessed his mind—at one time he thought she had been detected in her schemes for his rescue; then that her courage had failed, and she had abandoned him to his fate; or that her affection for her relatives had overcome her love for him. He had partially made known to his four fellow-prisoners his hopes of relief, cautioning them against sleeping, but enjoining upon them to keep perfectly quiet.

It was now past nine o'clock; and, with mingled feelings of disappointment, grief, and anger, he was just resigning all hopes, when the sentry at the door challenged. The next moment a person dressed in a long, loose cloak stood before him, whom he immediately recognized as his loved Isabella.

"I have brought you some supper and some wine," said the young lady, addressing him, as usual upon similar occasions, in Spanish; "I ought to have come before, but it was impossible."

So saying, she set her basket upon the stone bench, and, in so doing, whispered Morton:

"Every thing is ready; be patient, and be guided by me."

"But how are you about to manage these fellows? it will take all night to get them drunk, if that is your plan; for your soldiers, it cannot be denied, are extremely temperate, and will seldom do me the honor to empty more than a single bottle among the whole five."

"Hush, hush; I have a surer way than mere wine."

As she spoke she drew from her bosom a phial, containing a dark liquid. Morton started back in horror—(he thought he saw, in the composed and lovely countenance of the beautiful being before him, the cold-blooded, deliberate, practised assassin—)

"Good God! Isabella, is it possible? never, never will I owe my life and liberty to such abominable, such cowardly means!"

"Dismiss your suspicions," said Isabella, turning pale and trembling; "they are unworthy of you, and wholly unmerited by me. Not to save *your* life, which I value as I do my own, would I commit mur—the crime that you suspect. This phial contains a simple opiate, not half so dangerous or disagreeable as the laudanum and camphor of your ship's medicine chest. The sleep produced by it is speedy and deep, and lasts four or five hours."

Observing that Morton still looked distrustingly, she continued, with streaming eyes—

"Dear Charles, if you doubt me still, I will swallow the whole; its operation will not take place before I reach home, and will only cause long, deep sleep; but, in that case, your hopes of escape are cut off *forever*. To-morrow, or the next day, at farthest, you are to be sent to the capital"—her tears choked her utterance.

"Dearest Isabella," said Morton, taking her hands in both his, and pressing them to his bosom, "forgive my cruel suspicions, but I own you startled me exceedingly."

"Leave all to my management, and in half an hour all will be well."

In the mean time the seamen had "boarded" the basket, and spread its contents upon the stone bench, that did triple duty as a bed, a seat, and a table, as occasion required. The soldiers roused themselves at the gurgling sound of the wine, as it was decanted into cups made of the large end of an ox's horn, scraped thin, and capable of containing a pint or more. Isabella dexterously poured the contents of the phial into a cup, which was filled with wine, and Morton, taking it in his hand, approached the corporal with a nod of invitation. After holding it to his lips for some time, as if taking a deep draught, he passed it to the corporal; that officer, touching his cap *à la militaire*, drank and passed the horn, according to South American custom, to his comrades. The prisoners and Isabella watched its circulation with most painful anxiety, and soon had the felicity of beholding it turned bottom upwards over the mouth of the sentry at the door. Another bottle was opened, and poured, unobserved by the soldiers, into another cup, which, being handed to the sailors, was almost immediately passed back again, "a body without a soul." Another cup, medicated like the first, was prepared, and the prisoners, apparently busied with their supper, awaited with trepidation the effect of the medicine.

After the lapse of fifteen or twenty minutes, which seemed as many hours to the prisoners, the corporal betrayed palpable symptoms of somnolency. He had seated himself with his back to the wall, and his feet towards a small fire that was kept burning in the middle of the guard-room every night, to drive away the moschetoes, and had commenced a song, in a low voice. The first stanza he managed very respectably; but, before he had half finished the second, both the air and words seemed strangely deranged; his head sank upon his breast, and he snored repeatedly, instead of singing; he made an effort to arouse himself, uttered that ejaculation common to all ranks and both sexes of Spaniards, but which is too gross to be written, and, stretching himself at full length upon the floor, was sound asleep in an instant. His three comrades were not slow in following his example; wrapped in their *ponchos*, or South American cloaks, they "took ground" around the fire, and were soon asleep.

The sentry at the door, after two or three times stumbling over his own feet, and as often dropping his musket out of his arms from mere drowsiness, came into the guard-room to light a segar, which he eventually accomplished at the imminent risk of pitching head foremost into the fire. He resumed his station at the door, but was too sleepy to walk on his post; he seated himself on the stone bench, the butt of his musket resting upon the ground between his feet, and the muzzle leaning against his shoulder; the lighted segar dropped from his mouth; he leaned his head against the door-post, extended his feet and legs, and in a few seconds his nasal organ, in strains like the nocturnal song of one of our largest bull-frogs, gave notice that he was "absent without leave" to the land of Nod.

Isabella now arose, and, motioning to the prisoners to remain quiet, tripped backwards and forwards through the guard-room, to ascertain that the soldiers were asleep. Having satisfied herself on this point, she beckoned to them to follow her. In passing through the guard-room, Morton as well as his companions felt a strong inclination to possess themselves of the arms of the guard, which were piled in one corner. Their fair guide however entreated them to desist; but one of the seamen, in attempting, to use his own language, to "unship" one of the bayonets, made so much noise with the muskets, as alarmed himself as well as the rest; and the whole party sallied out unarmed.

Near the door they were met by another person, that alarmed the prisoners exceedingly; but it proved to be Transita, Isabella's Mexican servant, loaded with two "sizeable" bundles; for the annals of elopements, from the earliest ages down to the present day, have not recorded a single instance of a lady's running away from "cruel parents" or cross husband without the accompaniment of a sufficient quantity of baggage;

nay, I have heard of one young lady who accomplished a most perilous descent from her chamber window into the arms of an expecting lover, and returned for her favorite lap-dog, at the most imminent risk of detection and close imprisonment at the hands of her "ugly, old, cross papa."

Transita, like her mistress, was dressed in boy's clothes, a disguise that so effectually imposed upon the four sailors, that in a whispered conversation between them it it was decided that the two "young gentlemen" were the sons of the merchant to whom the cargo had been sold. Keeping close to the side of the plaza, the whole party advanced swiftly and silently without meeting a human being, and turned down the open space where Don Gregorio had met his horrid fate. As the dreadful scene rose to Isabella's memory, she could not repress a faint exclamation of horror, and hurried with increased speed down the narrow pathway on the edge of the cliff, to escape from the hideous recollection. Just as they were emerging from their narrow and crooked path into the street that terminated in the blind passage through the wood, they were startled by the regular, heavy tread of soldiers, apparently approaching them. It was a small patrol of a corporal and three men from the barrack at the water side, but who were not connected with the guard in the plaza. As they drew nigh, the party stood perfectly still, except that one of the tars drew forth his jack-knife, and another picked up a moderate-sized stone, observing in a whisper that if they came too nigh, he would try which was the hardest, a Spaniard's scull or that "ground nut," as he designated the stone which he held in his hand. The soldiers, however, passed on without seeing them, and in a few seconds their footsteps became inaudible.

CHAPTER XVIII

"She is won: we are gone, over bank, bush, and scaur;
They'll have fleet steeds that follow," quoth young
Lochinvar.

Marmion.

The liberated seamen once more pushed forward, no longer guided by Isabella, who had got as far as her knowledge of the place extended, and were again, in nautical language, "brought up all standing." A priest, returning from the death-bed of one of his flock, saw them gliding along silently and in "Indian file." His head being full of good wine, death, the devil, &c., and the place enjoying moreover the reputation of being haunted, his imagination magnified and multiplied the seven fugitives into a legion of devils, with horns, tails, and fiery breath complete. Under this impression he began to thunder forth a Latin form of exorcism: "In nomine sanctæ Trinitatis et purissimæ Virginis, exorcizo vos! Apage, Satana! Vade retro, diabole!" &c. &c. in such abominably bad Latin, that a devil or a ghost of the least classical taste would have incontinently fled to the Red Sea, without waiting to hear another syllable of the formula that sent him thither. The bawling of the priest awoke several of the neighbors, and sundry night-capped heads were protruded from the windows of the nearest houses; but the proprietors, catching a glimpse of the objects of the priest's alarm, and not caring to play bo-peep with the devil, closed and barred their casements, and betook them to their beads.

The party glided on in the same swift, silent pace; but the hindmost sailor, irritated by the continued vociferation of the priest, and stumbling at that moment over the carcase of a dog that had given up the ghost a few hours before, seized it by the hind leg, and flung it at the holy man with such true aim and force, as brought him to the ground. Luckily the monk swooned away with terror at this unexpected buffeting in the flesh from Satan, and his noise was consequently stopped. The next moment the party plunged into the bushy path, and were instantly lost to the view of the inhabitants, if indeed any were looking after them.

Advancing swiftly along the rough path, and losing their way two or three times, they at length heard the light dash of the surf upon the sand-beach; but, to their no small alarm, they also plainly heard, from time to time, the low hum of voices, though their language was not distinguishable. Fearing the worst, Morton advanced alone to reconnoitre, notwithstanding Isabella's earnest entreaties not to be left alone. Moving slowly and cautiously towards the point whence proceeded the voices, the soft sand rendering his footsteps inaudible, he approached as near as he durst, and listened for some minutes with the most fixed attention, to catch a word that would indicate the character and nation of the speakers, but in vain; and he was on the point of returning to his friends in despair, when he plainly distinguished the exclamation, "d— — n my eyes," uttered by some one at no great distance from where he stood. No Sontag or Malibran ever warbled a note that contained a hundredth part of the sweetness and music that was comprised in that simple and unsophisticated ejaculation; it decided in an instant, and beyond all possibility of doubt, who and what was the speaker. His joy was inconceivable, and he could scarce refrain from giving vent to it in a loud shout. Returning immediately, he communicated the joyful intelligence to his friends; and the whole party, with light hearts and rapid steps, advanced towards the beach. Just as they stepped from the shade and covert of the bushes, a pistol, the bright barrel of which glittered in the star-light, was presented to Morton's breast; and the holder thereof, in a grum voice, commanded him to "stand!"

"Heave to, and let's overhaul your papers," continued the speaker, who was immediately recognized, by the voice, as Jones, the boatswain of the Albatross.

"Hush, hush, don't speak so loud; 'tis I, 'tis Morton—Jones, is that you, my old boy?"

"God bless you, Mr. Morton, it is you indeed—I thought 'twas a raft of them thundering sojers bearing down upon us. I've been lying to, under the lee of this 'ere bush, for this two hours or more, waiting for you."

The parleying between their "look-out ship," as they called Jones, and the strangers, attracted the whole party of the Albatross to the spot; and Morton, to his surprise, found himself and his companions surrounded by at least thirty well-armed men. His friend Walker, the second mate of the ship, advanced, and testifying the sincerest affection, welcomed him once more to liberty and the company of his shipmates. Kind greetings and hearty welcomes were given by the seamen, in their blunt, straight-forward way, and not a few jokes were passed upon the four liberated tars by their light-hearted messmates.

"I say, Tom Wentworth, how much *grub* did the Don Degos allow you? a rat a-piece, or the hind leg of a jackass among the four of you?"

"Ay," said another, "and Sundays they had a jackass's head stewed in a lantern, and stuffed with sogers' coats."

"Yes," said a third, "and green-hide soup three times a week."

"Seasoned with brick-dust and pig-weeds," said a fourth, "by way of red pepper and cabbages."

"Well, never mind what they've had," said old Tom Jones, interposing, "one thing's sartain, they ha'n't had any steam, that's jist as clear as mud."

"You're idle there, old Tom Pipes; we've had as much good wine as we could lay our sides to. But howsomever, if you've got any white-eye in that black betty that you're rousing out of your pea-jacket pocket, I don't much care if I take a drop."

"Poor children!" said the boatswain, "they've been kept this whole week in a snug, warm *caliboose*, and they'll catch cold if they're out in the night air."

So saying, he offered his junk-bottle of New England to Morton, who declined it, and it was then passed to his four fellow-prisoners, who took a long, deliberate, steady aim at the stars through it in succession.

By this time the two whale-boats and yawls, that constituted the flotilla of the shore party, were hauled as close to the beach as the shoalness of the water would permit, and the embarkation commenced; Morton carrying the fair Isabella in his arms, and depositing her in the stern-sheets of the swiftest of the boats, in which he found ample store of boat-cloaks and pea-jackets to protect her from the night air and heavy dews. Her attendant, Transita, was about following her mistress, when Tom Jones, who had no suspicion that there were more than one "young gentleman" concerned in effecting the escape of his shipmates, or about taking passage in the ship, laid his huge hand upon her shoulder, exclaiming,

"Halloa! shipmate, where are you bound to, if the wind stands?"

"What are you about there, Jones?" shouted Morton from the boat, "she—he, I mean, is to go off with us. Take him through the surf."

"Ay, ay, sir; come, Mr. She—he, just get upon my shoulders, if you please; come, bear a hand before it snows—there, stow yourself away in the starn-sheets—there, that's the time of day—shove her bows off, Sam, and jump aboard—so, pull round your larboard oars—now give way together."

Their oars being all muffled, they glided, silently and swiftly, towards the offing, edging away a little to the south, or farther side of the bay, to avoid the possibility of observation from the shore. They had proceeded swiftly for some minutes, and had passed the point on which the battery stands without speaking a word, when the silence was broken by Morton,—

"Where is the ship, Jones? do you see any thing of her?"

The boatswain desisted rowing, and, holding his head down as near the water as possible, looked long and anxiously to the western horizon.

"I don't see her," said he, "unless that's her, here on our starboard bow."

"No, that's the rock."

By this time the other boats had come up, and all agreed that nothing could be seen of the ship. After a brief consultation, it was decided that their safest plan was to continue rowing to the westward, and that they would be sure of seeing the ship at day-break; whereas if daylight found them in the bay, they would most assuredly be seen, and chased by the boats from the shore.

Isabella, whom most powerful excitement had supported from the prison to the point of embarkation, had since then, reclining on the stern-sheets of the boat, and supported by her lover's arms, been in a state of stupor and silence; her thoughts were in a complete whirl, almost amounting to delirium; the kind and soothing voice of Morton she scarcely heard, and she only awoke to consciousness during the short deliberation just mentioned. In an agony of terror at the doubt and uncertainty that she heard expressed around her, she uttered the wildest exclamations, and struggled with Morton and her attendant, who endeavored in vain to pacify and sooth her. With unspeakable anguish Morton witnessed, for half an hour, the confusion of her intellects, till at length she sunk down exhausted, and wept bitterly. At this moment a voice from the yawl that had gone ahead, shouted, "There she is!"

"Where, where?" asked a dozen eager voices.

"Right ahead."

Every eye was instantly turned in that direction, and, to their unutterable joy, they saw, at the distance of about a mile, the light of a signal-lantern. Every oar was most vigorously plied, and in a few minutes the headmost boat was greeted with "Boat ahoy!" from Captain Williams— "Albatross," was the reply, and the boats dashed up to the lee gangway and fore-chains.

Isabella, whose buoyant spirit had recovered its spring when she saw the danger was over, was assisted up the side by her lover and two or three of the most careful men. As soon as Morton stepped upon deck, he was caught in the arms of his commander, who was inarticulate from emotion. Morton, quietly disengaging himself, presented his fair deliverer. The old seaman folded her in his arms, and kissing her cheek, drew her arm under his, and conducted her to the cabin, whither they were followed by Morton.

Under the superintendence of the second mate and boatswain the boats were now hoisted up and secured; the ship wore with her head to the westward, all sails set, and hot coffee, beef, bread, cheese, &c. provided liberally for the "shore party;" after which the watch was set, the deck "relieved" by Captain Williams, and the Albatross, with her white wings expanded, flew rapidly on her course before a fresh easterly breeze.

CHAPTER XIX

Master, let me take you a button hole lower; do you not see,
Pompey is uncasing for the combat? What mean you? you
will lose your reputation.
Love's Labor's Lost.

The rising sun the next day beheld the good ship Albatross, under the impulse of a very gentle breeze, gliding towards the west; the Andes, over which the sun was darting his levelled beams, were distinctly visible. The flapping of the topsails against their masts, the pattering of the reef-points, and the smoothness of the water, indicated an approaching calm.

"Go aloft, one of you," said Morton, who was the officer of the morning watch, "go aloft, and see if you can make out any sail astern of us under the land."

The seaman who obeyed this order, after *roosting* for fifteen or twenty minutes on the main royal yard, came down and reported that he could see nothing; but that the sun shone so brightly on the water that, if any thing was within the range of sight, the reflection of the sunbeams would render it invisible. Morton could not repress a vague apprehension that there was some vessel in chace, though it would have sorely puzzled him to give his whys and wherefores. After having pointed his glass for the fiftieth time towards the eastern horizon, without seeing any thing but smooth water and the dim, blue, cloudy-looking mountains, the man at the wheel notified him that it was "eight bells," or eight o'clock. Having gone below to compare the watch in the cabin with the half-hour glass in the binnacle, he returned to the quarter-deck and called out,

"Strike the bell eight—call the watch."

The bell was struck, and one of the watch on deck, after a preliminary thumping with the large end of a handspike upon the forecastle, vociferated down the fore scuttle,

"All the starboard watch, ahoy! Rouse out there, starbowlines—show a leg or an arm!"

This last phrase designates the manner in which "turning out" of a hammock is accomplished, which hammock, a person unacquainted with such kind of sleeping accommodations, would never dream contained a live man, until one or the other of the aforementioned limbs was protruded. In a few minutes the wheel was relieved, and the crew were clustering around the galley with their tin pots, joking, and laughing, and shouting "scaldings!" as they hurried forward with their respective allowances of hot coffee.

In the mean time the quarter-deck received an accession of company. Mr. Walker came up the companion-way, gaping and rubbing his eyes, and carrying his jacket on his arm. With a short "good morning!" to Morton he threw his jacket upon the hen-coop, proceeded to the lee gangway, drew a bucket of water, and commenced his morning's ablutions. Captain Williams next came on deck, and immediately looked round upon the weather with a troubled and disappointed air, for it was now almost quite a calm. Mr. Edwards and Dr. Bolton followed him—not that they had any business on deck, or cared much about leaving the cabin or their respective state-rooms oftener than was necessary; but it is not, or was not, in my sea-going days, esteemed genteel for passengers, or any other "idlers," to stay below while the steward was occupied with the mystery of arranging the breakfast-table. Lastly, and to the surprise of the whole company, Isabella, as lovely as the morning, and dressed in the proper habiliments of her sex, ascended the companion-ladder. She was greeted with paternal affection by the veteran commander, and with sparkling eyes and a silent pressure of the hand by Morton. She received and replied to their congratulations and compliments with crimsoned cheeks and downcast eyes. The supercargo and doctor, who had, with most commendable delicacy, kept out of the way the night before, were now introduced, and after a few minutes of general conversation, the steward informed Captain Williams that breakfast was ready.

The whole party, with the exception of Mr. Walker, who was now in his turn "officer of the deck," accordingly descended to the cabin, where they found the table covered with coffee and tea, *minus* milk; cold salt beef, cut into slices, of a thickness that would horrify a whole community of fashionable ladies and gentlemen, allowing that so exceedingly vulgar an article of "provent" as salt beef did not previously throw them into hysterics as soon as presented to their eyes, but which slices seemed to have been cut with the prospective intention of filling up that vacuum that Nature, as far as I am acquainted with her, seems to abhor more cordially than any other vacuum whatever; that void space, I mean, that is apt to be found in a healthy human stomach after a twelve-hour's fast. There was also a broiled chicken for the express use and behoof of their fair messmate; fried pork and potatoes; a large dish of fried fish, the produce of a fishing excursion the afternoon preceding; another of boiled eggs; a third composed of pilot-bread, soaked in hot water, toasted, and buttered; biscuit, butter, and cheese.

Breakfast proceeded much as sea breakfasts generally do—that is to say, the company ate heartily: even Isabella, who had sufficient excuse for low spirits and want of appetite, yielded to the demands of hunger the most unromantic, and, in vulgar language, "spoilt the looks" of the broiled fowl before her. The meal was drawing to a close, when the steward came below with information, that Mr. Walker had seen, from the main topmast head, with his glass, a square-rigged vessel right astern, and coming up with a fresh breeze. Captain Williams and Morton exchanged looks of intelligence, but said nothing; their fair passenger, fortunately, understood not a word of the steward's intelligence; and the merchant and doctor were of that happy and enviable description of men, who, when they sit down to a well-furnished table, seem to adopt, with a slight variation, the sentiment of the poet,

"Far from my thoughts, vain world, begone,
And let my *eating* hours alone,"

The two seamen, however anxious they might feel, finished their breakfast very composedly, and went on deck without hurry; Morton recommending to his fair deliverer to remain below for some time. In half an hour the chace was distinctly visible from the quarter-deck, and from the peculiar darkness of the water in that direction, it was evident that she had a good breeze. It was then that conjectures as to the character of the stranger were numerous, wild, and contradictory; no one thought for an instant that it was the Venganza, because they had seen her the day before with her fore-yard down and sent on shore—the idea that there might possibly be found a spare spar in the dock-yard that would answer *pro tem.* never, for an instant, presenting itself to their minds. A few minutes more, however, convinced them that it was indeed that "terrible ship with a terrible name;" and orders were immediately given to prepare for action as silently as possible. These orders were obeyed with joyous alacrity. A feeling of romantic gratitude to their lovely passenger was accompanied by a most chivalrous determination to "do or die" in her defence, and these sentiments pervaded the whole ship's company. Added to this exciting cause was that natural propensity to strife that Flora Mac Ivor says all men feel when placed in opposition to each other, or, as Titus Livius Patavinus hath it, they were "suopte ingenio feroces."

The clews of the topsails were lashed to the lower yard-arms; the topsail-yards slung with iron chains; round, grape, and cannister shot got up from the hold; the boarding-pikes taken down from the racks and laid at hand; the arm-chests unlocked, and their murderous contents of muskets, bayonets, pistols, cutlasses, and tomahawks or pole-axes produced; powder-horns and flasks, for priming the guns, filled and placed in readiness; rammers, sponges, and priming-wires distributed to the guns; preventer braces rove, and stoppers for the rigging sent up into the tops, or placed in different parts of the deck. The carpenter got ready his shot-plugs and top-maul; the armorer examined the locks of the fire-arms; the gunner paraded his wads, and opened the magazine beneath the cabin floor. Morton, to whom Captain Williams had deputed the charge of the two females, descended to the steerage, attended by two or three seamen, and hauled all the spare sails out of the sail-room, with which he formed a small hollow coil in the cable tier. These sails, being formed into long hard rolls and placed upon the cables, formed a rampart that, from its non-elasticity, would more effectually check the progress of a round shot than a greater thickness of oak plank.

Having finished the castle, he could not forbear passing into the cabin to see its future occupant. Isabella received him with a blush and a smile.

"What is the meaning of all this noise and bustle overhead?" said she.

"There is a strange ship in sight," said Morton, after a pause, "and we are almost sure that she has hostile intentions towards us." Isabella became pale as marble. "It is, in short, the man-of-war that was in St. Blas when we left there."

"Good God!" said the young lady, clasping her hands in agony, "what will become of us?"

"Do not allow yourself to be overcome with causeless alarm; we shall, if possible, run away; but if not, we must resort to certain arguments to convince her commander and crew of the impropriety and rudeness of their interfering in an affair that does not concern them."

"But if we are taken, what will become of you?"

"I suspect, dearest Isabella, that you will search in vain through the Albatross to find a single person, man or boy, that is prepared to admit the probability, nay, even the possibility, of such a conclusion. We are nominally inferior, but in reality superior, to our antagonist. In the mean time, I have been preparing a place of safety for you and Transita, where it is next to impossible that you should be in the way of danger."

"But you," said she, looking at him with tearful eyes.

"My life, my sweet girl, is in the hands of Him that gave it; and to His watchful care and boundless goodness I cheerfully and confidingly commit it."

"But if you are taken—such a thing is at least possible."

"Such an event is, as you say, possible. In that case, your Mexican friends must be content to work their revenge upon my dead body, for I am determined that the living Charles Morton shall never become an object for Spanish vengeance to exhaust its ingenuity upon. But I must leave you for the present. I will come below again in a few minutes, to conduct you to your citadel."

CHAPTER XX

Some writers make all ladies purloined,
And knights pursuing like a whirlwind;
But those, that write in rhyme, still make
The one verse for the other's sake.

Hudibras.

Morton and his companions had left the prison a few minutes past ten o'clock. It was nearly one when an officer, who was up and passing through the plaza for certain good reasons best known to himself, noticed, as he approached the guard-house, that there was an unusual degree of stillness about it; no sentry challenged as he drew near, and indeed there seemed to be none on post. Surprised at this, he entered the porch, or as it is called in New England, the "*pye*-azza," where he found the sentry seated, as before described, and snoring most lustily. Him he attempted to awaken by a very summary process; namely, by tumbling him from his seat upon the ground; but so stupified was the fellow with the drugged wine that he had drank, that after uttering certain unintelligible growlings, he again slept and snored. Passing into the interior, the officer found the corporal and his "brave compeers" as sound asleep and as motionless as the enchanted inhabitants of a fairy castle. After bestowing upon them several sound and hearty kicks, without producing any vivifying effects, he perceived that the door of the inner room, or prison, was wide open, and the room itself as empty as—an author's pockets. On further examination he found a basket, the remains of food, three or four empty bottles and drinking-cups, one or two full bottles, and a phial containing a small quantity of dark-colored liquid, with the qualities of which he did not think it prudent to make himself acquainted by experiment upon his own person; not possessing a particle of the philosophical courage and zeal of Sir Humphrey Davy, who gulped down poisonous gases till it became a matter of astonishment and mystery to his friends, as well as himself, how he contrived to find his way back into this world, after having strolled so far beyond its limits. The phial, however ignorant he was of the nature of its contents, explained, in connection with the empty bottles, the cause of the death-like sleep of the guard.

After deliberating for an extremely short space of time (for when a man has nobody near to bother him with advice, he makes up his mind with incredible despatch), he concluded that there would be no danger in leaving the guard-house just as he found it, for sundry reasons; in the first place, the present circumstances had probably existed some hours; secondly, as there was nothing there for the guard to watch over but the empty bottles, &c. said guard might as well sleep as be awake; thirdly—but by this time he was almost at his excellency's door, and it was hardly worth while to follow any farther a line of reasons that threatened to stretch out to the crack of day, if not of doom. After abundance of vociferating and thumping, he succeeded in rousing the governor from his slumbers, and bringing him to the window, night-capped and night-gowned "proper," as the heralds say. His excellency was thunderstruck at the intelligence, and in a few minutes his household was in motion.

His two daughters had no sooner learned that the prisoners had escaped, than they hastened to the chamber of their cousin, Isabella, to communicate the joyful intelligence. To their surprise and consternation no cousin Isabella was to be found; the chamber was in its usual state, but it was immediately obvious that the bed had not been pressed that night by its lovely occupant; one or two of the drawers of a bureau, in which she had formerly kept sundry articles of clothing, were open and empty; nor was this all; the doors of a little book-case, that stood upon a table in one corner of the room, and that formerly contained thirty or forty volumes, were also open, and every volume was gone.

This circumstance, which at once convinced the two young ladies that their cousin was decidedly deranged in mind, should have been mentioned and explained in its proper place. A fortnight previous to Morton's capture, Isabella consented to put herself under his protection, and having so done, retired to her chamber to deliberate upon the how and the what she should take with her. Her jewels, that had been left her by her mother, or given her by her uncle and other relatives, were numerous, costly, and easily portable; but jewels, though they ornament beauty, do not keep it warm. Her drawers were next opened, and sundry indispensable articles of dress were selected and set aside; but while she hesitated between certain elegant and valuable dresses and others more ordinary, that her natural good sense told her were more appropriate, her eyes rested upon a volume of Milton opened at the title-page, on which was written her mother's name by that beloved parent's hand: "My dear mother's books! how could I think of leaving them behind, or any thing that was ever hers!" She closed her drawers after having carelessly thrown aside, for "sea-service," the first dresses that came to hand—her whole thoughts occupied in devising means to save what, just at that moment, seemed of vastly superior consequence. The books, by Morton's advice, were subsequently carried, two or three at a time, to Juanita's house, and thence by him conveyed carefully on board the Albatross, and safely deposited in his chest. Having settled this affair so much to her satisfaction, she used the same means to transport the greater part of her most valuable clothes to the same place, till the unfortunate capture of her lover made it necessary to encumber herself and attendant with the remainder, upon the night of her elopement and their escape.

I pride myself not a little in being particular in an affair of such delicacy. Some writers wake their heroines at dead of night, drag them, half drest, out of a third story chamber window, lead them through a thousand perils by flood, fire, and field, till the mere matter-of-fact, common sense reader is convinced that the poor girls had neither a dry thread nor a clean one upon their persons; and no "change of raiment" so much as hinted at. I scorn so ungallant an action as to compel *my* heroine to make a voyage nearly round the world, or within thirty degrees of longitude of it, in such a draggle-tailed and sluttish condition; so that you see, madam, I have made this digression for the sole purpose of setting your mind at ease on the score of Isabella's gowns, frocks, hose, and those other articles of the "inner temple" whose names I dare not even think of, or whose existence it would be impolite and indelicate to hint at.

The alarming fact of his niece's absence the governor fortunately did not learn till morning, or rather till late in the forenoon, he having gone towards the guard-house before his daughters visited their cousin's chamber. When arrived there, Don Gaspar was convinced, by examination of the phial, that the soldiers were under the influence of a most powerful opiate; and, furthermore, that the prisoners had obtained that opiate and the wine that it was administered in, from some person out of the prison who had access to them; and he immediately vowed vengeance the most signal and summary against the traitor, offering, at the same time, a large reward for his, her, or their apprehension. Alas, poor man! he did not know that the traitor was of his own kith and kin, his own beloved niece.

His next movement was to send an officer at full gallop to the Venganza, or rather to the landing place, commanding her captain to despatch boats to the American ship in the outer harbor, and search for the fugitives. Don Diego Pinto, the commander of the Venganza, who had obtained a spare fore-yard from the dock-yard, rigged and swayed it aloft the night that he came in, instantly concluded that the escape had been effected by the American captain, and that the Albatross had immediately sailed. Impressed with this idea, he weighed anchor forthwith, and, favored by a fresh breeze from the land, was convinced by eight o'clock that morning that his conjecture was right.

How the governor bore the news of his niece's elopement we have never been able precisely to discover, but have understood vaguely that he displayed infinitely more warm and tender feelings than he had heretofore had credit for.

CHAPTER XXI

There was an ancient sage philosopher
That had read Alexander Ross over,
And swore the world, as he could prove,
Was made of fighting and of love.
Just so romances are, for what else
Is in them all but love and battles?
O' the first of these we've no great matter
To treat of, but a world o' the latter.

Hudibras.

The breeze that brought the Venganza within sight, was in a very short time felt likewise by the Albatross; but it gradually hauled to the southward, thereby giving the American the advantage of the wind, or weather-gage. Still it was evident that the Spaniard was the superior sailer, and that he might, if he chose, soon be alongside; but he seemed to be aware that preparations had been made by the Yankee commander and his crew to give him a very warm reception. Accordingly he shortened sail and tacked, with the hope of getting to windward; but in this he was foiled by the Albatross tacking also, and, in spite of all the Spaniard's manœuvring, retaining the advantage that the wind gave her.

The crew of the American were all this time quietly leaning on their guns, and watching the evolutions of their antagonist; and commenting upon every movement with as much composure as though their own ship was lying at anchor in a friendly port, and they were only looking at some ship beating into harbor.

"That old rattle-trap of a gardy coaster works tolerably well, only she's a month of Sundays swinging her head-yards, and getting her fore-tack down," said one of the seamen.

"You may well say that," said another, "and the same of his main-yard and main-tack, and jib-sheet to boot."

"Well, you can't blame him for not being in a hurry," said the boatswain, "he knows what he'll get when he hooks on to the old Albatross. When once we get fairly hold on him, I don't ask but half an hour to do his business for him: fifteen minutes to knock away some of his sticks, and send him off flanking, and fifteen minutes more to secure the guns and clear the decks up; and by that time it will be eight bells, and then we'll have our dinner and our grog, and be all ready to make sail on our course again."

"There she goes again! helm's a-tiller, jib-sheet's a-rope, and round she comes!"

"Ready about!" shouted Captain Williams, and the crew flew to their stations.

Both vessels were now heading to the westward; the Venganza, by superior sailing and frequent tacking, had gained considerably to windward; and it was evident that she would soon be alongside, though to leeward. In this situation of affairs, Captain Williams, seeing that flight was out of the question, called all hands aft.

"Lie aft there all of you, hurry aft there, men, at once," repeated the boatswain, adding, in a lower tone, "the old man's going to read us a page out of Hamilton Moore."

The men being all assembled upon the quarter-deck, Captain Williams advanced, and thus addressed them:

"Men, you see that fellow yonder that is following on after us, and know what he wants. He sails rather better than we do, and I don't see how we're going to get rid of him; and if we don't want to be plagued with him any longer, why we must fight him, that's all. I don't suppose that you will fight any the quicker or better for my making a speech to you, but I want you should know which leg you stand upon. We are nothing but a merchantman, and I don't suppose you are bound by the ship's articles to fight unless you see fit, but whether we fight or not, our fate is the same; if we are such d—d fools as to let that garlic-eating scarecrow make a prize of us without firing a gun, we shall be sent to the mines for life; but if we will only stand by each other, I'll be bail that we give him something that he can't eat. Now if you are all agreeable to that, say so, and give three cheers for the honor of the Yankee flag, and we'll fix his flint for him before the cook's dinner is ready."

This pertinent harangue was received with three roaring cheers, which were distinctly heard by the Spaniards, who were thereby convinced that the Americans were not the sort of men to be frightened into a surrender; and they, the Spaniards that is, "smelled the battle" by no means "afar off," but, on the contrary, rather nearer their noses than was altogether agreeable.

By way of commentary to his speech, the Yankee commander called to the steward to "bring up the case bottle, &c. and the molasses jug," observing, that; "although he knew that the Albatrosses didn't require any Dutch courage, the sun was over the fore-yard, and it was grog time in all Christian countries."

Jones, who by virtue of his office was always foremost at "splicing the main-brace," having compounded a tolerably stiff tumbler of blackstrap, turned to his shipmates, prefacing with the invariable commencement of a sailor's toast,

"*Here's hoping* that every shot we fire will make work for the doctor or carpenter."

This pithy "sentiment," as it would be called at the present day, was received with vast applause; and, having finished their grog, interspersed with similar toasts, the men quietly returned to their quarters.

During this scene Morton descended to the cabin and conducted his fair charge to her Gibraltar in the steerage. Isabella, weeping bitterly, clung to him, and Morton's heart, softened by the tears of one whom he loved so tenderly, seemed divested of all the elasticity of young hope and courage, and he began to regard the *possibility* of his being killed or taken prisoner as a *probability*; but he resisted the fast-coming weakness, and, pressing her to his bosom, tore himself from her arms, and hurried upon deck. Isabella was attended and consoled in her retirement by her faithful servant Transita, her "fidus Achates."

I hope my fair and also my classical readers will pardon me for giving the masculine title and name of a hero of antiquity to a lady's maid; but I could think of no other. History has immortalized Achates as a single friend, and Pylades and Orestes, and Damon and Pythias, as pairs of attached and inseparable friends; but, alas! neither ancient nor modern history has recorded the name of a single female, whose friendship was sufficiently ardent and pure to become proverbial. Even the Helena and Hermia of Shakspeare, whose friendship is so touchingly described by one of them, were not only imaginary creations of the poet's brain; but, as if to prove the impossibility of friendship existing between two ladies, he has made them actually pull caps in the very first act of the play in which they are introduced.

By this time the Venganza had ranged up within speaking distance, and hailed:

"Send the prisoners that you brought from San Blas on board my ship."

"We have no prisoners here—we are all freemen," was the answer.

"Send your first officer and the four men that were with him on board this ship, or I will fire into you."

"Well, I guess, then, you'll have to fire; for I can't spare either officer or men," replied Captain Williams drily.

"I repeat, for the last time, give up those men, or I will fire."

"Come after them yourself, then," roared back the irritated Yankee, losing all patience.

"D—n my buttons!" said Jones, from the midship or "slaughter-house" gun, "he'd better come aboard starn foremost, then, so's to be all ready for a run."

Don Diego Pinto, the commander of the Venganza, although a brave man, and one who had "done the state some service," by no means liked the aspect of affairs. He had had frequent opportunities of seeing the crew of the Albatross, and knew that, with the exception of Captain Williams, there was not a man on board over forty years of age; that they were all stout, active, powerful men, warmly attached to their officers, and living in perfect harmony with each other; that her guns were of uniform calibre— namely, nine pounders, and consequently no confusion could take place respecting cartridges or shot: on the other hand, he was a Spaniard, the first lieutenant a Portuguese; and the second a Frenchman; of three different nations, and three different dispositions, they never agreed: he knew, too, that his crew was composed of a few Spaniards, a few Portuguese, and the rest Chilians, Peruvians, and Mexicans, negroes, mulattoes, and Indians, quarrelling and stabbing from morning till night; that his guns were of all sorts, from twelve to four pounders inclusive; that, although he numbered eighty on board his ship, thirty well-armed men from the Albatross would take his ship from him in less than five minutes, if they were thrown upon his deck during the action. Under all these circumstances, he felt somewhat loth to commence operations, till, after considerable time had elapsed since Captain Williams's last angry reply, he took heart of grace, and opened an irregular and harmless fire.

"Thank God! he has spoken at last," said old Jones; "I was afraid he meant to keep us standing here, like mum-chance in a picture-shop, till seven bells in the afternoon with our hands in our pockets."

"Keep fast every thing," shouted the American Captain; "don't fire yet."

"Ay, ay, sir," answered the captains of the guns with perfect composure.

"Jemmy Bush," said the boatswain to one of his gun's crew, as he squinted along its side, "I'll bet you as much as you and I can drink, the first port we get into, that I hit that fellow's foremast the first shot."

"The devil thank you," said the tar; "'tisn't twenty yards from the muzzle of your gun."

"Starboard your helm—keep her away a little," said Captain Williams; "stand by—now's your time—fire!—luff! luff again!"

"Luff it is, sir," said the helmsman very deliberately.

The double-shotted broadside of the Albatross was followed by three thundering cheers. Her fire, although not exactly a raking one, had crossed the Spaniard's deck very obliquely, and the smoke blowing off immediately, gave the Americans an opportunity of seeing some of the effects of their shot. Two of the Venganza's foremost guns had been dismounted, and all the men stationed at them killed or wounded; there were huge gaps in her bulwarks; several of her weather fore-shrouds were shot away; and about ten feet from the deck there appeared upon the side of her foremast a large hole, caused by two or more shot striking nearly in the same place, and tearing off large splinters. There was silence for a few seconds, interrupted only, on board the Albatross, by the punching and thumping of rammers, as her crew were busily reloading their guns.

Mr. Walker, with the doctor and supercargo, all capital shots, constituted the marines or small-arm men of the ship. The doctor was not, however, unmindful of his medical duties; for he had prepared a place between decks, down the fore hatchway, where he had paraded his medicine-chest, instruments, and dressings; and, leaving them in charge of the cook, who acted as surgeon's mate *pro tem.*, he went on deck with his rifle, and was seen on the quarter-deck, with a case of pocket instruments tucked into the bosom of his jacket, loading, and firing, and bringing down a Spaniard at every discharge; for, like Apollo of old, who is represented as a good shot as well as a good doctor, he could send an enemy to his long home with a rifle-ball, or physic a friend with such success as might thereafter ensue:

"Mighty he was at both of these,
And styled of war as well as peace."

It has never been our lot to take part in a naval engagement as an agent, and we are thankful for it; for we are convinced, upon strong internal evidence, of our cowardice; but we have been present at sundry such actions, at a safe distance, as a spectator; and, from what we saw, we can venture to assure our readers, that, when two ships or fleets are exchanging their iron salutations, whether at long shot or close quarters, there is nothing peculiarly interesting to a mere spectator in the scene.

Isabella and her attendant had, all this time, remained quiet, but dreadfully frightened as soon as the firing commenced. Finding, after the lapse of fifteen or twenty minutes, that no danger had as yet come near them, they became more composed; the former most earnestly and sincerely imploring Divine protection, both for herself and for those who were exposed to danger for her sake. Still she could not avoid listening eagerly to every voice that was to be heard in the short intervals of comparative stillness.

The action had been now carried on between the two vessels nearly half an hour, at a distance of about forty yards, when a twelve-pound shot passed through the Albatross's larboard quarter, and, encountering the steward's pantry in its progress, made such a fearful jingling with the crockery ware, tin coffee-pots, and earthen jugs, that, overcome with extreme terror, both females left their city of refuge, and ran hastily up the after-hatchway ladder, and presented themselves on the quarter-deck. Just as they reached the deck, a shower of grape-shot flew whistling across the ship, one of which, passing through the hammock-nettings, struck a seaman in the forehead, and scattered his blood and brains in all directions. He reeled backwards two or three yards, and fell dead at Isabella's feet. Captain Williams immediately drew her away from the ghastly spectacle, and gave orders to carry the body forward on the other side of the deck. He then attempted to prevail upon her to go below; but she was too much terrified to listen to him, nor did she seem to understand him. After a minute or two, she became more composed, and eagerly inquired for Morton. Being informed that he was on the forecastle and unhurt, and doing his duty like a brave man and a good seaman, she expressed the most lively gratitude to Heaven, and permitted Captain Williams to conduct her to the starboard side, which was farthest from the enemy, and in great measure sheltered from shot by the long-boat and by the spare spars, &c. stowed amidships.

By this time the crew of the Venganza, as is often the case with cowards when driven to desperation, had become perfectly frantic, and also mutinous. With furious execrations, they compelled Captain Pinto to make a desperate attempt to board the American ship, and decide the action. For this purpose the helm of the guarda-costa was put hard down, and she immediately ran on board the Albatross, her bowsprit passing over that ship's larboard gangway, and coming in contact with the fore part of her mainmast, to which it was instantly lashed firmly by Mr. Walker, Jones, and two or three of the nearest seamen. In this state she was exposed to a murderous raking fire of grape and cannister shot, from such of the Albatross's guns as could be brought to bear upon her. Notwithstanding this, the Spaniards mustered in considerable force upon and about the heel of the bowsprit and cat-heads, armed with pistols, knives, and cutlasses. The Americans caught up their ten-foot boarding-pikes, and presented an impenetrable hedge of steel points; but, although his crew was fearfully thinned by a well directed discharge of canister-shot and bags of musket-balls from the two midship guns of the Albatross, Captain Pinto, at the head of about fifty men, the sole remnant of the original eighty, persisted in his attempt to board; and five or six of the most desperate actually "effected a lodgement," as militarists call it, in the main shrouds, where they were instantaneously transfixed by the long pikes of the Yankees, and fell shrieking into the water. At this moment the doctor, who had hitherto been engaged in dressing the hurts of the few wounded that thought proper to visit him in his temporary cockpit, hearing the bustle, caught up his rifle, and hastened to the *other* field of his usefulness.

"Here, doctor, doctor!" shouted old Jones as soon as he saw him, "here's a chance for you! here's the Spanish skipper looking as savage as a Yankee meat-axe—Gad! if you don't bear a hand, he'll cut his own throats, for want of some of ours."

"Where, where?" said the knight of the pillbox, skipping upon a gun.

"There, that notomy-looking thief with a sword two fathom long in his fist. Give him a blue pill, doctor; he looks as though he was billy-us."

The doctor raised his rifle—and Captain Diego Pinto, commander in his Most Catholic Majesty's navy, slept with his fathers.

A heavier sea than ordinary, a moment after this, lifted the Albatross, and forced her ahead: the bowsprit of her antagonist snapped close to the knight-heads; but, being held by the lashing, the guarda-costa was towed along, till a blow or two of a pole-axe severed the rope that connected the two vessels, and she dropped astern. The desperate and frantic courage of the Spaniards died with their commander; their first lieutenant had received a slight splinter-wound in the foot at the first fire of the Albatross, in consequence of which he went below, and had not been seen on deck since; the second lieutenant's orders were not attended to; and all was anarchy and confusion on board. A few minutes after she drifted from the Albatross, her foremast, already badly crippled and no longer supported by the bowsprit, fell over the larboard bow, dragging down with it the main topmast. At this the Yankees cheered. The Albatross soon after wore ship, and stood to the westward. Upon mustering the crew, it was ascertained that but one man was killed, and eight more or less wounded; her sails and rigging were much cut up; and the services of all hands were immediately put in requisition, to repair damages, and put the ship in condition to proceed on her voyage.

The first intelligence of the victory was conveyed to Isabella by Morton himself. As he approached her place of refuge with his head bound up with a bloody handkerchief, having received a slight wound in the left temple from a splinter, she uttered a scream of terror, and it was long before she could be convinced that the wound was trifling. As lady passengers are of no great use on deck when the ship's sails and rigging are hanging about her ears, she was conducted once more below.

In the mean time Jones, as he trudged backwards and forwards, thought he saw something amiss about the galley, which he entered, and a moment after backed out, exclaiming,

"D—n my two-and-twenty top-lights! if this here doesn't beat all my going down east!"

"What's the matter, Jones? what are you swearing about now?"

"Swearing? it's enough to make a minister pull off his wig, and rip right out in the middle of his sarmont!"

"Well, what *is* the matter?"

"Matter? why d—n my old shoes, Captain Williams, here is one of that bloody Don Dego's shot gone right through the galley-door, and through the side of the big copper, and knocked all the beef and hot water galley-west. By the piper that played before Moses when the children of Israel danced through the wilderness, I never see such a thing since I first went to sea, and I've seen shot fired afore to-day. And here's my two sweet potatoes," he continued, groping in the coppers with the cook's ladle, "that I popped in just as that fellow come alongside, all knocked to pieces. Here he is, d—n his eyes!" holding out a twelve-pound shot in his ladle; "here's the thundering thief that's spoilt our dinner, Captain Williams, stowed away in the bottom of the copper, as snug as a flea in a soger's blanket. The curse of the twelve geese that eat the grass off o' Solomon's grave upon you!" With these words he threw the shot overboard, and turned to Captain Williams with a most rueful countenance.

"Well, Jones, it's devilish unlucky I own, but I guess we can make out a dinner for to-day, and perhaps the armorer can patch it so that it will answer till we can get to Canton,"

"I hope so, sir," said Jones, with a deep sigh; "for if we don't have our reg'lar-cooked grub, we'll all get the scurvy, as sure as the devil's in London; though for that matter, I've been pretty much all over Lunnun, and never see nor heard nothin' on him, unless so be he's in the Tower, or the king's palace, or some one of them thunderin' great churches; and I've seen about all there was to be seen there, unless it may be them three places. But in my way of thinking, a ship might a d—d sight better go to sea without a medicine-chist, than without her proper cooking-utensils and coppers; because why? if a man don't get his reg'lar grub, his bowels gets out o' trim, and he gets belly-us, as our doctor calls it."

"Well, well, if we can't do any better, we'll burn out the big pitch-pot, and make a shift with that till we arrive in China."

"Aye, that indeed, so we can. By the hook-block! how our two snow-balls of cooks will swear! Well, thank God for every thing but bread, and that we get o' the baker." So saying, he rolled off towards the forecastle, to superintend the knotting of one of the fore shrouds, that had been shot away in the engagement.

CHAPTER XXII

But now, t' observe romantic method,
Let bloody steel awhile be sheathed:
And all those harsh and rugged sounds
Of bastinadoes, cuts, and wounds,
Exchanged to Love's more gentle style,
To let our reader breathe awhile.

Hudibras.

The damages done on board the Albatross were all repaired before sunset; the dead body of the poor fellow that was killed was committed to its watery tomb with becoming solemnity, and by the next morning the north-east trade-wind was blowing fresh and steady, and, as it usually does in both the Atlantic and Pacific, from almost due east. The ship, with booms rigged out and studding-sails set on both sides, dashed swiftly towards the west, rolling almost gunwales under at every motion, and initiating the two females into all the mysteries of sea-sickness. However, in two or three days the sea, that is always heaviest near the land, subsided into the long, regular undulation peculiar to the ocean, properly so called, and Isabella recovered from her sea-sickness, and, by keeping as much as possible in the open air, and walking the deck almost constantly, assisted at first by the arm of some one of the gentlemen, soon got her *sea-legs* on.

I would substitute some other phrase, if, by so doing, I could make myself intelligible; but as the case is, it is impossible to mince the matter—fashion has not yet, thank God, invaded the "Dictionary of Sea-Terms;" and ladies, when off soundings, must still be content to have "legs" like other folks—on shore they may vote it indecent to have even "ankles," for aught I care.

Captain Williams, having neither missionaries nor tracts on board, did not stop at the Sandwich Islands, nor did he even pass within sight of them; but holding on his course, on the fortieth day after leaving St. Blas, he saw Cape Espiritu Santo, the southern extremity of the island of Lugonia, or Lucon, one of the Philippine Islands. Passing through the Straits of Samar, he changed his course to the northward and westward, and steered for Macao, where he arrived six days afterwards.

The passage across the Pacific Ocean afforded the two lovers numerous moonlight quarter-deck walks. Morton, as first officer, had the first watch, from eight to twelve, every other night, and on these occasions was invariably accompanied by his fair bride elect, who, wrapped in a cloak or great coat, walked the deck leaning upon his arm; or, seated upon the hen-coop, listened with interest to his descriptions of American, or, more properly, New England, scenery, manners, and history; or gazed upon that lovely object, a moon-lit ocean in fine weather.

There is something peculiarly soothing in this scene—something in the soft light of the heavens, and in the dark and dimly-seen ocean, that induces a pleasing melancholy, a pensive tranquillity; the low, gentle murmuring of the waves calms the mind, tranquillizes its angry passions and boisterous feelings, and brings on those dreamy reveries that contemplative people are so fond of indulging. It is then, when the "grim-visaged" ocean has "smoothed his wrinkled front,"—when the winds of heaven are hushed to gentle airs, and the cloudless moon looks down upon the scene, tipping the crests of the lazy waves with silver,—that the memory and imagination of the wanderer are busy; it is then that the scenes of childhood and of manhood—the forms of friends, more loved because sundered from them by thousands of miles of water and land—all rise before him in original freshness and beauty.

Isabella also proposed to her lover to accompany him in his middle watch—that is, from midnight to four in the morning—but I grieve to say, that she proved worse on these occasions than an old man-of-war's man, not only "standing two calls," but, in fact, not "turning out" at all. She made some amends, however, by coming on deck at four o'clock frequently, to witness that splendid spectacle, sunrise at sea, which is particularly glorious between the tropics, not only on account of the extreme purity of the air, but from the shortness of the morning twilight; the sun rushing so suddenly from his salt water couch, as to come "within one" of catching the stars napping.

On arriving at Macao, Isabella was doomed to undergo another separation from her beloved Morton, whose qualities of head and heart she had had sufficient opportunities of studying and appreciating during the voyage from Mexico, and in the daily and familiar intercourse of a merchant-ship's cabin. As the Chinese eschew the society of foreign women even more rigorously than the children of Israel did that of "strange" ones— and, taking this notion of theirs "by and large" in connection with their laws, and manners, and tastes, we think they are perfectly right—Isabella was consequently landed at Macao, and placed in the care of a venerable and highly respectable Portuguese family, and after having arranged the means of as regular a correspondence as could be carried on in that country, where there are not quite so many mail-coaches and post-offices as with us, she saw with tearful eyes the whale-boat "shove off," containing in its stern-sheets Morton, a Chinese custom-house mandarin, two Chinese pigs, a hind-quarter of Chinese beef, a Chinese river pilot, and sundry baskets of Chinese fowls and vegetables.

Macao is beautifully situated upon a small island, near the mouth of the river Tigris, commanding a fine view towards the sea, and was, when I had the fortune to visit it, very clean and neat in its streets and the external condition of its houses—a circumstance the more remarkable, as its inhabitants are Portuguese and Chinese, two of the dirtiest people on the face of the earth: to these, of course, numerous other nations and parts of nations may be added; and among them, a very large proportion of the aristocratic and fastidious English, who prefer spitting in their pocket-handkerchiefs instead of the fire-place or the street; all the Spaniards; all the French in their houses, and food, and furniture; all the Dutch in their persons; all the Russians in every thing; nearly all the Irish and Scotch; and a very respectable modicum of my beloved countrymen, the Yankees, together with the greater part of the natives of the southern states, who, being nursed, brought up, and associating with negro slaves from the cradle to the grave, *smell* dirty, if they are not.

After an absence of about six weeks, Isabella one morning received a letter from Canton, informing her that the ship would commence "working" down the river that day, or, according to the date of the letter, two days previous, and that she would be off Macao on the second or third day from said date. Accordingly she made all necessary preparations for another and much longer voyage, and after dinner walked down to the water-side, accompanied by her Portuguese friends. They had been on the look-out for nearly half an hour, when a large ship hove in sight, evidently from Canton.

As she approached, steering apparently direct for the town, she suddenly tacked and stood out to sea, or directly away from it. The party had already made out with their glasses that the ship was indeed the Albatross; but poor Isabella, who had seen, on her passage from Mexico, nothing but fair winds, was exceedingly distressed by this last unintelligible manœuvre. Were they actually going away without her?—the thought was agony. The ship, that was but four miles off when first seen, was now at least eight, and her hull was fast sinking below the line of direct vision. Her companions, who had hitherto been occupied in silently admiring that most splendid effort of human genius, a ship under full sail, were suddenly startled by an exclamation betokening extreme anguish from their lovely friend—"They have gone! they have gone!" sobbed the unhappy girl.

The most affectionate kindness, and the most earnest assurances that the apparently unaccountable movement of the ship was no more than was absolutely necessary from the direction of the wind, were equally lost upon her—she "would not be comforted." In a few minutes the Albatross hove in stays (you need not hold your fan to your face, madam), and seemed to approach the shore as rapidly as she had before receded from it.

"Look up, my dear child," said M. de Silva; "see, your ship is flying in, and will soon be safely at anchor."

Isabella raised her head from the shoulder of Madam de Silva, and applying the glass to her tear-dimmed eye, was convinced of the folly of her grief. They sat down to watch the gallant ship as she rapidly approached the "roads." Before the sun was hid behind the hills in the rear of the town, they had the pleasure of seeing the Albatross commence reducing her sails; presently the topsails were clewed up, and the jib hauled down, the ship "rounded to," her anchor let go, and in a moment the men were seen clustering upon the lower and topsail yards. A minute or two afterwards Isabella plainly distinguished, by the help of her glass, the well-known whale-boat sweeping round the ship's stern, and rowing swiftly towards the shore. A deep blush announced that the glass had also informed her who was, in midshipman's language, the "sitter," the person in the stern-sheets, to wit, and she immediately proposed returning to the house. Morton, on landing, informed her that the ship would get under weigh the next morning at day-break, and that it would be most advisable, as the ship could approach no nearer than five miles to the town when beating out of the bay, to go on board as soon as possible that evening, to which she, of course, assented, and, having taken an affectionate leave of her Macao friends, who insisted upon supplying her with "sea-stores" enough to fit out half a dozen sail of Liverpool packets, she accompanied Morton to the boat.

The next morning at day-break she was startled from her slumbers by the clanking of the windlass-pauls, the voices of the officers, and the tramp of feet over her head; and, in a few minutes after, the rushing of the water under the cabin windows, and the "heeling" of the ship, announced that they were under weigh, and dashing out to sea with a fresh breeze. The passage home was, like most passages *from* the East Indies and China, rather monotonous from the long continuance of fair winds. Isabella gazed with delight upon the unrivalled scenery of the Straits of Sunda, where spring, summer, and autumn reign perpetually in a sort of triumvirate; the same field, nay, in some cases, the same tree, presenting, at one and the same time, blossoms, green fruit, and ripe fruit: infancy, maturity, and decay. She saw, too, in the night the volcano on the Island of Bourbon, afterwards False Cape and Table Mountain, but not the Flying Dutchman, the weather being unfortunately too fine to induce him to put to sea. Next came St. Helena, since so famous as the cage and then the tomb of that most furious and terrible of wild beasts, a great conqueror. Near the fifth degree of north latitude, the south-east trade-wind died away, and was succeeded by four days of light, variable, "baffling" winds, when the north-east trade set in strong from about east-by-north, its usual point near the equator, and they once more flew joyously on their north-west course. A few "regular built" *Mudian* (i. e. Bermudan) squalls served to vary the scene, and rendered the strong, steady gale from south-west, that succeeded them, peculiarly acceptable.

It was just sunrise one lovely morning, near the last of July, when Morton, who had the morning watch, directed one of the men to go aloft, and "take a look round." The seaman had gotten no higher than the fore-topsail-yard, when he shouted "land ho!" at the very top of his throat.

"Where away?"

"Broad on the larboard bow."

"What does it look like?"

"Low, white sand-beach."

"Cape Cod, by the mortal man that made horn spoons and poop lanterns!" said Jones, springing into the fore-rigging.

As the sun climbed higher in the heavens, the liquid blue plain appeared thickly studded with the white sails of vessels of all descriptions, and all steering to the westward. There was the majestic ship from India or Liverpool; brigs from the Mediterranean, from Portugal, South America, and the West Indies; schooners from the southern states, with flour, and from Maine, with boards; packet sloops from New York, Philadelphia, &c.; chebacco-boats from fishing on "Georgis;" and schooner-rigged pilot-boats, darting about under jib and mainsail, and boarding every vessel that carried the star-spangled "jack" at her fore-topgallant-mast head. Nothing could surpass the tranquil life of the scene: more than a hundred vessels, of all descriptions, were gradually but rapidly approaching a common focal point, the narrow entrance of Boston harbor, under the impulse of a fresh breeze from the south-east, that had not as yet brought forward its accompanying fogs and haze. The Albatross, her thin masts clothed from trucks to deck with snow-white canvass, dashed rapidly up the bay, the jack flying at her fore-royal-mast head, passing the low-decked molasses-loaded brigs from the West Indies, or the faster sailing topsail-schooners from the Chesapeake, inquiring the news, and furnishing matter for speculation to their crews.

On the passage from China to Boston, Morton expressed some impatience, particularly during the prevalence of calms or head winds; but

Isabella, like all young ladies similarly situated, was perfectly composed. Why is it, dear dissemblers, that you always *seem* to enter the holy state with either reluctance or lukewarm indifference? when every body, with half a head, *knows* that matrimony is the "hoc erat in votis," the grand object of all your wishes. Strange! that the laws of female modesty should decree it absolute indelicacy for a girl candidly to show her preference for a particular individual before the rest of his sex. Strange! that modern mothers should uniformly caution their daughters against marrying for love, as the most dangerous rock in their voyage through life. Solomon could find but four strange things in his day, and those four I do not care to repeat; if he had lived in these times, he might find a hundred and fifty connected with a single matrimonial engagement.

The Albatross arrived at Long Wharf early in the afternoon; and Morton, having deposited his dear messmate and watchmate in the house of a widowed sister of his father, went in search of a messenger to convey a letter to his father; for, unless I am much misinformed, the mail only went at that time once a week to New Bedford.

Though not "so terrible old" as I might be, I recollect when a journey from Boston to Providence, a distance *then* of forty-five miles, occupied three days: namely, the traveller, leaving Boston in the morning, arrived at Deadham about sunset, and "put up" at the "Gay tavern," or the "Widow Woodward's;" the second *hitch* carried him to Attleborough; and the third evening saw him snugly seated in the bar-room of the "Old Coffee House," Providence. But a journey to New York, as it was generally supposed that the traveller must "go down to the sea in ships" part of the way, that is, through Long Island Sound in a sloop, was one of the most momentous events of a long life. The traveller "concluded" upon it in the fall, occupied the entire winter and the months of March and April in collecting his dues, paying his debts, setting his house in order, and making his will, before the weather was settled.

Two Sundays before starting, a note was "put up" in his parish meeting-house, "desiring prayers," and early on Monday morning, to be sure of reaching Providence before the next Sabbath, he took a weeping farewell of his wife and family, and turned his horse's head towards the "neck," and his bereaved household betook them to their chambers, "sorrowing as those that had no hope" of seeing him again.

Morton's messenger, spurred on by the hopes of high pay, made such diligence that he actually arrived at Taunton the first night, the selectmen of which fair town were so indignant at what they conceived barbarous and unparalleled hard driving, that they talked of prosecuting the man; but it appearing from the report of a court of inquiry of ostlers that the horse did not seem distressed by his day's work, but had fallen to work upon his oats and hay, they "withdrew their motion."

Old Mr. Morton received the news of his son's arrival with the greatest joy. He sat out the next day in his own carriage, drawn by two noble bay horses, and arrived without "let or hindrance" in Boston. He expected to find Isabella a girl possessed of some considerable beauty, just sufficient to captivate a seaman who for months had seen no women more attractive than the squaws of the North-West Coast or South Sea Islands; and sailors, under such circumstances, are exceedingly susceptible, *me ipso testi*; he had made up his mind, too, that she could be no other than ignorant and ill-bred withal. When, then, her exquisite beauty, her lovely, retiring modesty of manner, free alike from affectation or sheepishness, her expressive and eloquent features, all burst upon his view at once, his heart was taken "by storm," —he clasped her to his bosom, and felt towards her in an instant as warm affection as though she was indeed his own child. The banns of matrimony were published immediately, after the manner of the descendants of the pilgrim roundheads, and the marriage solemnized as soon as the legal time had elapsed; and the happy party took up their abode in old Mr. Morton's house.

Morton's female friends and acquaintance at first seemed amazingly shy of the new-comer; but at a "numerous and highly respectable" petticoated caucus, a forlorn hope, after repeated declensions of the honor, was chosen to make the first "call." Their report was so very favorable that the newly-married couple were, in less than a fortnight, rather annoyed by too much company.

On the passage from Mexico to China, and thence home, Isabella had, in vulgar phrase, "taken a liking" to Jones, the boatswain, and formed, what was probably conceived, at that time, the visionary plan of breaking him from his intemperate habits. She communicated her scheme to her husband shortly after their marriage, who most cheerfully coincided in opinion with her. Jones was accordingly sent for, and regularly installed in the family. The eloquent representations of Mrs. Morton, and the promises of her husband and his father, had the wished-for effect—the old tar consented to "give up grog," and did so, making exceptions only in favor of the "glorious first of June," the anniversary of Lord Howe's victory off Ushant, at which Jones was present, the fourth of July, 'lection days, Thanksgiving days, and the birth of Mrs. Morton's first child. This last event took place, by what modern editors call a "singular coincidence," upon the first of June ensuing; and Jones was sorely puzzled how to "keep up" both days, and, in consequence, got very considerably "corned." It was, however, his last offence; he gradually adopted the temperate habits of the family, and continued in them to his death.

We have no farther particulars to communicate, except that Charles Morton was taken into partnership by his father, and became wealthy, and that his wife wrote a long and kind letter to her uncle, which was forwarded by the captain of an outward-bound whaleman, who delivered it into his own hands. The old Don did not answer it, however; and Isabella, in whose heart other affections had taken root, was not, perhaps, much grieved or indignant at his silence; the affection of her husband, her children, and her friends, soon obliterated all melancholy recollections.

THE PIRATE OF MASAFUERO

CHAPTER I

Gonzalo. Had I a plantation of this isle, my lord, And were
the king of it, what would I do?

Sebastian. 'Scape getting drunk, for want of wine.

Tempest.

In the Pacific Ocean, and within two days' sail of the coast of Chili,
lies the little island of Masafuero, or, as the word is generally divided by
the Spaniards who discovered it, Mas-a-fuero—that is, the farthest—to
distinguish it from Juan Fernandez, which lies nearer the main land, and
in sight of Masafuero. Juan Fernandez is well known to all the reading
community as having once been the temporary residence of Alexander
Selkirk, the original, or, as grammarians would call it, the *root*, of De Foe's
bewitching romance of Robinson Crusoe.

Masafuero is, on the contrary, remarkable for nothing more, that I know
of, than being very difficult of access, and overrun with wild goats. It is
situated in the latitude of thirty-three degrees and forty-five minutes, south,
and eighty degrees and thirty-six minutes, west longitude; for I love to be
particular in all such cases—not that I suppose my readers care a pin if I had
told them it was in the south-west horn of the new moon; but all authors,
when they put pen to paper, seem actuated by the kind and neighborly
spirit of the sagacious Dogberry—namely, to "bestow all their tediousness"
upon their readers; and I do not know that I have any prescriptive right—I
am sure I have no intention—to depart from so well-worn a track, or to fly
in the face of so many illustrious precedents.

This island is covered, from the water's edge to the summit, with trees,
and it is only for the sake of wood that it is ever visited by our whalemen,
who fell the trees on the brink of steep cliffs, and tumble them down, by
which process they are broken up into sufficiently short pieces to render
their carriage convenient. There are evident traces of most tremendous
earthquakes visible throughout the island; huge fissures and rents from the

tops of the highest hills to unknown and unexplorable depths, vast scattered masses of rock that have been shaken down from the cliffs, and many other similar appearances, announce that the most terrific convulsions of nature have rendered Masafuero a very unquiet residence, even to the poor goats, at different times. In its external appearance, and when seen at some distance, it bears considerable resemblance to the celebrated Isle of St. Helena, and is, like it, exceeding precipitous, and has but one approachable, and not always accessible, landing-place. Of this last trait in its character I can speak from experience and most feelingly, having visited the island in the year 1821, in a small brig, with the intention of getting off nine men, who had been left there some time previous for the purpose of collecting seal-skins, with which the island abounds, as well as with goats. Our attempt was rendered fruitless by the violence of the wind, which, for the time it lasted, exceeded any thing I had ever seen, except a *typhon* in the China seas, and *one* north-wester off Nantucket shoals.

Some of the men, whom I afterwards saw, informed me that they had, during their abode there, planted sundry garden seeds, such as beans, pumpkin, squash, and onion seeds; but this item of intelligence I look upon to be somewhat apocryphal; at any rate, I would not recommend to any one, who may chance to visit said island, to save his stomach for any pumpkin pies or baked beans he may obtain from it. There is undoubtedly fertile soil enough for a garden—but then the goats.

The island also enjoys the reputation of having once been the rendezvous of a gang of pirates, as a house, that has stood untenanted for any length of time, is sure to be peopled with ghosts. People seem to think it a pity that a tenement should remain unoccupied, so, out of sheer compassion for the proprietor, they stock it with unearthly tenants from roof to cellar, or like—for, now I am in the humor for comparisons, I might as well go on—it was like a man who keeps his business to himself and troubles nobody; his neighbors, knowing nothing about his occupations and habits, take it for granted that they are both bad and "contrary to the peace of the commonwealth."

Masafuero had, however, tolerably strong claims to the title of a "den of thieves;" for there could be no doubt that, during the stormy times that took place when South America shook off the Spanish yoke and put on fifty worse ones—when there was a revolution once a week, and murder and rapine every hour—many of the human vultures that flocked to the prey, from Europe and this country, made this little island a place of deposit for their ill-gotten wealth, and a rendezvous and city of refuge from the vengeance of some of the short-lived authorities. The celebrated Benavidas, a sort of "free companion," was, as sailors say, "in vogue," when I first visited the Pacific in 1821; and as he carried on business both by land and water, there is no doubt that he occasionally visited both Masafuero and Juan Fernandez.

But there were other "land rats and water rats" than Benavidas, who, it may be interesting to know, died suddenly one day of strangulation, in consequence of his cravat being tied too tight. Numbers of English and American seamen, at the first breaking out of the revolution, who happened to be on the spot, realised large sums by privateering, and by striking certain sudden and bold strokes, *à la Buccanier*, upon the rich Spanish towns and richer churches; and as "their sound went out into all lands," others flocked to the Pacific for the same purpose. But by this time the first agony was over: the new government, short-lived and ephemeral as it was, enacted certain wholesome laws, which, as they did not materially interfere with the political views of the parties that successively kicked each other down stairs, were generally permitted to stand. A navy was organised and plunder was legalised; privateering was placed under restrictions; and, as none of these butterfly republics were in existence long enough to take any further steps towards paying their seamen and soldiers than promising to, said seamen and soldiers very naturally betook themselves to their respective elements to look for prey. I have often wondered that the problem of our revolution was not followed by the same corollary. The two nations might be differently constituted—they were not differently situated.

Many stories are related of the daring exploits of these freebooters, both on the water and on the land; but there was generally a shade of difference in favor of the former, on the score of both courage and humanity; the "water rats" being almost exclusively English and Americans, and possessing both qualities by nature so strongly impressed, that they could never be entirely eradicated or smothered. The land robbers, on the other hand, were as exclusively native Chilenos, a mixture generally of Indian and Spaniard—a more detestable amalgamation the earth does not produce—if the devil was to cross the breed, it would rather improve it than otherwise. One of the most formidable, most blood-thirsty, and most successful of these pirates wound up his affairs not a great while before I arrived in the Pacific, Jack Ketch being his administrator.

CHAPTER II

Virtue? a fig! 'tis in ourselves that we are thus and thus.

Othello.

James Longford was the eldest son of a merchant in the neighborhood of New York, who furnished in his own conduct one of those very rare instances of a mercantile man contented with what he has amassed, and willing to retire to private life to enjoy it. 'Tis true that merchants pretend to say, after having heaped up something like a million, that they continue in business for the sake of the employment of time and excitement of mind that it affords, and not for the lucre of gain; "sed non ego credulus illis," or, in plain English, "they may tell that to the marines, the sailors won't believe them." The thirst for gain increases with its gratification, as I could quote more Latin to prove; and not only does gratification increase the appetite, but it seems to *pucker up* the heart, and contract the muscles of the hand, for your very rich man is almost invariably a very close and avaricious one, except when making public donations to institutions already bursting with wealth, when they know that their names and sums given will go the rounds of the public prints under the head of "munificent donations." How delicious is flattery, even when thrown down one's throat with a shovel!

But they are stingy in another way, that brings with it its own punishment—they starve themselves. I know of several of your half million folks, not a thousand miles from where I now sit, whose table does not cost them fifty cents a day, and that too with tolerably numerous families. I was once ill-advised enough to dine with a gentleman of this description, in a sister city, in consequence of his repeated and pressing invitations. We had part of a fore-quarter of very small mutton boiled, with a small modicum of potatoes; one man could have eaten the whole. To be sure, I had a glass of "London particular" Madeira after dinner, if it deserves the name, but as soon as I had done I made my excuses—"indispensable business—obliged to go out of town, &c." and fled to an eating-house, where I satisfied what Dan Homer emphatically calls the "thumos edodes," the madness of appetite, with something more to the purpose than lean mutton.

Mr. Longford was "none of them sort;"—he retired from business with only fifty thousand dollars, but with a clear conscience, adjusted books, and not a single cent of debt—he never refused his charity to deserving objects, and never signed a subscription paper for their relief,—he was never a member of a charitable society, and never contributed a cent to the Missionary funds, whether for the Valley of the Mississippi or the Island of Borneo, where there are nothing but monkeys, or Malays as incapable of being christianized as the monkeys. Had he lived at the present time, and in this section of the country, he would have been prayed *for* and prayed *at*, at least once a day, and been, besides, occasionally held up in the pulpit as a specimen of total depravity, and a child of perdition.

Yet, with all these defects, Mr. George Longford was a sincerely devout man, and a most firm believer in the Christian religion,—from a conviction of its truth, not merely because it was the fashion to believe it, or because his fathers believed it before him,—and a practical observer of its moral precepts. He read and studied the New Testament, because it contained a compendium of all his every-day duties as a rational and accountable being, and as a member of society, not because it was a magazine of polemical divinity and abstruse doctrines. The evening of such a man's life is calm and tranquil; his death is indeed the death of the righteous.

James was this man's eldest son;—I cannot say, as novel writers generally do, that "in him were centred the hopes and wishes of his fond parents,"—for they were not—they looked for support and comfort in their old age to their other children. James was a refractory and disobedient child from the very cradle. It is ridiculous to say that all men are born alike in dispositions and capacities; the great poet of nature, from whom I have, as usual, taken my text, says no; and I would sooner have a single line from him than folios of ingenious theories and metaphysical arguments from the profoundest philosophers. I have not much faith in innate ideas, but I confess that I have in innate dispositions, both good and bad.

James Longford's disposition was most decidedly bad by nature—he was constantly, even when a mere schoolboy, in mischief, and that, too, of a kind that marked a malicious and cruel temper. His father in vain exhausted kindness and severity, in the hope of subduing this most unhappy temper; but neither the infliction of punishment, that he deserved twenty times a day, nor the caresses of the tenderest parental affection, appeared to have the least influence in mollifying his stubborn and morose disposition—he seemed to be one of those whom St. Paul characterizes, in that tremendous first chapter of the Epistle to the Romans, as being "without natural affection." Notwithstanding all these faults, he had naturally a strong mind and good talents; so that by the time he had attained his eighteenth year he was, at one and the same time, one of the most ungovernable and ill-tempered boys and best scholars in Parson Crabtree's seminary of some fifty in number.

At this period his father placed him in the counting-room of a wealthy mercantile house in the city of New-York. Here his good education and natural quickness soon procured him the favorable notice of his employers, while his constant and active duties seemed to have smothered, at least for a time, his malicious temper. Before the expiration of a year he had acquired the good will and confidence of the merchants whom he served; but by this time the pleasures and temptations of the "Commercial Emporium" had begun to attract his inexperienced eyes, and his disposition seemed to have taken a new turn.

With all the stubborn wilfulness and unfeeling carelessness of consequences that characterized his temper, he plunged into all manner of vicious indulgences; but what seemed to attract him the most irresistibly, and fix him the most firmly, was a fondness for gambling. The "time-honored" black-legs of the billiard and roulette tables were, however, an overmatch for an inexperienced lad of nineteen, and, as might have been expected, he was soon stripped, thoroughly "cleaned out." It was then that the idea of replenishing his pockets from the counting-room trunk first presented itself to his mind, and, without much hesitation or compunction of conscience, he took small sums from time to time.

It is needless to trace his progress more minutely—he finished by forging a check for a thousand dollars, which forgery was subsequently detected.

Precisely the same "dull round" of vice is trodden, at least once a week, by the same class of young men. The merchants' clerks are certainly creatures of no imagination, or they would have struck out some new way of going to the devil; they evidently have not a spark of what an eminent Irish lawyer called "the poetry of wickedness;" they uniformly begin with plundering the money drawer, and end with forging checks.

Mr. Longford was advised of his son's guilt, and the affair was compromised by his paying the amount purloined. In utter despair the afflicted father placed his degenerate son on board an outward-bound Indiaman, a mode of proceeding often resorted to prematurely, for it generally does a boy's business if he is viciously inclined—a merchantman's forecastle is not a school of morality. Sending a refractory child to sea may be an excellent way of getting rid of him, but it is at the same time the most expeditious mode of sending him to the devil.

There is a great deal of talk about "godly captains;" but I never knew one that was not an infernal tyrant, and a most accomplished scoundrel.

If you wish to cure a boy of a fondness for the sea, send him a good long voyage with a godly captain, and I'll be bail that he comes home as lean as a weazel, and most thoroughly disgusted at the very thoughts of a ship. If you merely wish to get rid of him, send him to the coast of Guinea on a trading voyage, or to that Golgotha, New Orleans; a godly captain, by working him one half to death, and starving him the other, will put it out of his power to trouble you any more in this world. The Carmelites and other religious orders were once of opinion that the devil could be flogged out of the flesh, and for that purpose wore a couple of fathoms of two-inch rope about their loins: godly captains think he can be worked out, and so, perhaps, he can; but generally, in the two places that I have mentioned, he and the vital spark go out together.

I do not know whether I ought to regard it as a fortunate or unfortunate circumstance, that the first captain that I sailed with was a "ripper" for swearing and drinking. He was a professed infidel, a first-rate seaman, an excellent scholar, and took more care of the morals of his crew than many of those who have prayers twice a day; and ten thousand times more of their health, for he would not permit a man to expose himself for two minutes to the sun or rain in Batavia, and in consequence did not lose a man. He watched over my moral and physical health with a degree of zeal and tenderness that I have never, for an instant, experienced since, at the hands of those who call themselves my "friends." Indeed, the severest scolding he ever gave me, and I expected every moment he would knock me down in the street, was for walking, one deliciously cool morning, from Weltwreden to Batavia, a distance of four miles, when I had a carriage and two horses at my disposal.

Peace to his ashes! I have lived to see the grave close in succession over many of the few friends that I ever had. When I wandered about London streets, barefoot and half-naked, in the dead of a hard winter, just discharged from a hospital, and scarcely able to drag one foot after the other, my situation was comparatively enviable. I had no self-styled "friends" at my elbow, to mock me by talking about my "talents!" I knew that if I did not "bear a hand," and ship myself off *somewhere*, I should be taken up on the vagrant act, and sent to Bridewell. Burns says,

> "The fear o' death's a hangman's whip,
> That hauds the wretch in order."

I should be loth to admit that the fear of Bridewell operated as a stimulus upon my mind, for it did not often occur to me; but I longed to enjoy once more

"the glorious privilege
Of being independent;"

and he, who is earning an honest livelihood by his own exertions, and can shave with cold water, is, in my estimation, more truly independent than he, whose father has bequeathed him half a million. Reader! you may as well pardon this digression first as last, for it is ten chances to one that you fall in with a whole fleet of them before you have sailed through these pages. If I do not moralize as I go along, I shall not have a chance to do it any where else.

As the afflicted father returned, with melancholy steps and slow, towards his quiet home, he could not forbear feeling an emotion of regret at the thought of having parted with his son in such a manner. "Had I but placed him," he said to himself, "under the charge of the commander of one of our men-of-war, he would necessarily have been under such strict guardianship and discipline that his unfortunate habits might be entirely broken up; but now I fear that the liberty he will be allowed, or will take, in a merchant's ship, will be his ruin."

His home was more gloomy and sad that evening than it had ever been before; for though satisfied in the main with his own conduct, and hoping that the voyage would have most beneficial effects upon his son's behavior and disposition, he regretted most bitterly the necessity of the measure, and felt the keenest anxiety as to its results. That son was destined never to return.

The ship in which he was embarked was driven much farther to the westward than is usually the case with outward-bound Indiamen, and encountered one of those tremendous gales of wind, known to seamen by the local name of *pamperos*, from their blowing off the immense *pampas*, or plains, that constitute a large portion of the province of Buenos Ayres, or, as it is now called, the Argentine Republic. The ship was dismasted, and with difficulty succeeded in reaching the harbor of Buenos Ayres to refit.

The city of Buenos Ayres was at that time, and I believe it is not much better now, a nest and rendezvous of pirates, that, under the cover of the republican flag, and the assumed character of men-of-war or privateers, with forged commissions, committed the most barefaced and abominable acts of piracy. The British cruisers, by capturing and hanging a good number of them, struck a most wholesome terror into the rest; but our government, with a fraternal affection for every mean and insignificant patch of barren sand-beach that called itself a republic, more worthy the *sans-culotterie* of the French revolution, than becoming a great and polished nation, permitted them to sell their prizes and refit in our ports. Buenos Ayres was then a point towards which all the scoundrels, and thieves, and murderers, of Europe and the United States, were radiating as to a common centre.

Here, as might have been expected, Longford found plenty of congenial companions to "whet his almost blunted purpose" of vicious propensity and indulgence. In a drunken quarrel at the gaming-table, knives were drawn, and Longford stabbed his antagonist-to the heart. Murders are so exceedingly common in all the Spanish possessions and settlements in America, that but seldom or never is any inquiry set on foot with regard to them. The only *judicial* formality consists in laying the dead bodies on their backs, with a plate upon the breast of each to receive the contributions of those who are disposed to assist in defraying the expenses of burial. But the murdered person, in this case, was a man of considerable consequence in the Buenos Ayrean government, having the charge and management of certain public moneys, and in consequence, the "authorities" thought it worth their while to ask a few questions about his "taking off." Longford was well aware of these facts, and with considerable difficulty and danger made his escape to the other side of the river.

After remaining concealed for some time, he ventured down to Monte Video, where he found the English brig Swan, bound round Cape Horn. Her crew, deluded by the false and extravagant promises of privateering captains and owners, had all deserted. In this dilemma the captain was compelled to supply their places with such materials as could be picked up in the streets of Monte Video, and which were as bad as bad could be. Indeed, from the lawless state of all South America, it would have been next to impossible to have procured, "for love or money," twenty good and orderly seamen, from Darien to Patagonia. Among these vagabonds Longford recognised many of his gaming-table acquaintances at Buenos Ayres, who had left that city to get out of the way of certain impertinent questions that the police had taken the liberty to ask concerning the murder that has already been mentioned. These fellows had imbibed a notion that seems to be an easily-besetting one among sailors who enter on board a ship in the middle of her voyage, namely, that there is money on board; which notion is but too often followed by an exceedingly strong inclination to appropriate it to their own use and behoof. Sailors seem to understand but confusedly the tenth commandment, which forbids us to covet any thing that is our neighbor's.

The subject was discussed on the passage, the plan arranged, and the unsuspecting officers, passengers, and two lads, apprentices to the captain, murdered and thrown overboard. My readers would be, perhaps, but little edified by a more circumstantial narrative. There is so little variation in the details of shipwreck, acts of piracy, obituary notices, ordinations, commencements, murders, suicides, mammoth turnips, and Fourth of July celebrations, that printers would find it a great saving of time, money, and labor, to have regular and approved forms of each stereotyped, with blank spaces for names and dates.

This bloody deed was executed near the southern extremity of the then half province and half republic of Chili; and the murderers, with considerable difficulty, succeeded in running the ship between the island of Santa Marie and the main, and anchoring near the town or city of Aranco, which was then in the hands of Benavidas, above mentioned.

This sanguinary freebooter was then, under the auspices and with the assistance of the equally sanguinary royal governor of Chili, Sanchez, carrying on a most horrid and cruel war of extermination against the republican inhabitants of the southern part of Chili. Into the hands of this murderous ruffian and his ragamuffin gang the Swan was delivered; but the villany of her piratical crew was soon to receive its just punishment. Benavidas, who suspected them of having kept back no trifling part of the plunder, with very little privacy and no formality, shot them all but Longford, whom, for some unaccountable reason or other, he spared.

CHAPTER III

Orlando. Good day and happiness, dear Rosalind.

Jaques. Nay then, God be wi' you an you talk in blank verse.

As You Like It.

Our scene must now change somewhat abruptly from the shores of the Pacific to a very different part of this watery ball.

Great and manifold are the advantages that an author enjoys over his readers; for, however anxious those readers may be to arrive at the end of the story, they must either close the book with a "Pish!" or a "Pshaw!" or condescend to follow him, and resignedly await his leisure. He leads them where he pleases and at what pace he pleases; they must follow him: they are like passengers on board a packet beating into port with what sailors call "a good working breeze;" at one moment they seem to have almost reached the anchorage, when suddenly the skipper shouts "Helm's a-lee," the vessel heaves in stays and makes a long "stretch" off, till the spires and roofs of the wished-for haven seem fading away in the hazy distance.

The celebrated Hugh Peters, one of Cromwell's fanatical preachers, explaining to his audience why God was forty years leading the children of Israel through the wilderness, which was not more than forty days' march across, made a circumflex with his finger upon his pulpit cushion, and said, "he led them *crinkledum cum crankledum,*" I do not intend that my story shall make more "Virginia fence" than is absolutely necessary; but that it shall proceed, like a law-suit, "with deliberate speed."

In the vicinity of one of those beautiful villages that surround the great commercial city of Bristol, and upon the banks of the lovely Severn, stood the residence of a wealthy merchant. There was nothing about the house or grounds that denoted the occupant or owner to be of a mercantile turn; for there certainly is, very generally, something about merchants' houses that is prim and starch—something precise and formal about them, as though they had been planned according to the "Golden Rule of Three," and executed with reference to the multiplication table. It is a most melancholy fact, that the close, confined air of a counting-room is deadly poison to a taste for the fine arts, and, but too often, to every thing like liberality of feeling.

Effingham House was neither planned nor executed upon a grand or a mean scale; there was nothing extravagant or penurious, vast or contracted, about it; but it presented a happy combination of the comfortable, the elegant, and the neat. Such houses are very common indeed throughout New England; in the *old* country there is a constant repetition of the fable of the frog and the ox—the wealthy cit endeavoring to equal the haughty splendors of the nobleman.

The villa that we describe fronted upon a large and beautiful lawn, that gradually sloped towards the river, of which, and the lovely scenery beyond it, it commanded an enchanting view, and was spotted with noble oaks and elms, that appeared to have stood ever since the Conquest, or might, perhaps, have overshadowed the legions of Agricola. A carriage path, well gravelled and kept perfectly free from dirt and weeds, wound around among these primeval trees, occasionally emerging from their shade, as if to give the approaching stranger an opportunity to view every part of the delightful landscape.

Along this path a horseman was seen riding, one lovely afternoon in September. The air of the rider was that of a man to whom the scene was perfectly familiar, but who seemed busy with thoughts that made him inattentive to its beauties. His sunburnt countenance, and an indescribable something in his whole appearance, that the experienced eye of a member of the same fraternity only could discern, announced that he was one of those that "followed the seas."

He alighted, and, giving his horse to a servant, ran up the steps of the portico. A young lady, who was tending some flowers at a little distance, hearing his footsteps, sprang towards him with sparkling eyes and smiling countenance, exclaiming in a voice of most unequivocal tenderness, "George!" The seaman caught her offered hand, and covered it with kisses. The lady's cheek, brow, and throat were suffused with the deepest and most lovely crimson: she gently struggled to release her captive hand; but, finding that there was just one degree more force exerted to retain it than she exercised to withdraw it, she prudently gave up so hopeless a contest, and began very naturally to ask questions.

"Why, when did you arrive?—how long have you been gone? Oh! it seems an age since you left us—and how you are tanned!"

"I arrived this morning," at length answered the seaman; the mutual delight of their meeting rendering him, for a time, as inarticulate as it did her voluble; "and I have been gone six months. Time has stood still with me, dearest Julia, I assure you; and besides, I have had such a tedious passage home, that I began at last to think I was never to be blessed with another fair wind. I need not ask how you have been during that time," he continued, fixing his eyes upon her lovely countenance with unutterable affection.

No woman was ever insensible to a compliment, even an implied one, to her looks. Julia raised her liquid eyes to his with a blush and a smile so frank and unreserved, that his six months' absence and tedious homeward passage he would gladly endure twice ever again to meet.

There are moments in courtship—that part of it, I mean, where neither party has as yet whispered love to each other, or bothered the old folks about their consent; before, in short, it has become an "understood thing" all over town—there are such moments, when the lady throws off all reserve, and by a look, a smile, a blush, a half-articulate word, repays her lover for months, if he is fool enough to court so long, of prudish and affected shyness, past or future. These moments occur but seldom, even in the most patriarchal courtships, and it is well that it is so. Love is a fiery steed, and should always be ridden with a curb bridle, both before and after marriage. (I am sorry that I cannot think of a nautical metaphor, or I assure you, reader, that I would never have gone into the stable to look for one.) The ancients, and their opinion is decisive, ever held the "semi-reducta Venus" the most beautiful.

Leaving these turtles to bill and coo over a cup of tea, and to the enjoyment of a lover's walk along the lovely banks of the Severn, we will proceed to enlighten the reader as to who and what they are, and to discuss sundry other equally important topics.

As the good ship Bristol Trader was lazily rolling along in a southerly direction, with a light breeze and fine weather, and in the latitude of about thirty-nine or forty north, she fell in with the wreck of a schooner, of about eighty or ninety tons burthen, dismasted and apparently half full of water, in which most unpleasant situation she did not appear long to have been. The Bristol Trader hove to, and sent her boat alongside, in hopes of obtaining something valuable from the wreck, either cargo, or provisions, or rigging—if a wreck yields nothing else, there is always plenty of fish around it. As the boat approached, the attention of the crew was attracted by the appearance of some person on board, who made the most animated and intelligible signs to them to come alongside. The boat's crew redoubled their exertions, and, upon coming on board, found a boy of about fourteen years, the only living human being. The poor little fellow seemed almost exhausted with fatigue and hunger; but being carried on board the ship and refreshed, he informed his deliverers that his name was George Allerton— that the schooner belonged to a port in New England, and was homeward bound from Fayal with a quantity of wine and fruit—that she had been capsized, in a sudden and violent squall, three days previous, when all the crew but himself and one other were swept overboard—that she had righted after cutting away the masts, but with a great deal of water in the hold, and that the other man had accidentally fallen overboard, and was drowned.

It happened that the owner of the ship, Mr. Effingham, was on board. He was going to Rio de Janeiro, partly on account of his health, but chiefly to look after and secure a large amount of property belonging to the firm of which he was senior partner, and which was jeopardised by certain disturbances in Brazil. Like all passengers on board a ship, he could find but little or nothing to do to pass away the time, and being a married man and a father, his sympathies and good feelings were powerfully excited and strongly attracted towards this "waif of the sea," their new passenger. The boy, on the other hand, to a very handsome face added a mild and amiable disposition, and, like all New-England boys, an education vastly superior to boys of the same age and standing in Great Britain. George's parents were respectable in some sort—that is to say, their moral and religious characters were beyond reproach, but their social reputation was very bad indeed—they were poor. It has been said by an English traveller, that in all other countries pleasure, rank, literary renown, &c. are the objects upon which men place their affections; but, in the United States, the pursuit of wealth is an imperious duty; and, of course, if a man fails in this duty, his good name as a member of society soon becomes most deplorably out at elbows.

Before the end of the voyage, young Allerton had made himself master of Mr. Effingham's affections, and being of that happy age when all places are nearly alike, provided they are comfortable, he readily consented to remain with his protector, and was accordingly regularly inducted into the old gentleman's family as a member of it. He was the playmate of Mr. Effingham's daughter, six years younger than himself, and the companion of her rambles abroad. The old man wished to take him into his counting-room as a clerk, but the boy's predilection for the sea frustrated that scheme, and the senior, after some reflection and persuasion, yielded to it. Accordingly Master George, having served a noviciate as apprentice, stepped over the intermediate state of "able seaman," and became second mate, then first mate, and lastly captain, or more properly master. During the whole of this time, he was employed in the West India trade, in which most of the Bristol merchants are engaged more extensively than in any other. He never came home from a voyage without bringing some curiosity to little Julia,—as he continued to call her, even after she had attained her eighteenth year,—and never failed writing frequently to his parents, and sending them the whole or a greater part of his wages: a line of conduct that raised him incredibly in the old gentleman's favor, and made a deep impression upon the young mind of Julia.

While George was passing through the different grades of his profession, the young lady was advancing through the different grades of physical and intellectual beauty and improvement. The "pretty child" that played in her father's parlor, the "elegant girl of the boarding-school", had now become a most lovely and accomplished young lady. She had lost her mother when young, and the whole force of her filial affection had centred upon her father. Brought up in unreserved intimacy with her father's new *protégé*, she always regarded him as a brother, or rather as her equal. She always anxiously awaited his return from sea, though she did not, in her more youthful days, exactly understand why. When her beauty brought wealth and rank to her feet, she could not avoid comparing their possessors with the nautical absentee.

"Sir Reginald Bentley is not half so handsome a man as George; Lord Dormington, although he has travelled over all Europe, and has besides a seat in the House of Lords, is not, after all, half so well informed as George; the Honorable Adolphus Fitz William dresses very expensively and fashionably, but his clothes do not fit him so well as George's; and as for that wine-swilling brute, Squire Foxley, I would not be condemned to marry such a man for the world." So she dismissed them all, "cum multis aliis."

On the other hand, her father had acquired as much affection for George as for a son, and treated him as such; though he never dreamed that his daughter might from his behavior be led one day to select him as a husband. When his daughter rejected one wealthy or titled suitor after another, he thought nothing strange of it; Sir Reginald was a gambler, his lordship a fool, Fitz William a dandy, Foxley a sot, and so of the rest; he only saw in her rejection of them proofs that she possessed more good sense and prudence than he was generally willing to admit that any of her sex possessed.

About two years before the events mentioned in the beginning of this chapter, George had sailed on his first voyage as master of the ship Hebe. He had been gone about five months, and Julia, with a feeling that she did not pretend to understand or think to analyze, had been day after day inquiring about him, when one evening her father informed her that the Hebe had arrived safely in London. The joy that she felt and expressed in the most lively manner, was damped by the farther intelligence that he was to return to Barbadoes as soon as possible, without visiting Effingham House. When she retired to her chamber, she seated herself by the window, and seriously began to ask herself why she felt such pleasure at hearing of his safe arrival, and why the disappointment at not seeing him was so exceedingly painful. Her own good sense answered the question, after a short reflection.

"It is, it must be love; I *do* love him, and that most sincerely;" and she gave way to a burst of irrepressible but soothing tears. "And why should I not?" she reasoned, "is he not every thing that heart can desire—handsome, well educated, and generous? and does not my father love him as a son? But my father may not consent," she continued, again weeping, "and I must endeavor to conquer an affection that has been growing silently but rapidly for years; it is impossible, I know, but I will make the attempt."

The old man, too, could not but notice the different effects of the two items of intelligence he had that evening communicated. "What could ail Julia when I told her that George was going to sea again without coming home? the poor girl was ready to cry: he's a fine young fellow, that's certain, and they've been brought up together like brother and sister; so I suppose it is natural that she loves him like a brother: I have half a mind to write to him to scamper across the country, and see us for a couple of days; but I dare say he's too busy." With these reflections the merchant dropped asleep, and dreamed of "Africa and golden joys."

Upon Captain Allerton's subsequent return, Julia's determination to avoid him and to stifle her attachment to him vanished, like most resolutions of the kind that young ladies are in the habit of forming, and she gave herself up to the illusions of that bewitching passion, without knowing—and, when enjoying his society, certainly without thinking—how it would end; and as for her father, he, good easy man, had done thinking about it altogether: not that his affection for her was in any wise abated, but his mind was taken up with something else more engrossing, and, as perhaps he thought, more important, than watching the actions of two young people.

After tea, Captain Allerton and Julia took a walk upon the banks of the river, along a secluded green lane, that had often witnessed similar rambles. After a long pause, during which each seemed too busy with their own peculiar train of thinking to regard the silence of the other, they stopped, as if by mutual consent.

"And so, Julia, your father, after losing so much money in South America, is going there, to see if he can grapple any of it up from the mines of Mexico, or wherever else it has sunk."

"He is certainly going to South America, but I never knew that he had lost much money by his speculations there."

"Nor do I say that he has, but as every body else has, I do not see how he can have escaped;" and then added, after a short pause, and in an embarrassed and tremulous voice, "are you, tell me, Julia, are you going with him?"

"Me! no, George; what could put such a wild thought into your head?"

"And what then is to become of you during his absence, that must necessarily be a long one?"

"I shall remain with my aunt Selwyn in Bristol, till she returns to Clifton."

"Julia, you know that I love you, and you have given me reason to believe that I am far from indifferent to you; then why not, my dearest girl, give me the right to protect and provide for you at once, instead of delegating it to a maiden aunt, who, whatever may be her good qualities, has, as you know, always regarded me with dislike and jealousy."

"I cannot, George, without my father's consent."

"Your hand, then, goes where he chooses to bestow it, let your affections be where they will."

"It is a duty that I owe to him to attend to his wishes, and listen to his advice."

"So then, if he advises you to marry the fool Dormington, or the brute Foxley, you obey unhesitatingly?"

"George, this is unkind; you are supposing an extreme case."

"But you say you will obey him; you repeat that it is your duty to listen to his advice in all cases."

"I will never marry without his consent, but I will never marry any one that I dislike."

"That is intimating, rather obliquely, to be sure, that you may alter your mind."

"O George, George," said the weeping girl, "why will you continue to torment me and yourself with these jealous doubts and suspicions? why will you not rather ask my father's consent? you know his affection for you."

"Yes, propose such a question, and what is the reply? a peremptory refusal, and an immediate dismissal from his employment. Now that his mind is so much taken up with his new scheme, such a proceeding would be little short of madness. Be mine, then, at once."

"I dare not."

"But suppose, what is by no means impossible, nay, rather likely to happen, that he should determine to fix himself in Mexico, or Lima, or some other South American city, as foreign partner of the house?"

"I cannot believe such an event possible, but if it should—" she turned away her head.

"Do I interpret your silence right, Julia? would you indeed be mine? speak to me, Julia." She made no other answer than a sigh, but still kept her head averted. By this time they had reached the house.

As soon as they were seated in the drawing-room, the lover again urged her to "make signal of his hope;"—she raised her eyes, swimming in tears, in which an affirmative was plainly to be read. The entrance of a servant prevented the happy lover from proceeding to extremities upon her lips, "according to the statute in such case made and provided;" and a very excellent statute it is too. Whether the "quashing of proceedings" by the inopportune appearance of the servant was agreeable to either party, I leave to wiser heads than mine to determine.

Many very well-meaning people, who pass for men of sense in every other respect, are apt, when they feel matrimonially inclined, to think it indispensably necessary to court the old folks, "hammer and tongs," as the vulgar saying is, in the first place, and, having obtained their good graces, to proceed very leisurely in their approaches to the young lady. This may be a very prudent mode of managing matters, for aught I know, but to me it savors rather of cold-blooded calculation, than ardent or even passably warm affection. It is, besides, a gross and unpardonable insult to the said young lady, whom it places immediately upon a level with a horse, a pig, a cow, a load of hay, a chest of drawers, or any other article of trade. It is like a man-of-war going in to engage an enemy's battery, and heaving to, to "blaze away" at two old dismantled hulks that are lying high and dry at the harbor's mouth.

CHAPTER IV

Parolles. My lord, I am a man whom fortune hath cruelly scratched.

Lafeu. Well, what would you have me to do? 'tis too late to pare her
nails now.

All's Well That Ends Well.

There never was yet fair woman but she made mouths in a glass.

King Lear.

Julia Effingham was the only child of a rich merchant, who, like many others in these latter days, when scheming and speculation have superseded the good, old-fashioned habits of steady industry and unmoveable perseverance in the art of acquiring wealth, was dazzled by the one thousand and one bubbles that the South American revolution set afloat. He dipped pretty largely into Mexican mines, and was bit; he undertook to improve the breed of horses in Peru, and was bit; he attempted to establish steam cotton-factories in Colombia, and was bit; he bought largely into a Chilian Steam-boat Company, and was bit; till, finally, he resolved to visit South America himself, "to see," as he expressed it, "where the devil his fifty thousand pounds had gone to." He could obtain no tidings of a single farthing on the Atlantic side of that continent; but he learned one thing most thoroughly and satisfactorily, as thousands have done besides him, that if he had gone there in the first place, and seen the nakedness of the land, and the deplorable and remediless ignorance and superstition of the people, his fifty thousand pounds would have snugly remained in the three per cents. and India bonds. He was determined, however, now that he was fairly afloat, to "go the whole figure," and see the worst, if there was any thing worse to come. Accordingly he took passage for Valparaiso, where he found how, why, and wherefore his steam-boat concern had become a decided take-in; it is not very profitable running a boat of that kind in a country where wood sells at three cents per pound on the beach, and where the people have no idea of travelling except in the saddle.

Chili, then under the directorship of O'Higgins, was the only South American province that seemed to have changed for the better, by renouncing its allegiance to "Ferdinand the Beloved." Its ports were thrown open to foreign commerce; its navy was respectable, for the ships, the officers, and the seamen were English or Americans; its inhabitants had become quite civilized and tame, for the murdered foreigners in the streets of Valparaiso did not average much more than one or two per night; which, compared with Havana and Buenos Ayres, gave Chili a preponderance of refinement scarcely credible. Mr. Effingham was highly delighted with the country; and indeed Chili, setting aside the inhabitants, for the salubrity and mildness of its climate, the fertility of its soil, and the variety and delicacy of its fruits and vegetables, is certainly one of the finest countries in the world. He found many Englishmen established in various sections of the country, and the better sort of inhabitants very much disposed to treat them with kindness and urbanity.

He had been about eighteen months in St. Jago when he sent for his daughter, who now constituted the whole of his family; his English business he knew was safe in the management of his partner, and he sat himself down with the determination of making a magnificent fortune very much at his ease. Poor man! he little dreamed that the whole of South America is as infamous for revolutions as it is for earthquakes.

Having said thus much concerning the father of Julia Effingham, it is but fair to give the reader some idea of the lady herself. Indeed, in strict gallantry, I suspect that I ought to have introduced her first, but she has already been upon the stage, and "made her obedience," as sailors call it, to the audience; and, besides, age has claims that ought to be attended to.

In person, then, Julia was not remarkably tall, (I don't like tall women; "a man never ought to look *up* to his wife for a kiss or for advice;") her form had all that graceful and delicate roundness and fullness of outline so irresistibly pleasing to the eye. "Man," says an elegant writer upon natural history, contrasting the two sexes, "man is most angular, woman most round." Euclid himself could not have detected any thing angular in the faultless form of Julia Effingham; nothing resembling his "Asses' Bridge," or his "Windmill" problems, in the fall of her shoulders, the bend of her snowy neck, the delicate round of her chin, the delicious fulness of her ripe lip, the easy turn of her rosy cheeks, the graceful curve of her brow. Her nose was indeed a straight Grecian one, but not geometrically straight.

It must be admitted, by the way, that there are more decidedly *good* noses among women than among men. The latter are aquiline, Roman, parrot, pug, snub, thick, thin, long, short, peaked, bottle—some with a bump in the middle, some with a cleft, or fissure, and some with a button, or knob, at the end, like that on a man-of-war's boat-hook. In short, to describe all the various kinds of noses masculine, it would be necessary for philologians to create a new batch of adjectives, as the king of England does occasionally of peers.

I have already said, or meant to be understood to say, that Miss Effingham was somewhat inclined to *embonpoint*. I do not pretend to know the reason of this: perhaps leanness and emaciation were not considered *genteel* when she happened to be educated, as they are unfortunately by too many of my fair countrywomen; perhaps she never thought much about it; for I have always observed that very beautiful women, who prefer revolving in the quiet circle of domestic happiness and usefulness, are seldom or never very anxiously solicitous about their beauty; and the consequence is, that they *are* more beautiful, and stand the attacks of time far better, than those who choose a life of fashionable display, and court public admiration. Ladies may lace tight, eat pickles, and drink vinegar, to make them genteel; but it is free exercise in the open air, and simplicity of diet, provided it is nutritious, that confer gentility and grace, and preserve beauty. Will any man, married or single, and in the possession of his senses, say that he likes the looks of a horse whose ribs are visible and *countable* at half a mile's distance? I am confident the answer will be, no.

Still there is a wonderful resemblance between a lean woman and a lean horse, in more points than one; the lady does not, indeed, go upon all fours, but I can never see a very *genteel* female, laced into the shape of an hour-glass, without wishing, from the bottom of my heart, that she had an extra pair of le—ahem!—ancles, to support her feeble and tottering frame.

As I am growing old, and am, moreover, somewhat peculiarly circumstanced, I suppose that I must put up with such a wife as it pleases God to send me; but were I ten or fifteen years younger, and "well to do," I would accept of no descendant of mother Eve, as a helpmate and partner for life, who did not cut at least two inches on the ribs. The Turks, who are practical men of taste in these things; the Chinese, who pretend to the highest antiquity in civilization; the naked Africans and South Sea Islanders, beyond dispute the most unsophisticated of all father Adam's children, and who, like Job, "retain their integrity" pretty stiffly, considering the missionaries, the "march of intellect," and other untoward circumstances, are all of them most decidedly in favor of something substantial in wedlock; no man of taste, in either of these nations, ever dreams of comfort and happiness in matrimony, unless he clasps to his bosom an armful of wife. They choose their wives as we do lobsters—the heaviest are the best.

I am a firm believer in the maxim that mind and matter exert a mutual influence upon each other, and one of the most obvious deductions from that datum that occurs to my mind is, that the acidities of the disposition are not only neutralized but absolutely shut up by the embonpoint of the body. People blessed with healthy plumpness are indolent as well as good-natured, and it is a laborious piece of business for such folks to get in a passion.

The wealth and fondness of Julia's father, and her own natural good sense, had made her mistress of all those elegant and fashionable accomplishments that constitute the education of a lady of fortune; and she had a grace and sweetness in every thing she did that reminded the beholder of that exquisitely beautiful line in Ariosto:

"She walked—she spoke—she sang—and heaven was there."

This description may not be according to certain received axioms concerning female beauty; but I never could bear to contemplate a fair face and graceful form as painters do, who measure woman's loveliness by certain fixed and arbitrary rules, as surveyors of lumber do boards. Nothing makes me more fidgetty than to hear a man compare every beautiful face he sees with a certain standard, even if that standard is the Venus de Medicis herself; this face is not good, for it is not exactly oval; that nose is altogether wrong, for it is not Grecian; a chin is not this, or a mouth is not that, &c. Portrait painters are much addicted to this kind of criticism; and whenever I find myself in company with one of these two-foot-rule critics, I make my escape from him as I would from a plague hospital.

At the time of our narrative, Julia's father had been absent somewhat more than two years. He had sent for her to join him at Valparaiso, a summons that she prepared to obey with no small trepidation. "The course of true love," which is somewhat notorious for "never running smooth," seemed at this moment about to encounter a "head sea." Her absence from England she knew must be a long one, perhaps an eternal one; the separation from Allerton weighed much heavier upon her spirits than she was willing to admit, and altogether her prospects of happiness seemed darkened for ever.

The same conveyance that brought Julia's letters also brought instructions to the other partners of the house to fit out two vessels for the Pacific, one of which was to be entrusted to the command of Captain Allerton; but Mr. Effingham omitted to designate which of the two was to be honored by being for some months the floating home of his fair daughter; either intending it should be left to her option, or taking it for granted that his partner, well aware of the intimacy of Allerton's standing in her father's family, would of course place Julia on board the ship commanded by George. But that partner was a crafty old fox, who had long since seen the growing affection of the two young people, and, with all that eagerness to destroy happiness, that they are past enjoying, that characterizes the majority of old people, decided that Miss Julia should, for a time, entrust her person and fortunes to the fatherly care of Captain Burton, a sedate old Cornish man of sixty years of age, who had no more idea of love than he had of the Chaldee language.

CHAPTER V

Should a man full of talk be justified? O that ye would altogether hold your peace; and it should be your wisdom. Job, Ch. xi. 2; xiii. 5.

Voyages across the Atlantic are now performed every day by old and young women and children, and described by them so much more elegantly and scientifically, and with so much more correct knowledge of the technicalities necessary for such descriptions, than it is possible that seafaring men can ever attain, that if one of the latter, in a moment of mental hallucination, was to undertake to convey an idea of the element that has been his home for years, he would be hissed off the stage as another Munchausen. For this reason nautical men, who have laid aside the marlinspike and taken up the pen, very prudently avoid that portion of the literary arena, leaving Daddy Neptune's dominions to be explored and described by landsmen.

It is in obedience to public opinion in this respect, I suppose, that our Secretaries of the Navy are almost uniformly chosen from the "mass of the people," at the greatest possible distance from high-water mark; men who have never seen a piece of water that they could not jump across, or a ship, except in the newspaper, till they came to Washington. "Let the sea make a noise, and the fulness thereof; let the floods clap their hands" for joy, that the Cooks and the Falconers, the Ansons and the Byrons, of olden time, are at length banished from the department of nautical literature, and no *oceanic* description will be listened to unless said or sung by a *ci-devant* midshipman or a half-boy, half-woman poet, who lies in his berth, and sees, through the four-inch-plank deadlight of a packet, the full moon rising in the west. James Fenimore Cooper, Esq.—I give the man his entire name and title, as he seems to insist upon it upon all occasions—the "American Walter Scott," is undisputably at the very head of his *trade* at the present day for nautical descriptions; his terrestrial admirers have pronounced him "a practical seaman;" and, of course, the only man in these United States that can give any, even an approximate idea of the sea, and "those that go down in ships." I have at my pen's end six or eight very desperate "cases" of his knowledge of "practical seamanship" and maritime affairs, which may be found in the "Red Rover" and "Water Witch" *passim*; but those animals, vulgarly called critics, but more politely and properly at present, reviewers, whom the New York Mirror defines to be "great dogs, that go about unchained and growl at every thing they do not comprehend," these dogs have dragged the lion's hide partly off, and ascertained, what every man, to whom the Almighty has vouchsafed an ordinary share of common sense, had all along suspected, that it covered an ass. James Fenimore Cooper, Esquire's "Letter to his Countrymen" was an explosion of folly and absurdity that has blown his name up so high, that there is little or no chance of its coming down again "this king's reign." Whether he was or was not hired to write it to support the present administration, as some folks suspect, is not my affair. I will, therefore, resume the thread of my discourse, which was only "belayed" for a few minutes, to indulge in the rare pleasure of grumbling a little at seeing

"Fools rush in where angels fear to tread."

Julia Effingham was embarked on board the large, burthensome, and not alarmingly fast sailing brig Avon—John Burton, master; while the ship under the command of Captain Allerton was called the Hyperion. Both vessels were nearly of the same tonnage, though there was much difference in their rates of sailing, the Hyperion having been built as near the model of a swift American ship as the English naval architect's conscience would let him, which, however, did not allow him any greater latitude than such as made a very obvious difference in their appearance and rate of speed. Miss Effingham was accompanied by her maid, Miss Dolly, alias Dorothea, Hastings. Nothing material occurred for the first six weeks of their voyage, by which time they had nearly reached the equator, except that Allerton improved every opportunity afforded by light breezes and calms to visit the Avon; which visits Captain Burton, honest man! supposed were intended for himself.

But at this period—that is, six weeks after leaving the Lizard Point, and while the two ships were in that peculiarly disagreeable strip of salt water that lies between the southern limits of the northeast trade-wind and the northern edge of the south-east, and is affected by neither—there came on one night one of those very black and threatening squalls, that look as though they would blow the ocean out of its bed, and frequently do not blow at all. Captain Burton, who thought a squall was a squall all over the world, and who was better acquainted with the Grand Banks and the Bay of Biscay than with the tropics, took in all sail, while the Hyperion, with topgallant-sails lowered, ran gallantly before it, and made upwards of fifty miles before the breeze left her. The Avon was in her turn shortly after favored with a fine breeze, but the two ships did not meet again till they had passed Cape Horn.

In the mean time, Mr. Effingham began to discover that Chili was not paradise, nor its inhabitants saints; many thefts, robberies, and frauds, were practised upon him, for which he could obtain no redress from the contemptible magistrates; an earthquake, that did a great deal of damage, was followed by a sweeping epidemic, which, as it affected only the natives, was imputed by the priests to magic art and diabolical witchcraft on the part of the heretical foreign residents. A riot was the consequence, and the foreigners were only able to secure their lives and property by a combination of their numbers, and the most determined firmness of purpose. In short, the harassed merchant found out at last that he had blundered into one of those self-styled republics, so many of which have sprung up and passed away since the commencement of the nineteenth century, where infant Liberty is nursed by mother Mob.

These vexatious circumstances, and the prospect of an approaching revolution, that threatened to be a bloody one, completely changed his sentiments with regard to all South American governments, and he bitterly regretted having sent for his daughter to join him.

It was too late now to remedy that mis-step; but he determined, as soon as she arrived, to re-embark for England as soon as possible, and in consequence he lost no time in disposing of his merchandize, and transmitting his funds to the coast, and thence to the spirit-room of a British frigate. Having thus "set his house in order," and adjusted his Chilian books, he left St. Jago, and took up his abode for the time being in Valparaiso, waiting impatiently for the arrival of the Hyperion and Avon, that were now daily expected.

CHAPTER VI

Finally, my dear hearers.

Old Sermons.

Nothing material occurred to the good brig Avon after parting company, as aforesaid, with her consort, the Hyperion; a circumstance that I regret not a little, as it deprives me of my only chance for describing a storm at sea. They only experienced one tornado, and fifteen gales of wind, before joining the other ship. The tornado was no great things after all—the brig ran merrily before it, under a reefed foresail and close-reefed main-topsail. The crew were all on deck during the whole night it lasted, in case of their services being required. But the females below had by far the worst of it—they were "turned in" to berths that the ship-joiner had built with reference rather to the accommodation of an able-bodied man, than a delicate young lady; and in consequence, poor Julia was dashed first against the vessel's side, and then against the front berth-board, as the brig rolled gunwales under at every motion, till she began to think with the Frenchman, that she "should get some sleeps, no, not never." In this dilemma she thought of taking her maid, Miss Dorothea Hastings, into the berth with her, where the two females, operating mutually as "checks" to each other, eventually made out a very passable night's rest. As for the gales of wind, they were the merest flea-bites in creation, though one of them borrowed the brig's fore-topmast, and another walked away with her jib-boom.

During this period, Benavidas had been taken a second time; and as his captors did not choose to risk shooting him again, which they had already practised upon him once without success, they hanged him. His gang were nearly all killed or taken at the same time, and the prisoners summarily dealt with.

Longford and about thirty more made their escape in a small schooner; and as they well knew that they would experience no other mercy, if taken, than a high gallows and short halter, they shaped a course for the island of Masafuero, which they determined to make their head-quarters, and to commit depredations upon all vessels that passed which were not too well armed. They effected a landing with some difficulty, and found, as they expected, considerable quantities of provisions and stores, that had been deposited among the deep fissures of the rocks by Benavidas some time previous, when his affairs on the continent began to assume a smoky appearance. Here the scattered but desperate remnant of his lawless followers found a temporary respite from the harassing pursuit of the Chilenos, that resulted every day in the capture and immediate execution of some of their number.

The landing-place at Masafuero, with the open ground beyond it, surrounded on three sides by broken rocks or high mountains, makes a very beautiful appearance from the offing—anchorage, I believe, there is none. It is a gentle slope, fronting the northern or sunny side of the horizon, smooth, and of most delightful verdure. Perhaps it appeared more lovely to me, who had been groping among the ices of the ant-arctic circle for five months previous. The men whom we had left to get seal-skins assured me the soil was very rich and deep, and the herbage green and luxuriant. Since commencing these chapters, I have been informed that the island is very frequently visited by our whalemen for supplies of wood and young goat's flesh, which last is a savory morsel to men who have been many months tumbling and rolling about on the long regular swell of the Pacific. The waters that surround the island are almost literally filled with fine fish, to which sailors have given the general name of "snappers," and which differ from any fish among us, more particularly in their propensity to bite as greedily at a bare hook as a baited one.

It was here that the pirates lay *perdue*, waiting when the devil, who always befriends such gentry, should send them a defenceless prey. They were unable to anchor, as I have already noticed that there was no anchorage, and were accordingly continually on the move, sometimes extending their researches fifty or sixty miles to the eastward of Juan Fernandez, which lies about that distance nearer the main than Masafuero.

As they were lying to one morning, off the north-western side of Fernandez, they were suddenly startled by the unexpected appearance of a large brig that came out from behind the western extremity of the island, and edged away towards the northward and eastward under all sail. It was the first vessel they had seen since they had set up the piratical business on their own account and risk, except an English "jackass frigate," that chased them at the rate of one mile to the schooner's five. The Vincedor, which was the name of the schooner, also kept away and made sail, but kept yawing about in a manner that excited the suspicions of the people on board the brig, and it was evident that the manœuvre would soon bring the schooner alongside. The brig now hoisted the English ensign, but continued on her way without deviating from her course. The schooner also made an attempt to "talk bunting," or show colors; but she had nothing of the kind on board but some old ragged signals that formerly belonged to the ill-fated brig Swan; and one of these was accordingly run up to the end of the main gaff. Captain Burton, for it was indeed he and the brig Avon, after attentively examining the stranger, gave it as his opinion that she was a pirate, and directed his men to stand to their guns.

In a few minutes the schooner, having closed with the Avon, fired a shot across her bows, which being unnoticed, another was fired that passed through her foresail, to which the brig replied with three guns loaded with grape, that took fatal effect upon the exposed and crowded deck of the Vincedor. The pirates then kept up a heavy and well-directed fire of small arms upon the Avon, and Captain Burton, seeing several of his best men killed and wounded, reluctantly gave orders to haul up the courses and back the main yard, still keeping his colors flying.

Longford and about twenty ruffians like himself immediately came on board; and their first question to Captain Burton was, how he had dared to fire upon their schooner?

"Because," said the sturdy old seaman, "I knew you to be pirates, and I was determined not to surrender this vessel without some resistance."

During this speech, Longford raised his pistol, and at its conclusion fired; and the brave old sailor, shot through the body, and mortally wounded, fell at his feet. This was the signal for a general massacre of the crew; and while the bloody act was perpetrating, Longford ran down into the cabin, to secure certain articles of plunder that he did not choose to share with his partners in crime and blood.

Before the pirate came alongside the Avon, Captain Burton, suspecting her real character, had requested Julia to go below for a while, on pretence that he was going to tack ship, and she would be in the way, as women always are at sea, of the head-braces and main-boom. As the blunt old veteran never used much ceremony upon such occasions, she thought no more about it, but went below as she was bid. The firing, however, had terrified her exceedingly; and Miss Dorothy Hastings, who was sent out as a vidette as far as the upper step of the companion-ladder, came scampering back to the main body with intelligence that the stranger was a pirate, and immediately proceeded to enumerate the outrages that they might certainly calculate upon being subjected to. Almost sinking with terror, Julia listened with a scarce-beating heart to the increased trampling of feet on deck, the oaths of the pirates, and the report of a pistol; and when the murderer Longford, splashed with poor Burton's blood, suddenly appeared before her, she uttered a wild shriek, and sank senseless upon the cabin floor.

But vengeance was on its way, and close at hand. While the pirates were busily engaged in murdering the unhappy crew of the Avon, which they did not accomplish without considerable loss to themselves, for the gallant fellows fought most desperately, the Hyperion hove in sight from behind Fernandez, following the track of her consort. Captain Allerton had heard the firing, and, suspecting all was not right, had "packed on" a press of sail, and soon came within short musket-shot of the schooner, whose hull received eight or ten round shot, but her sweeps and superiority of sailing on a wind, enabled her to escape. Allerton then steered for the brig, the disordered state of whose sails, her braces loose and yards flying about as the wind and sea pleased, convinced him that the pirates had been on board, and it was with a horrible dread of what might have taken place that he drew near. When within half a mile of the Avon, he saw a boat shove off from alongside, that a single look at his glass convinced him contained none of the brig's crew. Satisfied that they were part of the schooner's piratical crew, he sent all his men forward armed with muskets, with orders to give them a volley as soon as they came near enough to be sure of their mark. This was done, and the next moment the boat was sunk by the ship passing over her, and not one of the blood-stained wretches escaped. The Hyperion then shortened sail, and hove to.

To return to the Avon's cabin. When Longford saw a lovely young woman lying insensible before him, when he expected no such person's existence on board, his better feelings prevailed—he thought of his mother, his sisters, his home, and the bright prospects he had forever darkened by his own folly and vice, and he leaned against the bulk-head in bitter agony. He neither heard nor heeded the repeated calls of one of his comrades, announcing the rapid approach of the Hyperion, his thoughts were in a complete whirl, nor was he roused from his gloomy reflections but by the voices of Allerton and his boat's crew, as they came alongside. Then he started and ran up the companion-way, but escape was impossible. He drew a pistol from his belt; but before he could even put himself in an attitude of defence, he was cloven to the teeth by a blow of Allerton's cutlass.

Without stopping to see if there was more of them, George ran instantly below, and found his Julia still insensible, and Miss Hastings kicking her heels and screaming, after the most approved recipe for performing hysterics. Allerton sprinkled the young lady's face with water and vinegar, and ransacked the medicine-chest for hartshorn and ether, but without success, till at length he thought of bleeding, at which he was sufficiently expert when his patients had been sailors. The snow-white, round arm was instantly bared and bandaged; the vein rose, and was pierced by the lancet with as much skill as Sangrado himself could have displayed; but the operator, although he knew how much blood a tough seaman could afford to lose, was completely at a loss when his patient was a delicate young lady; and, having, to his joy, witnessed the success of his phlebotomy in restoring her to life and consciousness, slacked the bandage and stopped the bleeding.

For a few minutes Julia's senses seemed completely bewildered; she stared wildly around, and uttered the most incoherent ravings; when George, who seemed to retain his presence of mind most wonderfully, wisely reflecting that human nature was about the same, whether in breeches or petticoats, poured out a glass of wine, and compelled his patient to swallow a large share of it. The wine produced the most happy effects. In a few minutes she looked up in his face with an intelligent glance, and in a soft voice murmured his name.

In the mean time it would be unpardonable in us to leave Miss Dorothea Hastings any longer. Allerton had been followed into the cabin by several of his men, one of whom, compassionating the situation of the young woman, who was, in truth, a plump, rosy-cheeked lass, and having seen cold water thrown into the faces of people in fits, caught up a gallon pitcher filled with the element, and dashed it into her countenance. The remedy effectually restored her to consciousness and herself, by rousing her indignation against the perpetrator of such an ungallant action.

A German theorist of the present age has much such a way of curing all human diseases; that is, he drives one disorder out of the system by introducing another more powerful—in some cases similar, in others directly opposite; as for instance, he attacks pulmonary consumption with insanity, gout with the "seven-years-itch," small-pox with its partial namesake, pleurisy with inflammatory rheumatism, &c., and so *vice versa* in all cases; no doubt the theory is a good one, and so was that which proposed to keep a horse upon nothing.

In the course of an hour Julia declared herself sufficiently restored to accompany George to his own ship, whither she was accordingly removed, and a cabin fitted up for her accommodation.

In the process of burying the murdered crew of the Avon, four of her men were found alive, severely but not dangerously wounded; and a fifth, who had lowered himself over the bows, and clung to the bob-stays. Six of the pirates were also found dead on her decks, their brains dashed out by the handspikes with which the seamen had defended themselves till shot down in detail.

By the time all necessary arrangements and changes had been made, it was dark; and the Avon, with the second officer and six men from the Hyperion, jogged along in the wake of that ship, which carried a lantern at her gaff-end for her direction. Miss Dorothy, being comfortably established in the Hyperion's cabin, complained of "feeling bad somehow." Her mistress had *turned in* long before, and was sound asleep under the influence of a composing medicine, prescribed by her physician and lover. Perhaps Miss Hastings thought the same medicine might do *her* good; perhaps she meant the complaint as a hint to Mr. Brail, the mate, to have pity upon her. The seaman took the hint, real or imaginary, and declared he could compound a draught as composing as any prescribed in the "book of directions," and accordingly mixed a tumbler of hot grog, well sweetened with loaf-sugar; but he forgot he was not mixing for himself, and put in the same quantity of pure Antigua as though the "charge" was intended for his own throat and brain of proof. Miss Dolly drank the potent mixture, which effectually dispelled the remains of her hysterical squall; and in a few minutes after retiring to her berth, she was fast in the arms of Morpheus, if Morpheus ever goes to sea.

Our story must now gallop a little. Mr. Effingham was delighted with George's gallant conduct, though he was too late to save poor Burton and his men; the cargoes of both vessels were sold, and the old gentleman, with his daughter, returned to England with Allerton. Shortly after their arrival, the hall of Effingham House witnessed the performance of that ceremony, which, in the English prayer-books, "begins with 'dearly beloved,' and ends with 'amazement;'" but "the bishops, priests, and deacons, and all other clergy," who were engaged in altering and adapting the Book of Common Prayer to the Episcopal church in this country, finding nothing very amazing in matrimony, have omitted the short sermon that usually closed its performance, and the form, like most religious forms, now ends modestly with a simple Amen.

In three days after the murder on board the Avon, the schooner was driven ashore upon Masafuero in a "norther," a violent gale so called in that sea, from its uniformly blowing from the northward; and of the eight on board, seven perished. The wretched survivor, after suffering every thing but death from starvation, escaped in a whaler to the main, was recognised, identified as one of Benavidas' gang, and shot before he had been on shore two hours.